"With his exquisite control of language and unsparing vision, Trevor serves up the pain of ordinary life with such precision that it feels like a physical ache to comprehend it. . . . What you have in this collection then, is something small and perfect."
> —*The Washington Post Book World*

"A dazzling collection of short stories."
> —Geordie Greig, The *Sunday Times* Pick of the Year (London)

"Like the Old Masters, Trevor creates moments that are evocative and incandescent. His messages linger and hang in the air."
> —*People* magazine

"William Trevor is among the most accessible of Britain's most distinguished contemporary writers. His prose is enviably simple and clear. He writes for the reader rather than for himself or his literary peers. . . . If you don't know his work, *After Rain* would be a fine place to get acquainted."
> —*Providence Sunday Journal*

"William Trevor shows himself as a master of domestic horror. . . . Behind closed doors, people live lives of quiet happiness or despair, and within their own walls unspeakable horrors scuttle around."
> —Clare Boylan, *The Independent* (London)

"The stories here are among Trevor's finest."
> —John Banville, *The New York Review of Books*

"A poet of prose fictions . . . Whether he is writing about a boy who believes he has been kissed by the ghost of a female saint, or the two rival wives of a blind piano-tuner . . . or a pair of petty thieves plying their trade in the suburbs of Dublin, the manner of these stories is specific and shocking and matter-of-fact. . . . Trevor at the top of his form."
> —Robert Nye, *The Times* (London)

"A wonderfully affecting new collection of twelve stories by the Anglo-Irish master. . . . Dependably brilliant work from one of Chekhov's most accomplished disciples."
> —*Kirkus Reviews*

"Few writers have so deftly crafted as important or widely praised a body of work that continually illuminates the darkest corners of the human psyche as it grapples with despair and heartbreak."
—*The Miami Herald*

"Trevor writes of the piercing tragedies and grand dramas of everyday life in a tone through which the echoes of Chekhov and Maupassant are clearly audible. Like theirs, Trevor's view of the world is melancholy and unsparing.... But like them, too, his work is supported by a fundamental optimism, a belief in the indomitability of the human spirit and rare sustaining power of love."
—Jane Shilling, *Sunday Telegraph* (London)

"Trevor is that rare thing, a writer who can be serious without being ponderous, who can be somber without being depressing.... *After Rain* is the work of a master storyteller at the top of his form."
—*The Raleigh News & Observer*

"There are two frequently expressed opinions about William Trevor. One is that he is the best writer in the world. The other, more modest claim, is that he is the best writer of short stories.... After reading one of his novels ... there is no resisting the temptation to simply call him the best and be done with it. But after reading his short stories ... the feeling is apt to take hold that the more modest claim of best writer of short stories is so demonstrable that there is no need to try to go further."
—*Newark Star Ledger*

"This collection of stories is archetypal Trevor—entertaining, uplifting, sobering." —Penelope Lively, *Spectator* (London)

"There are few contemporary writers who can match the quiet dignity with which Trevor imbues his writing, or his command of the short story form.... *After Rain* shows Trevor as a brilliant master of his craft."
—*Publishers Weekly*

"In a season crowded with accomplished short stories, Trevor's are the best of the bunch, a dozen marvels of subtle brilliance by one of the century's most underappreciated stylists."
—*Time Out New York*

PENGUIN BOOKS

AFTER RAIN

William Trevor was born in Mitchelstown, Co. Cork, in 1928, and spent his childhood in provincial Ireland. He attended a number of Irish schools and, later, Trinity College, Dublin. He is a member of the Irish Academy of Letters. Among his books are *The Old Boys* (1964), winner of the Hawthornden Prize; *The Children of Dynmouth* (1976) and *Fools of Fortune* (1983), both winners of the Whitbread Award; *The Silence in the Garden* (1989), winner of the Yorkshire Post Book of the Year Award; and *Two Lives* (1991; comprising the novellas *Reading Turgenev*, shortlisted for the Booker Prize, and *My House in Umbria*), which was named by *The New York Times* as one of the ten best books of the year. His eight volumes of stories were brought together in *The Collected Stories* (1992), chosen by *The New York Times* as one of the ten best books of the year. Many of his stories have appeared in *The New Yorker* and other magazines. He has also written plays for the stage, and for radio and television. In 1977 William Trevor was named honorary Commander of the British Empire in recognition of his services to literature. His most recent novel, *Felicia's Journey* (1994), won the Whitbread Book of the Year Award and the Sunday Express prize. It was a national bestseller. William Trevor lives in Devon, England.

By the Same Author

After
Rain

—

WILLIAM
TREVOR

PENGUIN BOOKS

PENGUIN BOOKS

Published by the Penguin Group
Penguin Putnam Inc., 375 Hudson Street,
New York, New York 10014, U.S.A.
Penguin Books Ltd, 27 Wrights Lane, London W8 5TZ, England
Penguin Books Australia Ltd, Ringwood, Victoria, Australia
Penguin Books Canada Ltd, 10 Alcorn Avenue,
Toronto, Ontario, Canada M4V 3B2
Penguin Books (N.Z.) Ltd, 182–190 Wairau Road,
Auckland 10, New Zealand

Penguin Books Ltd, Registered Offices:
Harmondsworth, Middlesex, England

First published in the United States of America by Viking Penguin,
a division of Penguin Books USA Inc. 1996
Published in Penguin Books 1997

3   5   7   9   10   8   6   4

"The Piano Tuner's Wives," "Timothy's Birthday," "After Rain," "Widows,"
"Lost Ground," and "A Day" first appeared in *The New Yorker*; "Child's Play"
in *The Oldie*; "A Bit of Business" in *Antaeus*; "Gilbert's Mother" in *Harper's*;
and "The Potato Dealer" in *Spectator*.

THE LIBRARY OF CONGRESS HAS CATALOGUED THE HARDCOVER AS FOLLOWS:
Trevor, William, 1928–
[Short stories. Selections]
After rain: stories/William Trevor.
p.   cm.
ISBN 0-670-87007-2 (hc.)
ISBN 0 14 02.5834 5 (pbk.)
I. Title.
PR6070.R4A6   1996
823´.914—dc20   96–17282

Printed in the United States of America
Set in Bulmer

Contents

After
Rain

The Piano Tuner's Wives

Violet married the piano tuner when he was a young man. Belle married him when he was old.

There was a little more to it than that, because in choosing Violet to be his wife the piano tuner had rejected Belle, which was something everyone remembered when the second wedding was announced. 'Well, she got the ruins of him anyway,' a farmer of the neighbourhood remarked, speaking without vindictiveness, stating a fact as he saw it. Others saw it similarly, though most of them would have put the matter differently.

The piano tuner's hair was white and one of his knees became more arthritic with each damp winter that passed. He had once been svelte but was no longer so, and he was blinder than on the day he married Violet – a Thursday in 1951, June 7th. The shadows he lived among now had less shape and less density than those of 1951.

'I will,' he responded in the small Protestant church of St Colman, standing almost exactly as he had stood on that other afternoon. And Belle, in her fifty-ninth year, repeated the words her one-time rival had spoken before this altar also. A decent interval had elapsed; no one in the church considered that the memory of Violet had not been honoured, that her passing had not been distressfully mourned. '. . . and with all my worldly goods I thee endow,' the piano tuner stated, while his new wife thought she would like to be standing beside him in white instead of suitable wine-red. She had not attended the first wedding, although she had been invited. She'd kept herself occupied that day, whitewashing the chicken shed, but even so she'd wept. And tears or not, she was more beautiful – and younger by almost five years – than the bride who so vividly occupied her thoughts as she battled with her jealousy. Yet he had preferred Violet – or the prospect of the house that would one day become hers, Belle told herself bitterly in the chicken shed, and the little bit of money there was, an easement in a blind man's existence. How understandable, she was reminded later on, whenever she saw Violet guiding him as they walked, whenever she thought of Violet making everything work for him, giving him a life. Well, so could she have.

As they left the church the music was by Bach, the organ played by someone else today, for usually it was his task. Groups formed in the small graveyard that was scattered around the small grey building, where the piano tuner's father and mother were buried, with ancestors on his father's side from previous generations. There would be tea and a few drinks for any of the wedding guests who cared to make the journey to the house, two miles away, but some said goodbye now, wishing the pair happiness. The piano tuner shook hands that were familiar to him, seeing in his mental eye faces that his first wife had described for him. It was the depth of summer, as in 1951, the sun warm on his forehead and his cheeks, and on his body through the heavy wedding clothes. All his life he had known this graveyard, had first felt the letters on the stones as a child, spelling out to his mother the names of his father's family. He and Violet had not had children themselves, though they'd have liked them. He was her child, it had been said, a statement that was an irritation for Belle whenever she heard it. She would have given him children, of that she felt certain.

'I'm due to visit you next month,' the old bridegroom reminded a woman whose hand still lay in his, the owner of a Steinway, the only one among all the pianos he tuned. She played it beautifully.

He asked her to whenever he tuned it, assuring her that to hear was fee enough. But she always insisted on paying what was owing.

'Monday the third I think it is.'

'Yes, it is, Julia.'

She called him Mr Dromgould: he had a way about him that did not encourage familiarity in others. Often when people spoke of him he was referred to as the piano tuner, this reminder of his profession reflecting the respect accorded to the possessor of a gift. Owen Francis Dromgould his full name was.

'Well, we had a good day for it,' the new young clergyman of the parish remarked. 'They said maybe showers but sure they got it wrong.'

'The sky –?'

'Oh, cloudless, Mr Dromgould, cloudless.'

'Well, that's nice. And you'll come on over to the house, I hope?'

'He must, of course,' Belle pressed, then hurried through the gathering in the graveyard to reiterate the invitation, for she was determined to have a party.

*

Some time later, when the new marriage had settled into a routine, people wondered if the piano tuner would begin to think about retiring. With a bad knee, and being sightless in old age, he would readily have been forgiven in the houses and the convents and the school halls where he applied his skill. Leisure was his due, the good fortune of company as his years slipped by no more than he deserved. But when, occasionally, this was put to him by the loquacious or the inquisitive he denied that anything of the kind was in his thoughts, that he considered only the visitation of death as bringing any kind of end. The truth was, he would be lost without his work, without his travelling about, his arrival every six months or so in one of the small towns to which he had offered his services for so long. No, no, he promised, they'd still see the white Vauxhall turning in at a farm gate or parked for half an hour in a convent play-yard, or drawn up on a verge while he ate his lunch-time sandwiches, his tea poured out of a Thermos by his wife.

It was Violet who had brought most of this activity about. When they married he was still living with his mother in the gate-lodge of Barnagorm House. He had begun to tune pianos – the two in Barnagorm House, another in the town of Barnagorm, and one in a farmhouse he walked to four miles away. In those days he was a charity because he was blind, was now and again asked to repair the sea-grass seats of stools or chairs, which was an ability he had acquired, or to play at some function or other the violin his mother had bought him in his childhood. But when Violet married him she changed his life. She moved into the gate-lodge, she and his mother not always agreeing but managing to live together none the less. She possessed a car, which meant she could drive him to wherever she discovered a piano, usually long neglected. She drove to houses as far away as forty miles. She fixed his charges, taking the con-sumption of petrol and wear and tear to the car into account. Effi-ciently, she kept an address book and marked in a diary the date of each next tuning. She recorded a considerable improvement in earnings, and saw that there was more to be made from the playing of the violin than had hitherto been realized: Country-and-Western evenings in lonely public houses, the crossroads platform dances of summer – a practice that in 1951 had not entirely died out. Owen Dromgould delighted in his violin and would play it anywhere, for profit or not. But Violet was keen on the profit.

So the first marriage busily progressed, and when eventually Violet inherited her father's house she took her husband to live there. Once a farmhouse, it was no longer so, the possession of the land that gave it this title having long ago been lost through the fondness for strong drink that for generations had dogged the family but had not reached Violet herself.

'Now, tell me what's there,' her husband requested often in their early years, and Violet told him about the house she had brought him to, remotely situated on the edge of the mountains that were blue in certain lights, standing back a bit from a bend in a lane. She described the nooks in the rooms, the wooden window shutters he could hear her pulling over and latching when wind from the east caused a draught that disturbed the fire in the room once called the parlour. She described the pattern of the carpet on the single flight of stairs, the blue-and-white porcelain knobs of the kitchen cupboards, the front door that was never opened. He loved to listen. His mother, who had never entirely come to terms with his affliction, had been impatient. His father, a stableman at Barnagorm House who'd died after a fall, he had never known. 'Lean as a greyhound,' Violet described his father from a photograph that remained.

She conjured up the big, cold hall of Barnagorm House. 'What we walk around on the way to the stairs is a table with a peacock on it. An enormous silvery bird with bits of coloured glass set in the splay of its wings to represent the splendour of the feathers. Greens and blues,' she said when he asked the colour, and yes, she was certain it was only glass, not jewels, because once, when he was doing his best with the badly flawed grand in the drawing-room, she had been told that. The stairs were on a curve, he knew from going up and down them so often to the Chappell in the nursery. The first landing was dark as a tunnel, Violet said, with two sofas, one at each end, and rows of unsmiling portraits half lost in the shadows of the walls.

'We're passing Doocey's now,' Violet would say. 'Father Feely's getting petrol at the pumps.' Esso it was at Doocey's, and he knew how the word was written because he'd asked and had been told. Two different colours were employed; the shape of the design had been compared with shapes he could feel. He saw, through Violet's eyes, the gaunt façade of the McKirdys' house on the outskirts of Oghill. He saw the pallid face of the stationer in Kiliath. He saw his mother's eyes closed in death, her hands crossed on her breast. He saw the mountains, blue on some days, misted away to grey on others. 'A primrose isn't flamboyant,' Violet said. 'More like straw or country butter, with a spot of colour in the middle.' And he would nod, and know. Soft blue like smoke, she said about the mountains; the spot in the middle more orange than red. He knew no more about smoke than what she had told him also, but he could tell those sounds. He knew what red was, he insisted, because of the sound; orange because you could taste it. He could see red in the Esso sign and the orange spot in the primrose. 'Straw' and 'country butter' helped him, and when Violet called Mr Whitten gnarled it was enough. A certain Mother Superior was austere. Anna Craigie was fanciful about the eyes. Thomas in the sawmills was a streel. Bat Conlon had the forehead of the Merricks' retriever, which was stroked every time the Merricks' Broadwood was attended to.

*

Between one woman and the next, the piano tuner had managed without anyone, fetched by the possessors of pianos and driven to their houses, assisted in his shopping and his housekeeping. He felt he had become a nuisance to people, and knew that Violet would not have wanted that. Nor would she have wanted the business she built up for him to be neglected because she was no longer there. She was proud that he played the organ in St Colman's Church. 'Don't ever stop doing that,' she whispered some time before she whispered her last few words, and so he went alone to the church. It was on a Sunday, when two years almost had passed, that the romance with Belle began.

Since the time of her rejection Belle had been unable to shake off her jealousy, resentful because she had looks and Violet hadn't, bitter because it seemed to her that the punishment of blindness was a punishment for her too. For what else but a punishment could you call the dark the sightless lived in? And what else but a punishment was it that darkness should be thrown over her beauty? Yet there had been no sin to punish and they would have been a handsome couple, she and Owen Dromgould. An act of grace it would have been, her beauty given to a man who did not know that it was there.

It was because her misfortune did not cease to nag at her that Belle remained unmarried. She assisted her father first and then her brother in the family shop, making out tickets for the clocks and watches that were left in for repair, noting the details for the engraving of sports trophies. She served behind the single counter, the Christmas season her busy time, glassware and weather indicators the most popular wedding gifts, cigarette lighters and inexpensive jewellery for lesser occasions. In time, clocks and watches required only the fitting of a battery, and so the gift side of the business was expanded. But while that time passed there was no man in the town who lived up to the one who had been taken from her.

Belle had been born above the shop, and when house and shop became her brother's she continued to live there. Her brother's children were born, but there was still room for her, and her position in the shop itself was not usurped. It was she who kept the chickens at the back, who always had been in charge of them, given the responsibility on her tenth birthday: that, too, continued. That she lived with a disappointment had long ago become part of her, had made her what she was for her nieces and her nephew. It was in her eyes, some people noted, even lent her beauty a quality that enhanced it. When the romance began with the man who had once rejected her, her brother and his wife considered she was making a mistake, but did not say so, only laughingly asked if she intended taking the chickens with her.

That Sunday they stood talking in the graveyard when the

handful of other parishioners had gone. 'Come and I'll show you the graves,' he said, and led the way, knowing exactly where he was going, stepping on to the grass and feeling the first gravestone with his fingers. His grandmother, he said, on his father's side, and for a moment Belle wanted to feel the incised letters herself instead of looking at them. They both knew, as they moved among the graves, that the parishioners who'd gone home were very much aware of the two who had been left behind. On Sundays, ever since Violet's death, he had walked to and from his house, unless it happened to be raining, in which case the man who drove old Mrs Purtill to church took him home also. 'Would you like a walk, Belle?' he asked when he had shown her his family graves. She said she would.

*

Belle didn't take the chickens with her when she became a wife. She said she'd had enough of chickens. Afterwards she regretted that, because every time she did anything in the house that had been Violet's she felt it had been done by Violet before her. When she cut up meat for a stew, standing with the light falling on the board that Violet had used, and on the knife, she felt herself a follower. She diced carrots, hoping that Violet had sliced them. She bought new wooden spoons because Violet's had shrivelled away so. She painted the upright rails of the banisters. She painted the inside of the front door that was never opened. She disposed of the stacks of women's magazines, years old, that she found in an upstairs cupboard. She threw away a frying-pan because she considered it unhygienic. She ordered new vinyl for the kitchen floor. But she kept the flowerbeds at the back weeded in case anyone coming to the house might say she was letting the place become run-down.

There was always this dichotomy: what to keep up, what to change. Was she giving in to Violet when she tended her flowerbeds? Was she giving in to pettiness when she threw away a frying-pan and three wooden spoons? Whatever Belle did she afterwards doubted herself. The dumpy figure of Violet, grey-haired as she had been in the end, her eyes gone small in the plumpness of her face, seemed irritatingly to command. And the unseeing husband they shared, softly playing his violin in one room or another, did not know that his first wife had dressed badly, did not know she had thickened and become sloppy, did not know she had been an unclean cook. That Belle was the one who was alive, that she was offered all a man's affection, that she plundered his other woman's possessions and occupied her bedroom and drove her car, should have been enough. It should have been everything, but as time went on it seemed to Belle to be scarcely anything at all. He had become set in ways that had been allowed and hallowed in a marriage of nearly forty years: that was what was always there.

A year after the wedding, as the couple sat one lunchtime in the car which Belle had drawn into the gateway to a field, he said:

'You'd tell me if it was too much for you?'

'Too much, Owen?'

'Driving all over the county. Having to get me in and out. Having to sit there listening.'

'It's not too much.'

'You're good the way you've patience.'

'I don't think I'm good at all.'

'I knew you were in church that Sunday. I could smell the perfume you had on. Even at the organ I could smell it.'

'I'll never forget that Sunday.'

'I loved you when you let me show you the graves.'

'I loved you before that.'

'I don't want to tire you out, with all the traipsing about after pianos. I could let it go, you know.'

He would do that for her, her thought was as he spoke. He

wasn't much for a woman, he had said another time: a blind man moving on towards the end of his days. He confessed that when first he wanted to marry her he hadn't put it to her for more than two months, knowing better than she what she'd be letting herself in for if she said yes. 'What's that Belle look like these days?' he had asked Violet a few years ago, and Violet hadn't answered at first. Then apparently she'd said: 'Belle still looks a girl.'

'I wouldn't want you to stop your work. Not ever, Owen.'

'You're all heart, my love. Don't say you're not good.'

'It gets me out and about too, you know. More than ever in my life. Down all those avenues to houses I didn't know were there. Towns I've never been to. People I never knew. It was restricted before.'

The word slipped out, but it didn't matter. He did not reply that he understood about restriction, for that was not his style. When they were getting to know one another, after that Sunday by the church, he said he'd often thought of her in her brother's jeweller's shop, wrapping up what was purchased there, as she had wrapped for him the watch he bought for one of Violet's birthdays. He'd thought of her putting up the grilles over the windows in the evenings and locking the shop door, and then going upstairs to sit with her brother's family. When they were married she told him more: how most of the days of her life had been spent, only her chickens her own. 'Smart in her clothes,' Violet had added when she said the woman he'd rejected still looked a girl.

There hadn't been any kind of honeymoon, but a few months after he had wondered if travelling about was too much for her he took Belle away to a seaside resort where he and Violet had many times spent a week. They stayed in the same boarding-house, the Sans Souci, and walked on the long, empty strand and in lanes where larks scuttered in and out of the fuchsia, and on the cliffs. They drank in Malley's public house. They lay in autumn sunshine on the dunes.

'You're good to have thought of it.' Belle smiled at him, pleased because he wanted her to be happy.

'Set us up for the winter, Belle.'

She knew it wasn't easy for him. They had come to this place because he knew no other; he was aware before they set out of the complication that might develop in his emotions when they arrived. She had seen that in his face, a stoicism that was there for her. Privately, he bore the guilt of betrayal, stirred up by the smell of the sea and seaweed. The voices in the boarding-house were the voices Violet had heard. For Violet, too, the scent of honeysuckle had lingered into October. It was Violet who first said a week in the autumn sun would set them up for the winter: that showed in him, also, a moment after he spoke the words.

'I'll tell you what we'll do,' he said. 'When we're back we'll get you the television, Belle.'

'Oh, but you –'

'You'd tell me.'

They were walking near the lighthouse on the cape when he said that. He would have offered the television to Violet, but Violet must have said she wouldn't be bothered with the thing. It would never be turned on, she had probably argued; you only got silliness on it anyway.

'You're good to me,' Belle said instead.

'Ah no, no.'

When they were close enough to the lighthouse he called out and a man called back from a window. 'Hold on a minute,' the man said, and by the time he opened the door he must have guessed that the wife he'd known had died. 'You'll take a drop?' he offered when they were inside, when the death and the remarriage had been mentioned. Whiskey was poured, and Belle felt that the three glasses lifted in salutation were an honouring of her, although this was not said. It rained on the way back to the boarding-house, the last evening of the holiday.

'Nice for the winter,' he said as she drove the next day through rain that didn't cease. 'The television.'

When it came, it was installed in the small room that once was called the parlour, next to the kitchen. This was where mostly they sat, where the radio was. A fortnight after the arrival of the television set Belle acquired a small black sheepdog that a farmer didn't want because it was afraid of sheep. This dog became hers and was always called hers. She fed it and looked after it. She got it used to travelling with them in the car. She gave it a new name, Maggie, which it answered to in time.

But even with the dog and the television, with additions and disposals in the house, with being so sincerely assured that she was loved, with being told she was good, nothing changed for Belle. The woman who for so long had taken her husband's arm, who had guided him into rooms of houses where he coaxed pianos back to life, still claimed existence. Not as a tiresome ghost, some unforgiving spectre uncertainly there, but as if some part of her had been left in the man she'd loved.

Sensitive in ways that other people weren't, Owen Dromgould continued to sense his second wife's unease. She knew he did. It was why he had offered to give up his work, why he'd taken her to Violet's seashore and borne there the guilt of his betrayal, why there was a television set now, and a sheepdog. He had guessed why she'd re-covered the kitchen floor. Proudly, he had raised his glass to her in the company of a man who had known Violet. Proudly, he had sat with her in the dining-room of the boarding-house and in Malley's public house.

Belle made herself remember all that. She made herself see the bottle of John Jameson taken from a cupboard in the lighthouse, and hear the boarding-house voices. He understood, he did his best to comfort her; his affection was in everything he did. But Violet would have told him which leaves were on the turn. Violet would have reported that the tide was going out or coming in. Too late Belle realized that. Violet had been his blind man's vision. Violet had left her no room to breathe.

*

One day, coming away from the house that was the most distant they visited, the first time Belle had been there, he said:

'Did you ever see a room as sombre as that one? Is it the holy pictures that do it?'

Belle backed the car and straightened it, then edged it through a gateway that, thirty years ago, hadn't been made wide enough.

'Sombre?' she said on a lane like a riverbed, steering around the potholes as best she could.

'We used wonder could it be they didn't want anything colourful in the way of a wallpaper in case it wasn't respectful to the pictures.'

Belle didn't comment on that. She eased the Vauxhall out on to the tarred road and drove in silence over a stretch of bogland. Vividly she saw the holy pictures in the room where Mrs Grenaghan's piano was: Virgin and Child, Sacred Heart, St Catherine with her lily, the Virgin on her own, Jesus in glory. They hung against nondescript brown; there were statues on the mantelpiece and on a corner shelf. Mrs Grenaghan had brought tea and biscuits to that small, melancholy room, speaking in a hushed tone as if the holiness demanded that.

'What pictures?' Belle asked, not turning her head, although she might have, for there was no other traffic and the bog road was straight.

'Aren't the pictures still in there? Holy pictures all over the place?'

'They must have taken them down.'

'What's there then?'

Belle went a little faster. She said a fox had come from nowhere, over to the left. It was standing still, she said, the way foxes do.

'You want to pull up and watch him, Belle?'

'No. No, he's moved on now. Was it Mrs Grenaghan's daughter who played that piano?'

'Oh, it was. And she hasn't seen that girl in years. We used say the holy pictures maybe drove her away. What's on the walls now?'

'A striped paper.' And Belle added: 'There's a photograph of the daughter on the mantelpiece.'

Some time later, on another day, when he referred to one of the sisters at the convent in Meena as having cheeks as flushed as an eating apple, Belle said that that nun was chalky white these days, her face pulled down and sunken. 'She has an illness so,' he said.

Suddenly more confident, not caring what people thought, Belle rooted out Violet's plants from the flowerbeds at the back, and grassed the flowerbeds over. She told her husband of a change at Doocey's garage: Texaco sold instead of Esso. She described the Texaco logo, the big red star and how the letters of the word were arranged. She avoided stopping at Doocey's in case a conversation took place there, in case Doocey were asked if Esso had let him down, or what. 'Well, no, I wouldn't call it silvery exactly,' Belle said about the peacock in the hall of Barnagorm house. 'If they cleaned it up I'd say it's brass underneath.' Upstairs, the sofas at each end of the landing had new loose covers, bunches of different-coloured chrysanthemums on them. 'Well no, not *lean*, I wouldn't call him that,' Belle said with the photograph of her husband's father in her hand. 'A sturdy face, I'd say.' A schoolteacher whose teeth were once described as gusty had false teeth now, less of a mouthful, her smile sedate. Time had apparently drenched the bright white of the McKirdys' façade, almost a grey you'd call it. 'Forget-me-not blue,' Belle said one day, speaking of the mountains that were blue when the weather brought that colour out. 'You'd hardly credit it.' And it was never again said in the piano tuner's house that the blue of the mountains was the subtle blue of smoke.

*

Owen Dromgould had run his fingers over the bark of trees. He could tell the difference in the outline of their leaves; he could tell the thorns of gorse and bramble. He knew birds from their song, dogs from their bark, cats from the touch of them on his legs. There were the letters on the gravestones, the stops of the organ, his violin. He could see red, berries on holly and cotoneaster. He could smell lavender and thyme.

All that could not be taken from him. And it didn't matter if, overnight, the colour had worn off the kitchen knobs. It didn't matter if the china light-shade in the kitchen had a crack he hadn't heard about before. What mattered was damage done to something as fragile as a dream.

The wife he had first chosen had dressed drably: from silence and inflexions – more than from words – he learned that now. Her grey hair straggled to her shoulders, her back was a little humped. He poked his way about, and they were two old people when they went out on their rounds, older than they were in their ageless happiness. She wouldn't have hurt a fly, she wasn't a person you could be jealous of, yet of course it was hard on a new wife to be haunted by happiness, to be challenged by the simplicities there had been. He had given himself to two women; he hadn't withdrawn himself from the first, he didn't from the second.

Each house that contained a piano brought forth its contradictions. The pearls old Mrs Purtill wore were opals, the pallid skin of the stationer in Kiliath was freckled, the two lines of oaks above Oghill were surely beeches? 'Of course, of course,' Owen Dromgould agreed, since it was fair that he should do so. Belle could not be blamed for making her claim, and claims could not be made without damage or destruction. Belle would win in the end because the living always do. And that seemed fair also, since Violet had won in the beginning and had had the better years.

A Friendship

Jason and Ben – fair-haired, ten and eight respectively – found that a bucketful of ready-mixed concrete was too heavy to carry, so they slopped half of it out again. Sharing the handle of the bucket, they found they could now manage to convey their load, even though Ben complained. They carried it from the backyard, through the kitchen and into the hall, to where their father's golf-bag stood in a corner. The bag, recently new, contained driver, putter and a selection of irons, as well as tees, balls and gloves in various side pockets. A chair stood in front of the bag, on to which both boys now clambered, still precariously grasping the bucket. They had practised; they knew what they were doing.

After five such journeys the golf-bag was half full of liquid concrete, the chair carried back to the kitchen, and small splashes wiped from the tiles of the hall. Then the workmen who were re-building the boiler-shed returned from the Red Lion, where they had spent their lunchtime.

'We know nothing about it,' Jason instructed his brother while they watched the workmen shovelling more sand and cement into the concrete-mixer.

'Nothing about it,' Ben obediently repeated.

'Let's go and watch *Quick Draw*.'

'OK.'

When their mother returned to the house half an hour later, with her friend Margy, it was Margy who noticed the alien smell in the hall. Being inquisitive by nature she poked about, and was delighted when she discovered the cause, since she considered that the victim of the joke would benefit from the inroads it must inevitably make on his pomposity. She propped the front door open for a while so that the smell of fresh concrete would drift away. The boys' mother, Francesca, didn't notice anything.

'Come on!' Francesca called, and the boys came chattering into the kitchen for fish fingers and peas, no yoghurt for Ben because someone had told him it was sour milk, Ribena instead of hot chocolate for Jason.

'You did your homework before you turned on that television?' Francesca asked.

'Yes,' Ben lied.

'I bet you didn't,' Margy said, not looking up from the magazine she was flipping through. Busy with their food, Francesca didn't hear that.

Francesca was tall, with pale, uncurled hair that glistened in the sunlight. Margy was small and dark, brown-eyed, with thin, fragile fingers. They had known one another more or less all their lives.

'Miss Martindale's mother died,' Ben divulged, breaking the monotony of a silence that had gathered. 'A man interfered with her.'

'My God!' Francesca exclaimed, and Margy closed the magazine, finding little of interest in it.

'Miss Martindale saw him,' Jason said. 'Miss Martindale was just arriving and she saw this figure. First she said a black man, then she said he could be any colour.'

'You mean, Miss Martindale came to school today after something like that?'

'Miss Martindale has a sense of duty,' Jason said.

'Actually she was extremely late,' Ben said.

'But how ghastly for the poor woman!'

Miss Martindale was a little thing with glasses, Francesca told her friend, not at all up to sustaining something like this. Ben said all the girls had cried, that Miss Martindale herself had cried, that her face was creased and funny because actually she'd been crying all night.

Margy watched Jason worrying in case his brother went too far. They could have said it was Miss Martindale who'd been murdered; they had probably intended to, but had changed it to her mother just in time. It wouldn't have worked if they'd said Miss Martindale because sooner or later Miss Martindale would be there at a parents' evening.

'*Neighbours* now,' Jason said.

'Started actually,' Ben pointed out.

Margy lit a cigarette when she was alone with Francesca, and suggested a drink. She poured gin and Cinzano Bianco for both of them, saying she didn't believe there was much wrong with Miss Martindale's mother, and Francesca, bewildered, looked up from the dishes she was washing. Then, without a word, she left the kitchen and Margy heard her noisily reprimanding her sons, declaring that it was cruel and unfeeling to say people were dead who weren't. Abruptly, the sound of the television ceased and there were footsteps on the stairs. Margy opened a packet of Mignons Morceaux.

Francesca and Margy could remember being together in a garden when they were two, meeting there for the first time, they afterwards presumed, Francesca smiling, Margy scowling. Later, during their schooldays, they had equally disliked a sarcastic teacher with gummy false teeth, and had considered the visiting mathematics man handsome, though neither of them cared for his subject. Later still Francesca became the confidante of Margy's many love affairs, herself confiding from the calmer territory of marriage. Margy brought mild adventure into Francesca's life, and Francesca recognized that Margy would never suffer the loneliness she feared herself, the vacuum she was certain there would be if her children had not been born. They telephoned one another almost every day, to chat inconsequentially or to break some news, it didn't matter which. Their common ground was the friendship itself: they shared some tastes and some opinions, but only some.

When Philip – father of Jason and Ben – arrived in the house an hour later Francesca and Margy had moved to the sitting-room, taking with them the gin, the Cinzano Bianco, what remained of the Mignons Morceaux, and their glasses.

'Hi, Philip,' Margy greeted him, and watched while he kissed Francesca. He nodded at Margy.

'Margy's going to make us her paella,' Francesca said, and Margy knew that when Philip turned away it was to hide a sigh. He didn't like her paella. He didn't like the herb salad she put together to go with it. He had never said so, being too polite for that, but Margy knew.

'Oh, good,' Philip said.

He hadn't liked the whiff of cigarettes that greeted him when he opened the hall-door, nor the sound of voices that had come from the sitting-room. He didn't like the crumpled-up Mignons Morceaux packet, the gin bottle and the vermouth bottle on his bureau, Margy's lipstained cigarette-ends, the way Margy was lolling on the floor with her shoes off. Margy didn't have to look to see if this small cluster of aversions registered in Philip's tight features. She knew it didn't; he didn't let things show.

'They've been outrageous,' Francesca said, and began about Miss Martindale's mother.

Margy looked at him then. Nothing moved in his lean face; he didn't blink before he turned away to stand by the open french windows. *Golf and gardening* he gave as his hobbies in *Who's Who*.

'Outrageous?' he repeated eventually, an inflection in his tone – unnoticed by Francesca – suggesting to Margy that he questioned the use of this word in whatever domestic sense it was being employed. He liked being in *Who's Who*: it was a landmark in his life. One day he would be a High Court judge: everyone said that.

One day he would be honoured with a title, and Francesca would be also because she was his wife.

'I was really furious with them,' Francesca said.

He didn't know what all this was about, he couldn't remember who Miss Martindale was because Francesca hadn't said. Margy smiled at her friend's husband, as if to indicate her understanding of his bewilderment, as if in sympathy. It would be the weekend before he discovered that his golf-clubs had been set in concrete.

'Be cross with them,' Francesca begged, 'when you go up. Tell them it was a horrid thing to say about anyone.'

He nodded, his back half turned on her, still gazing into the garden.

'Have a drink, Philip,' Margy suggested because it was better usually when he had one, though not by much.

'Yes,' Philip said, but instead of going to pour himself something he walked out into the garden.

'I've depressed him,' Francesca commented almost at once. 'He's not in the house more than a couple of seconds and I'm nagging him about the boys.'

She followed her husband into the garden, and a few minutes later, when Margy was gathering together the ingredients for her paella in the kitchen, she saw them strolling among the shrubs he so assiduously tended as a form of relaxation after his week in the courts. The boys would be asleep by the time he went up to say goodnight to them and if they weren't they'd pretend; he wouldn't have to reprimand them about something he didn't understand. Of course all he had to do was to ask a few questions, but he wouldn't because anything domestic was boring for him. It was true that when Mrs Sleet's headscarf disappeared from the back-door pegs he asked questions – precise and needling, as if still in one of his court-rooms. And he had reached a conclusion: that the foolish woman must have left her headscarf on the bus. He rejected out of hand Francesca's belief that a passing thief had found the back door open and reached in for what immediately caught his eye. No one would want such an item of clothing, Philip had maintained, no thief in his senses. And of course he was right. Margy remembered the fingernails of the two boys engrained with earth, and guessed that the headscarf had been used to wrap up Mabel, Ben's guinea-pig, before confining her to the gerbil and guinea-pig graveyard beside the box hedge.

Smoking while she chopped her herb salad – which he would notice, and silently deplore, as he passed through the kitchen – Margy wondered why Philip's presence grated on her so. He was handsome in his way and strictly speaking he wasn't a bore, nor did he arrogantly impose his views. It was, she supposed, that he was simply a certain kind of man, inimical to those who were not of his ilk, unable to help himself even. Several times at gatherings in this house Margy had met Philip's legal colleagues and was left in no doubt that he was held in high regard, that he commanded both loyalty and respect. Meticulous, fair, precise as a blade, he was feared by his court-room opponents, and professionally he did not have a silly side: in his anticipated heights of success, he would surely not become one of those infamous elderly judges who flapped about from court to court, doling out eccentric sentences, lost outside the boundaries of the real world. On the other hand, among a circle of wives and other women of his acquaintance, he was known as 'Bad News', a reference to the misfortune of being placed next to him at a dinner party. On such occasions, when he ran out of his stock of conversational questions he tried no more, and displayed little interest in the small-talk that was, increasingly desperately, levelled at him. He had a way of saying, flatly, 'I see' when a humorous anecdote, related purely for his entertainment, came to an end. And through all this he was not ill at ease; others laboured, never he.

As Margy dwelt on this catalogue of Philip's favourable and less favourable characteristics, husband and wife passed by the kitchen window. Francesca smiled through the glass at her friend, a way of saying that all was well again after her small *faux pas* of nagging too soon after her husband's return. Then Margy heard the french windows of the sitting-room being closed and Philip's footsteps passed through the hall, on their way to the children's bedroom.

Francesca came in to help, and to open wine. Chatting about other matters, she laid out blue tweed mats on the Formica surface of the table, and forks and other cutlery and glasses. It wasn't so much Philip, Margy thought; had he been married to someone else, she was sure she wouldn't have minded him so. It was the marriage itself: her friend's marriage astonished her.

*

Every so often Margy and Francesca had lunch at a local bistro called La Trota. It was an elegant rendezvous, though inexpensive and limited in that it offered only fish and a few Italian cheeses. Small and bright and always bustling, its decorative tone was set by a prevalence of aluminium and glass, and matt white surfaces. Its walls were white also, its floor colourfully tiled – a crustacea pattern that was repeated on the surface of the bar. Two waitresses – one from Sicily, the other from Salerno – served at the tables. Usually, Francesca and Margy had Dover sole and salad, and a bottle of Gavi.

La Trota was in Barnes, not far from Bygone Antiques, where Margy was currently employed. In the mornings Francesca helped in the nearby Little Acorn Nursery School, which both Jason and Ben had attended in the past. Margy worked in Bygone Antiques because she was, 'for the time being' as she put it, involved with its proprietor, who was, as she put it also, 'wearily married'.

On the Tuesday after Philip's discovery of the concrete in his golf-bag they lunched outside, at one of La Trota's three pavement tables, the June day being warm and sunny. Two months ago, when Margy had begun her stint at Bygone Antiques, Francesca was delighted because it meant they would be able to see more of one another: Margy lived some distance away, over the river, in Pimlico.

'He was livid of course,' Francesca reported. 'I mean, they said it was a *joke.*'

Margy laughed.

'I mean, how could it be a joke? And how could it be a joke to say Miss Martindale's mother was dead?'

'Did Mrs Sleet's headscarf ever turn up?'

'You don't think they stole Mrs Sleet's headscarf?'

'What I think is you're lucky to have lively children. Imagine if they never left the straight and narrow.'

'How lovely it would be!'

Francesca told of the quarrel that had followed the discovery of the golf-bag, the worst quarrel of her marriage, she said. She had naturally been blamed because it was clear from what had occurred that the boys had been alone in the house when they shouldn't have been. Philip wanted to know how this had happened, his court-room manner sharpening his questioning and his argument. How long had his children been latchkey children, and for what reason were they so?

'I wish I'd had girls,' Francesca complained pettishly. 'I often think that now.'

Their Dover soles arrived. 'Isn't no help,' the Sicilian waitress muttered crossly as she placed the plates in front of them. 'Every day we say too many tables. Twice times, maybe hundred times. Every day they promise. Next day the same.'

'Ridiculous.' Margy smiled sympathetically at the plump Sicilian girl. 'Poor Francesca,' she sympathized with her friend, taking a piece of lettuce in her fingers.

But Francesca, still lost in the detail of the rumpus there had been, hardly heard. An hour at the very least, Philip was arguing all over again; possibly two hours they must have been on their own. It was absurd to spend all morning looking after children in a nursery school and all afternoon neglecting your own. That Jason and Ben had been sent back early that day, that she had been informed of this beforehand and had forgotten, that she would naturally have been there had she remembered: all this was mere verbiage apparently, not worth listening to, much less considering. Mrs Sleet left the house at one o'clock on the dot, and Francesca was almost always back by three, long before the boys returned. Jason and Ben were not latchkey children; she had made a mistake on a particular day; she had forgotten; she was sorry.

'If you're asked to do anything,' had been the final shaft, 'it's to see to the children, Francesca. You have all the help in the house you ask for. I don't believe you want for much.' The matter of Andy Konig's video had been brought up, and Jason's brazen insistence at the time that it was for Social Studies. Andy Konig's video wouldn't have been discovered if it hadn't become stuck in the video-player, repeating an endless sequence of a woman undressing in a doctor's surgery. 'You didn't even look to see what was on it,' had been the accusation, repeated now, which of course was true. It was over, all this was followed by; they would forget it; he'd drive to the Mortlake tip with the golf-bag, there'd be no television for thirty days, no sweets, cake or biscuits. 'I would ask you to honour that, Francesca.' As the rumpus subsided, she had sniffed back the last of her tears, not replying.

'Oh Lord!' she cried in frustration at La Trota. 'Oh Lord, the guilt!'

Cheering her friend up, Margy insisted that they change the subject. She recounted an episode that morning in the antique shop, a woman she knew quite well, titled actually, slipping a Crown Derby piece into a shopping bag. She touched upon her love affair with the shop's proprietor, which was not going well.

One of these days they should look up Sebastian, she idly suggested. 'It's time I settled down,' she murmured over their cappuccinos.

'I'm not sure that Sebastian . . .' Francesca began, her concentration still lingering on the domestic upset.

'I often wonder about Sebastian,' Margy said.

*

Afterwards, in the antique shop, it was cool among the polished furniture, the sofa-tables and revolving libraries, the carved pew ends and sewing cabinets. The collection of early Victorian wall clocks – the speciality of the wearily married proprietor – ticked gracefully; occupying most of the window space, the figure of Christ on a donkey cast shadows that were distorted by the surfaces they reached. A couple in summer clothes, whom Margy had earlier noticed in La Trota, whispered among these offerings. A man with someone else's wife, a wife with someone else's husband: Margy could tell at once. 'Of course,' she'd said when they asked if they might look around, knowing that they wouldn't buy anything: people in such circumstances rarely did. 'Oh, isn't that pretty!' the girl whispered now, taken with a framed pot-lid – an 1868 rifle contest in Wimbledon, colourfully depicted.

'Forty-five pounds I think,' Margy replied when she was asked the price, and went away to consult the price book. One day, she believed, Francesca would pay cruelly for her passing error of judgement in marrying the man she had. Hearing about the fuss over the golf-bag, she had felt that instinct justified: the marriage would go from bad to worse, from fusses and quarrels over two little boys' obstreperousness to fusses and quarrels about everything else, a mound of pettiness accumulating, respect all gone and taking with it what once had seemed like love. Too often Margy had heard from married men the kind of bitter talk that was the evidence of this, and had known she would have heard still worse from the wives they spoke of. Yet just as often, she fairly admitted, people made a go of it. They rarely said so because of course that wasn't interesting, and sometimes what was making a go of it one day was later, in the divorce courts, called tedium.

'Look in again,' she invited the summery couple as they left without the pot-lid.

'Thanks a lot,' the man said, and the girl put her head on one side, a way of indicating, possibly, that she was grateful also.

Margy had mentioned Sebastian at lunch, not because she wished to look him up on her own account but because it occurred to her that Sebastian was just the person to jolly Francesca out of her gloom. Sebastian was given to easy humour and exuded an agreeableness that was pleasant to be exposed to. Since he had once, years ago, wanted to marry Francesca, Margy often imagined what her friend's household would have been like with Sebastian there instead.

'Hullo,' her employer said, entering the shop with a Regency commode and bringing with him the raw scent of the stuff he dabbed on his underarms, and a whiff of beer.

'Handsome,' Margy remarked, referring to the commode.

*

It was Francesca who telephoned Sebastian. 'A voice from the past,' she said and he knew immediately, answering her by name. He was pleased she'd rung, he said, and all the old telephone inflections, so familiar once, registered again as their conversation progressed. 'Margy?' he repeated when Francesca suggested lunch for three. He sounded disappointed, but Francesca hardly noticed that, caught up with so much else, wondering how in fact it would affect everything if, somehow or other, Sebastian and Margy hit it off now, as she and Sebastian had in the past. She knew Sebastian hadn't married. He had been at her wedding; she would have been at his, their relationship transformed on both sides then. Like Margy, Francesca imagined, Sebastian had free-wheeled through the time that had passed since. At her wedding she had guessed they would lose touch, and in turn he had probably guessed that that was, sensibly, what she wanted. Sebastian, who had never honoured much, honoured that. When marriage occurs, the past clams up, lines are drawn beneath a sub-total.

'Well, well, well,' he murmured at La Trota, embracing Margy first and then Francesca. There were flecks of grey in his fair hair; his complexion was a little ruddier. But his lazy eyes were touched with the humour that both women remembered, and his big hands seemed gentle on the table.

'You haven't changed a bit,' Sebastian said, choosing Francesca to say it to.

*

'Oh heavens, I've said the wrong thing!' a woman exclaimed in horror at a party, eyes briefly closed, a half-stifled breath drawn in.

'No, not at all,' Philip said.

'It's just that –'

'We see Sebastian quite often, actually.'

He wondered why he lied, and realized then that he was saving face. He had been smiling when the woman first mentioned Sebastian, when she'd asked how he was these days. Almost at once the woman had known she was saying the wrong thing, her expression adding more and more as she stumbled on, endeavouring to muddle with further words her original statement about trying unsuccessfully to catch Francesca's and Sebastian's attention in Wigmore Street.

'So very nice,' the woman floundered, hot-faced. 'Sebastian.'

A mass of odds and ends gathered in Philip's mind. 'The number of this taxi is 22003,' he had said after he'd kissed Francesca in it. Their first embrace, and he had read out the number from the enamel disc on the back of the driver's seat, and neither of them had since forgotten it. The first present Francesca gave him was a book about wine which to this day he wouldn't lend to people.

No one was as honest as Francesca, Philip reflected as the woman blundered on: it was impossible to accept that she had told lies, even through reticence. Yet now there were – as well – the odds and ends of the warm summer that had just passed, all suddenly transformed. Dates and the order of events glimmered in Philip's brain; he was good at speedy calculation and accurately recalling. Excuses, and explanations, seemed elaborate in the bare light of the hindsight that was forced upon him. A note falling to the floor had been too hastily retrieved. There were headaches and cancellations and apologies. There'd been a difference in Francesca that hadn't at the time seemed great but seemed great now.

'Yes, Sebastian's very nice,' Philip said.

*

'It's over,' Francesca said in their bedroom. 'It's been over for weeks, as a matter of fact.'

Still dressed, sitting on the edge of their bed, Francesca was gazing at the earrings she'd just taken off, two drops of amber in the palm of her hand. Very slowly she made a pattern of them, moving them on her palm with the forefinger of her other hand. In their bedroom the light was dim, coming only from a bedside lamp. Francesca was in the shadows.

'It doesn't make much difference that it's over,' Philip said. 'That's not the point.'

'I know.'

'You've never told lies before.'

'Yes, I know. I hated it.'

Even while it was happening, she had sometimes thought it

wasn't. And for the last few lonely weeks it had felt like madness, as indeed it had been. Love was madness of a kind, Margy had said once, years ago, and Francesca at that time hadn't understood: being fond of Sebastian in the past, and loving Philip, had never been touched by anything like that. Her recent inexplicable aberration felt as if she had taken time off from being herself, and now was back again where she belonged, not understanding, as bouts of madness are never understood.

'That's hardly an explanation,' her husband said when she endeavoured to relate some of this.

'No, I know it isn't. I would have told you about it quite soon; I couldn't not tell you.'

'I didn't even notice I wasn't loved.'

'You are loved, Philip. I ended it. And besides, it wasn't much.'

A silence grew between them. 'I love you,' Sebastian had said no longer ago than last June, and in July and in August and September also. And she had loved him too. More than she loved anyone else, more than she loved her children: that thought had been there. Yet now she could say it wasn't much.

As though he guessed some part of this, Philip said : 'I'm dull compared to him. I'm grey and dull.'

'No.'

'I mooch about the garden, I mooch about on golf courses. You've watched me becoming greyer in middle age. You don't want to share our middle age.'

'I never think things like that. Never, Philip.'

'No one respects a cuckold.'

Francesca did not reply. She was asked if she wanted a divorce. She shook her head. Philip said:

'One day in the summer you and Margy were talking about a key when I came in, and you stopped and said, "Have a drink, darling?" I remember now. Odd, how stuff's dredged up. The key to Margy's flat, I think?'

Francesca stood up. She placed her amber earrings in the drawer of their bedside table and slowly began to undress. Philip, standing by the door, said he had always trusted her, which he had said already.

'I'm sorry I hurt you, Philip.' Tiredly, she dropped into a cliché, saying that Sebastian had been banished as a ghost may be, that at last she had got him out of her system. But what she said had little relevance, and mattered so slightly that it was hardly heard. What was there between them were the weekends Philip had been in charge of the children because Francesca needed a rest and had gone, with Margy, to some seaside place where Margy was looking after a house for people who were abroad. And the evenings she helped to paint Margy's flat. And the mornings that were free after she gave up helping in the Little Acorn Nursery School. Yes, that key had been Margy's, Francesca said. Left for her under a stone at the foot of a hydrangea bush in Pimlico, in a block of flats' communal garden: she didn't add that. Found there with a frisson of excitement: nor that, either.

'I'm ashamed because I hurt you,' she said instead. 'I'm ashamed because I was selfish and a fool.'

'You should have married him in the first place.'

'It was you I wanted to marry, Philip.'

Francesca put on her nightdress, folded her underclothes, and draped her tights over the back of a chair. She sat for a moment in front of her dressing-table looking-glass, rubbing cold cream into her face, stroking away the moisture of tears.

'You have every right to turn me out,' she said, calmly now. 'You have every right to have the children to yourself.'

'D'you want that?'

'No.'

He hated her, Francesca thought, but she sensed as well that this hatred was a visitation only, that time would take it away. And she guessed that Philip sensed this also, and resented it that something as ordinary as passing time could destroy the high emotions he was experiencing now. Yet it was the truth.

'It happened by chance,' Francesca said, and made it all sound worse. 'I thought that Margy and Sebastian – oh well, it doesn't matter.'

They quarrelled then. The tranquillity that had prevailed was shattered in a moment, and their children woke and heard the raised voices. Underhand, hole-in-corner, shabby, untrustworthy, dishonourable, grubby: these words had never described Francesca in the past, but before the light of morning they were used. And to add a garnish to all that was said, there was Margy's treachery too. She had smiled and connived even though there was nothing in it for her.

Francesca countered when her spirit returned, after she'd wept beneath this lash of accusation, and the condemnation of her friend. Philip had long ago withdrawn himself from the family they were: it was an irony that her misbehaviour had pulled him back, that occasionally he had had to cook beans and make the bacon crispy for their children, and see that their rooms were tidied, their homework finished. At least her lies had done that.

But there was no forgiveness when they dressed again. Nothing was over yet. Forgiveness came later.

*

There was a pause after Francesca made her bleak statement in La Trota. Margy frowned, beginning to lean across the table because the hubbub was considerable that day. No longer working at Bygone Antiques, she had come across London specially.

'Drop me?' Margy said, and Francesca nodded: that was her husband's request.

The restaurant was full of people: youngish, well-to-do, men together, women together, older women with older men, older men with girls, five businessmen at a table. The two waitresses hurried with their orders, too busy to mutter their complaints about the overcrowding.

'But why on earth?' Margy said. 'Why should you?'

Expertly the Sicilian waitress opened the Gavi and splashed some into their glasses. '*Buon appetito,*' she briskly wished them, returning in a moment with the sole. They hadn't spoken since Margy had asked her questions.

'He has a right to something, is that it?' Margy squeezed her chunk of lemon over the fish and then on to her salad. 'To punish?'

'He thinks you betrayed him.'

'*I* betrayed him? *I?*'

'It's how Philip feels. No, not a punishment,' Francesca said. 'Philip's not doing that.'

'What then?'

Francesca didn't reply, and Margy poked at the fish on her plate, not wanting to eat it now. Some vague insistence hovered in her consciousness: some truth, not known before and still not known, was foggily sensed.

'I don't understand this,' Margy said. 'Do you?'

A salvaging of pride was a wronged husband's due: she could see that and could understand it, but there was more to this than pride.

'It's how Philip feels,' Francesca said again. 'It's how all this has left him.'

She knew, Margy thought: whatever it was, it had been put to Francesca in Philip's court-room manner, pride not even mentioned. Then, about to ask and before she could, she knew herself: the forgiving of a wife was as much as there could be. How could a wronged husband, so hurt and so aggrieved, forgive a treacherous friend as well?

'Love allows forgiveness,' Francesca said, guessing what

Margy's thoughts were, which was occasionally possible after years of intimacy.

But Margy's thoughts were already moving on. Every time she played with his children he would remember the role she had played that summer: she could hear him saying it, and Francesca's silence. Every present she brought to the house would seem to him to be a traitor's bribe. The summer would always be there, embalmed in the friendship that had made the deception possible – the key to the flat, the seaside house, the secret kept and then discovered. What the marriage sought to forget the friendship never would because the summer had become another part of it. The friendship could only be destructive now, the subject of argument and quarrels, the cause of jealousy and pettiness and distress: this, Philip presented as his case, his logic perfect in all its parts. And again Margy could hear his voice.

'It's unfair, Francesca.'

'It only seems so.' Francesca paused, then said: 'I love Philip, you know.'

'Yes, I do know.'

In the crowded bistro their talk went round in muddled circles, the immediacy of the blow that had been struck at them lost from time to time in the web of detail that was their friendship, lost in days and moments and occasions not now recalled but still remembered, in confidences, and conversation rattling on, in being different in so many ways and that not mattering. Philip, without much meaning to, was offering his wife's best friend a stature she had not possessed before in his estimation: she was being treated with respect. But that, of course, was neither here nor there.

'What was her name,' Margy asked, 'that woman with the gummy teeth?'

'Hyatt. Miss Hyatt.'

'Yes, of course it was.'

There was a day when Margy was cross and said Francesca was

not her friend and never would be, when they were six. There was the time the French girl smoked when they were made to take her for a walk on the hills behind their boarding-school. Margy fell in love with the boy who brought the papers round. Francesca's father died and Margy read Tennyson to cheer her up. They ran out of money on their cycling tour and borrowed from a lorry driver who got the wrong idea. Years later Francesca was waiting afterwards when Margy had her abortion.

'You like more cappuccinos?' the Sicilian waitress offered, placing fresh cups of coffee before them because they always had two each.

'Thanks very much,' Francesca said.

In silence, in the end, they watched the bistro emptying. The two waitresses took the tablecloths off and lifted the chairs on to the tables in order to mop over the coloured patterns of shellfish on the tiled floor. Quite suddenly a wave of loneliness caused Margy to shiver inwardly, as the chill news of death does.

'Perhaps with a bit of time,' she began, but even as she spoke she knew that time would make no difference. Time would simply pass, and while it did so Francesca's guilt would still be there; she would always feel she owed this sacrifice. They would not cheat; Francesca would not do that a second time. She would say that friends meeting stealthily was ridiculous, a grimier deception than that of lovers.

'It's all my fault,' Francesca said.

Hardly perceptibly, Margy shook her head, knowing it wasn't. She had gone too far; she had been sillily angry because of a children's prank. She hadn't sought to knock a marriage about, only to give her friend a treat that seemed to be owing to her, only to rescue her for a few summer months from her exhausting children and her exhausting husband, from Mrs Sleet and the Little Acorn Nursery School, from her too-safe haven. But who was to blame, and what intentions there had been, didn't matter in the least now.

'In fairness,' Francesca said, 'Philip has a point of view. Please say you see it, Margy.'

'Oh yes, I see it.' She said it quickly, knowing she must do so before it became impossible to say, before all generosity was gone. She knew, too, that one day Francesca would pass on this admission to her husband because Francesca was Francesca, who told the truth and was no good at deception.

'See you soon,' the Sicilian waitress called out when eventually they stood up to go.

'Yes,' Margy agreed, lying for her friend as well. On the pavement outside La Trota they stood for a moment in a chill November wind, then moved away in their two different directions.

Timothy's Birthday

They made the usual preparations. Charlotte bought a small leg of lamb, picked purple broccoli and sprigs of mint. All were Timothy's favourites, purchased every year for April 23rd, which this year was a Thursday. Odo ensured that the gin had not gone too low: a gin and tonic, and then another one, was what Timothy liked. Odo did not object to that, did not in fact object to obtaining the gin specially, since it was not otherwise drunk in the house.

They were a couple in their sixties who had scarcely parted from each other in the forty-two years of their marriage. Odo was tall, thin as a straw, his bony features receding into a freckled dome on which little hair remained. Charlotte was small and still pretty, her grey hair drawn back and tidy, her eyes an arresting shade of blue. Timothy was their only child.

Deciding on a fire, Odo chopped up an old seed-box for kindling and filled a basket with logs and turf. The rooks were cawing and chattering in the high trees, their nests already in place – more of them this year, Odo noticed, than last. The cobbles of the yard were still damp from a shower. Grass, occasionally ragwort or a dock, greened them in patches. Later perhaps, when Timothy had gone, he'd go over them with weed-killer, as he did every year in April. The outhouses that bounded the yard required attention also, their wooden doors rotted away at the bottom, the whitewash of their stucco gone grey, brambles growing through their windows. Odo resolved that this year he would rectify matters, but knew, even as the thought occurred, that he would not.

'Cold?' Charlotte asked him as he passe   through the kitchen, and he said yes, a little chilly outside. The kitchen was never cold because of the range. A long time ago they had been going to re-place it with a secondhand Aga Charlotte had heard about, but when it came to the point Odo hadn't wanted to and anyway there hadn't been the funds.

In the drawing-room Odo set the fire, crumpling up the pages of old account books because no newspaper was delivered to the house and one was rarely bought: they had the wireless and the television, which kept them up with things. The account books were of no use to anyone, belonging entirely to the past, to the time of Odo's grandfather and generations earlier. Kept for the purpose in a wall-cupboard by the fireplace, their dry pages never failed to burn well. *Slating: £2. 15s.,* Odo read as he arranged the kindling over the slanted calligraphy. He struck a match and stacked on logs and turf. Rain spattered against the long-paned windows; a sudden gust of wind tumbled something over in the garden.

Charlotte pressed rosemary into the slits she'd incised in the lamb. She worked swiftly, from long experience knowing just what she was doing. She washed the grease from her fingertips under a running tap and set aside what remained of the rosemary, even though it was unlikely that she would have a use for it: she hated throwing things away.

The oven was slow; although it was still early, the meat would have to go in within half an hour, and potatoes to roast – another Timothy favourite – at eleven. The trifle, gooey with custard and raspberry jam and jelly – a nursery pudding – Charlotte had made the night before. When Timothy came he chopped the mint for the mint sauce, one of the first of his childhood tasks. He'd been a plump little boy then.

*

'I can't go,' Timothy said in the flat that had recently been left to him by Mr Kinnally.

Eddie didn't respond. He turned the pages of the *Irish Times*, wishing it were something livelier, the *Star* or the *Express*. With little interest he noticed that schools' entrance tests were to be abolished and that there was to be a canine clean-up, whatever that was, in Limerick.

'I'll drive you down,' he offered then. His own plans were being shattered by this change of heart on the part of Timothy, but he kept the annoyance out of his voice. He had intended to gather his belongings together and leave as soon as he had the house to himself: a bus out to the N4, the long hitch-hike, then start all over again. 'No problem to drive you down,' he said. 'No problem.'

The suggestion wasn't worth a reply, Timothy considered. It wasn't even worth acknowledgement. No longer plump at thirty-three, Timothy wore his smooth fair hair in a ponytail. When he smiled, a dimple appeared in his left cheek, a characteristic he cultivated. He was dressed, this morning, as he often was, in flannel trousers and a navy-blue blazer, with a plain blue tie in the buttoned-down collar of his plain blue shirt.

'I'd get out before we got there,' Eddie offered. 'I'd go for a walk while you was inside.'

'What I'm saying is I can't face it.'

There was another silence then, during which Eddie sighed without making a sound. He knew about the birthday tradition because as the day approached there had been a lot of talk about it. The house called Coolattin had been described to him: four miles from the village of Baltinglass, a short avenue from which the entrance gates had been removed, a faded green hall-door, the high grass in the garden, the abandoned conservatory. And Timothy's people – as Timothy always called them – had been as graphically presented: Charlotte's smile and Odo's solemnity, their fondness for one another evident in how they spoke and acted, their fondness for Coolattin. Charlotte cut what remained of Odo's hair, and Timothy said you could tell. And you could tell, even when they were not in their own surroundings, that they weren't well-to-do: all they wore was old. Hearing it described, Eddie had visualized in the drawing-room the bagatelle table between the windows and Odo's ancestor in oils over the fireplace, the buttoned green sofa, the rugs that someone had once brought back from India or Egypt. Such shreds of grace and vigour from a family's past took similar form in the dining-room that was these days used only once a year, on April 23rd, and in the hall and on the staircase wall, where further portraits hung. Except for the one occupied by Odo and Charlotte, the bedrooms were musty, with patches of grey damp on the ceilings, and plaster fallen away. Timothy's, in which he had not slept for fifteen years, was as he'd left it, but in one corner the wallpaper had billowed out and now was curling away from the surface. The kitchen, where the television and the wireless were, where Odo and Charlotte ate all their meals except for lunch on Timothy's birthday, was easily large enough for this general purpose: a dresser crowded with crockery and a lifetime's odds and ends, a long scrubbed table on the flagged floor, with upright kitchen chairs around it. As well, there were the two armchairs Odo had brought in from the drawing-room, a washing-machine Timothy had given his mother, wooden draining-boards on either side of the sink, ham hooks in the panelled ceiling, and a row of bells on springs above the door to the scullery. A cheerful place, that kitchen, Eddie estimated, but Timothy said it was part and parcel, whatever he meant by that.

'Would you go, Eddie? Would you go down and explain, say I'm feeling unwell?'

Eddie hesitated. Then he said:

'Did Mr Kinnally ever go down there?'

'No, of course he didn't. It's not the same.'

Eddie walked away when he heard that reply. Mr Kinnally had been far too grand to act as a messenger in that way. Mr Kinnally had given Timothy birthday presents: the chain he wore on his wrist, shoes and pullovers. 'Now, I don't want you spending your money on me,' Timothy had said a day or two ago. Eddie, who hadn't been intending to, didn't even buy a card.

In the kitchen he made coffee, real coffee from Bewley's, measured into the percolator, as Timothy had shown him. Instant gave you cancer, Timothy maintained. Eddie was a burly youth of nineteen, with curly black hair to which he daily applied gel. His eyes, set on a slant, gave him a furtive air, accurately reflecting his nature, which was a watchful one, the main chance being never far out of his sights. When he got away from the flat in Mountjoy Street he intended to go steady for a bit, maybe settle down with some decent girl, maybe have a kid. Being in the flat had suited him for the five months he'd been here, even if – privately – he didn't much care for certain aspects of the arrangement. Once, briefly, Eddie had been apprenticed to a plumber, but he hadn't much cared for that either.

He arranged cups and saucers on a tray and carried them to the sitting-room, with the coffee and milk, and a plate of croissants. Timothy had put a CD on, the kind of music Eddie didn't care for but never said so, sonorous and grandiose. The hi-fi was Bang and Olufsen, the property of Mr Kinnally in his lifetime, as everything in the flat had been.

'Why not?' Timothy asked, using the telecommander on the arm of his chair to turn the volume down. 'Why not, Eddie?'

'I couldn't do a thing like that. I'll drive you –'

'I'm not going down.'

Timothy reduced the volume further. As he took the cup of coffee Eddie offered him, his two long eye-teeth glistened the way they sometimes did, and the dimple formed in his cheek.

'All I'm asking you to do is pass a message on. I'd take it as a favour.'

'The phone –'

'There's no phone in that place. Just say I couldn't make it due to not feeling much today.'

Timothy broke in half a croissant that had specks of bacon in it, the kind he liked, that Eddie bought in Fitz's. A special favour, he softly repeated, and Eddie sensed more pressure in the words. Timothy paid, Timothy called the tune. Well, two can play at that game, Eddie said to himself, and calculated his gains over the past five months.

*

The faded green hall-door, green also on the inside, was sealed up because of draughts. You entered the house at the back, crossing the cobbled yard to the door that led to the scullery.

'He's here,' Charlotte called out when there was the sound of a car, and a few minutes later, as Odo arrived in the kitchen from the hall, there were footsteps in the scullery passage and then a hesitant knock on the kitchen door. Since Timothy never knocked, both thought this odd, and odder still when a youth they did not know appeared.

'Oh,' Charlotte said.

'He's off colour,' the youth said. 'A bit naff today. He asked me would I come down and tell you.' The youth paused, and added then: 'On account you don't have no phone.'

Colour crept into Charlotte's face, her cheeks becoming pink. Illness worried her.

'Thank you for letting us know,' Odo said stiffly, the dismissive note in his tone willing this youth to go away again.

'It's nothing much, is it?' Charlotte asked, and the youth said seedy, all morning in the toilet, the kind of thing you wouldn't trust yourself with on a car journey. His name was Eddie, he explained, a friend of Timothy's. Or more, he added, a servant really, depending how you looked at it.

Odo tried not to think about this youth. He didn't want

Charlotte to think about him, just as for so long he hadn't wanted her to think about Mr Kinnally. 'Mr Kinnally died,' Timothy said on this day last year, standing not far from where the youth was standing now, his second gin and tonic on the go. 'He left me everything, the flat, the Rover, the lot.' Odo had experienced relief that this elderly man was no longer alive, but had been unable to prevent himself from considering the inheritance ill-gotten. The flat in Mountjoy Street, well placed in Dublin, had had its Georgian plasterwork meticulously restored, for Mr Kinnally had been that kind of person. They'd heard about the flat, its contents too, just as Eddie had heard about Coolattin. Timothy enjoyed describing things.

'His tummy played up a bit once,' Charlotte was saying with a mother's recall. 'We had a scare. We thought appendicitis. But it wasn't in the end.'

'He'll rest himself, he'll be all right.' The youth was mumbling, not meeting the eye of either of them. Shifty, Odo considered, and dirty-looking. The shoes he wore, once white, the kind of sports shoes you saw about these days, were filthy now. His black trousers hung shapelessly; his neck was bare, no sign of a shirt beneath the red sweater that had some kind of animal depicted on it.

'Thank you,' Odo said again.

'A drink?' Charlotte offered. 'Cup of coffee? Tea?'

Odo had known that would come. No matter what the circumstances, Charlotte could never help being hospitable. She hated being thought otherwise.

'Well. . .' the youth began, and Charlotte said:

'Sit down for a minute.' Then she changed her mind and suggested the drawing-room because it was a pity to waste the fire.

Odo didn't feel angry. He rarely did with Charlotte. 'I'm afraid we haven't any beer,' he said as they passed through the hall, both coffee and tea having been rejected on the grounds that they would be troublesome to provide, although Charlotte had denied that. In the drawing-room what there was was the sherry that stood near the bagatelle, never touched by either of them, and Timothy's Cork gin, and two bottles of tonic.

'I'd fancy a drop of Cork,' the youth said. 'If that's OK.'

Would Timothy come down another day? Charlotte wanted to know. Had he said anything about that? It was the first time his birthday had been missed. It was the one occasion they spent together, she explained.

'Cheers!' the youth exclaimed, not answering the questions, appearing to Odo to be simulating denseness. 'Great,' he complimented when he'd sipped the gin.

'Poor Timothy!' Charlotte settled into the chair she always occupied in the drawing-room, to the left of the fire. The light from the long-paned windows fell on her neat grey hair and the side of her face. One of them would die first, Odo had thought again in the night, as he often did now. He wanted it to be her; he wanted to be the one to suffer the loneliness and the distress. It would be the same for either of them, and he wanted it to be him who had to bear the painful burden.

*

Sitting forward, on the edge of the sofa, Eddie felt better when the gin began to glow.

'Refreshing,' he said. 'A drop of Cork.'

The day Mr Kinnally died there were a number of them in the flat. Timothy put the word out and they came that night, with Mr Kinnally still stretched out on his bed. In those days Eddie used to come in the mornings to do the washing-up, after Mr Kinnally had taken a fancy to him in O'Connell Street. An hour or so in the mornings, last night's dishes, paid by the hour; nothing of the other, he didn't even know about it then. On the day of the death Timothy shaved the dead face himself and got Mr Kinnally into his tweeds. He sprayed a little Krizia Uomo, and changed the slippers for lace-ups. He made him as he had been, except of course for the closed eyes, you couldn't do anything about that. 'Come back in the evening, could you?' he had requested Eddie, the first time there'd been such a summons. 'There'll be a few here.' There were more than a few, paying their respects in the bedroom, and afterwards in the sitting-room Timothy put on the music and they just sat there. From the scraps of conversation that were exchanged Eddie learned that Timothy had inherited, that Timothy was in the dead man's shoes, the new Mr Kinnally. 'You'd never think of moving in, Eddie?' Timothy suggested a while later, and afterwards Eddie guessed that that was how Timothy himself had been invited to Mountjoy Street, when he was working in the newsagent's in Ballsbridge, on his uppers as he used to say.

'As a matter of fact,' Eddie said in the drawing-room, 'I never touch a beer.'

Timothy's father – so thin and bony in Eddie's view that when he sat down you'd imagine it would cause him pain – gave a nod that was hardly a nod at all. And the mother said she couldn't drink beer in any shape or form. Neither of them was drinking now.

'Nothing in the gassy line suits me,' Eddie confided. It wasn't easy to know what to say. Timothy had said they'd ask him to stop for a bite of grub when they realized he'd come down specially; before he knew where he was they'd have turned him into the birthday boy. Odo his father's name was, Timothy had passed on, extraordinary really.

'Nice home you got here,' Eddie said. 'Nice place.'

A kind of curiosity had brought him to the house. Once Timothy had handed him the keys of the Rover, he could so easily have driven straight to Galway, which was the city he had decided to make for, having heard a few times that it was lively. But instead he'd driven as directed, to Baltinglass, and then by minor roads to Coolattin. He'd head for Galway later: the N80 to Portlaoise was what the map in the car indicated, then on to Mountmellick and Tullamore, then Athlone. Eddie didn't know any of those towns. Dublin was his place.

'Excuse me,' he said, addressing Timothy's father, lowering his voice. 'D'you have a toilet?'

*

Charlotte had years ago accepted her son's way of life. She had never fussed about it, and saw no reason to. Yet she sympathized with Odo, and was a little infected by the disappointment he felt. 'This is how Timothy, wishes to live,' she used, once, gently to argue, but Odo would look away, saying he didn't understand it, saying – to Timothy, too – that he didn't want to know. Odo was like that; nothing was going to change him. Coolattin had defeated him, and he had always hoped, during Timothy's childhood, that Timothy would somehow make a go of it where he himself had failed. In those days they had taken in overnight guests, but more recently too much went wrong in the house, and the upkeep was too burdensome, to allow that to continue without financial loss. Timothy, as a child, had been both imaginative and practical: Odo had seen a time in the future when there would be a family at Coolattin again, when in some clever way both house and gardens would be restored. Timothy had even talked about it, describing it, as he liked to: a flowery hotel, the kitchen filled with modern utensils and machines, the bedrooms fresh with paint, new wallpapers and fabrics. Odo could recall a time in his own childhood when visitors came and went, not paying for their sojourn, of course, but visitors who paid would at least be something.

'You'll have to ask him if he wants to stay to lunch,' Charlotte said when Timothy's friend had been shown where the downstairs lavatory was.

'Yes, I know.'

*

'I'd fix that toilet for you,' Eddie offered, explaining that the flow to the bowl was poor. Nothing complicated, corrosion in the pipe. He explained that he'd started out as a plumber once, which was why he knew a thing or two. 'No sweat,' he said.

When lunch was mentioned he said he wouldn't want to trouble anyone, but they said no trouble. He picked up a knife from the drinks table and set off with his gin and tonic to the downstairs lavatory to effect the repair.

'It's very kind of you, Eddie.' Timothy's mother thanked him and he said honestly, no sweat.

When he returned to the drawing-room, having poked about in the cistern with the knife, the room was empty. Rain was beating against the windows. The fire had burnt low. He poured another dollop of gin into his glass, not bothering with the tonic since that would have meant opening the second bottle. Then the old fellow appeared out of nowhere with a basket of logs, causing Eddie to jump.

'I done it best I could,' Eddie said, wondering if he'd been seen with the bottle actually in his hand and thinking he probably had. 'It's better than it was anyway.'

'Yes,' Timothy's father said, putting a couple of the logs on to the fire and a piece of turf at the back. 'Thanks very much.'

'Shocking rain,' Eddie said.

Yes, it was heavy now, the answer came, and nothing more was said until they moved into the dining-room. 'You sit there, Eddie,' Timothy's mother directed, and he sat as she indicated, between the two of them. A plate was passed to him with slices of meat on it, then vegetable dishes with potatoes and broccoli in them.

'It was a Thursday, too, the day Timothy was born,' Timothy's mother said. 'In the newspaper they brought me it said something about a royal audience with the Pope.'

1959, Eddie calculated, fourteen years before he saw the light of day himself. He thought of mentioning that, but decided they wouldn't want to know. The drop of Cork had settled in nicely, the only pity was they hadn't brought the bottle in to the table.

'Nice bit of meat,' he said instead, and she said it was Timothy's favourite, always had been. The old fellow was silent again. The old fellow hadn't believed him when he'd said Timothy was off colour. The old fellow knew exactly what was going on, you could tell that straight away.

'Pardon me a sec.' Eddie rose, prompted by the fact that he knew where both of them were. In the drawing-room he poured himself more gin, and grimaced as he swallowed it. He poured a smaller measure and didn't, this time, gulp it. In the hall he picked up a little ornament that might be silver: two entwined fish he had noticed earlier. In the lavatory he didn't close the door in the hope that they would hear the flush and assume he'd been there all the time.

'Great,' he said in the dining-room as he sat down again.

The mother asked about his family. He mentioned Tallaght, no reason not to since it was what she was after. He referred to the tinker encampment, and said it was a bloody disgrace, tinkers allowed like that. 'Pardon my French,' he apologized when the swearword slipped out.

'More, Eddie?' she was saying, glancing at the old fellow since it was he who was in charge of cutting the meat.

'Yeah, great.' He took his knife and fork off his plate, and after it was handed back to him there was a bit of a silence so he added:

'A new valve would be your only answer in the toilet department. No problem with your pressure.'

'We must get it done,' she said.

It was then – when another silence gathered and continued for a couple of minutes – that Eddie knew the mother had guessed also: suddenly it came into her face that Timothy was as fit as a fiddle. Eddie saw her glance once across the table, but the old fellow was intent on his food. On other birthday occasions

47

Timothy would have talked about Mr Kinnally, about his 'circle', which was how the friends who came to the flat were always described. Blearily, through a fog of Cork gin, Eddie knew all that, even heard the echo of Timothy's rather high-pitched voice at this same table. But talk about Mr Kinnally had never been enough.

''Course it could go on the way it is for years,' Eddie said, the silence having now become dense. 'As long as there's a drop coming through at all you're in business with a toilet cistern.'

He continued about the faulty valve, stumbling over some of the words, his speech thickened by the gin. From time to time the old man nodded, but no sign came from the mother. Her features were bleak now, quite unlike they'd been a moment ago, when she'd kept the conversation going. The two had met when she walked up the avenue of Coolattin one day, looking for petrol for her car: Timothy had reported that too. The car was broken down a mile away; she came to the first house there was, which happened to be Coolattin. They walked back to the car together and they fell in love. A Morris 8, Timothy said; 1950 it was. 'A lifetime's celebration of love,' he'd said that morning, in the toneless voice he sometimes adopted. 'That's what you'll find down there.'

It wouldn't have been enough, either, to have had Kinnally here in person. Kinnally they could have taken; Kinnally would have oozed about the place, remarking on the furniture and the pictures on the walls. Judicious, as he would have said himself, a favourite word. Kinnally could be judicious. Rough trade was different.

'There's trifle,' Eddie heard the old woman say before she rose to get it.

*

The rain came in, heavier now, from the west. A signpost indicated Athlone ahead, and Eddie remembered being informed in a classroom that this town was more or less the centre of Ireland.

He drove slowly. If for any reason a police car signalled him to stop he would be found to have more than the permitted quantity of alcohol in his bloodstream; if for any reason his clothing was searched he would be found to be in possession of stolen property; if he was questioned about the car he was driving he would not be believed when he said it had been earlier lent to him for a purpose.

The Rover's windscreen wipers softly swayed, the glass of the windscreen perfectly clear in their wake. Then a lorry went by, and threw up surface water from the road. On the radio Chris de Burgh sang.

The sooner he disposed of the bit of silver the better, Athlone maybe. In Galway he would dump the car in a car park somewhere. The single effect remaining after his intake of gin was the thirst he experienced, as dry as paper his mouth was.

He turned Chris de Burgh off, not trying another channel. It was one thing to scarper off, as Timothy had from that house: he'd scarpered himself from Tallaght. To turn the knife was different. Fifteen years later to make your point with rough trade and transparent lies, to lash out venomously: how had they cocked him up, how had they hurt him, to deserve it? All the time when there had been that silence they had gone on eating, as if leaving the food on their plates would be too dramatic a gesture. The old man nodded once or twice about the valve, but she had given no sign that she even heard. Very slightly, as he drove, Eddie's head began to ache.

'Pot of tea,' he ordered in Athlone, and said no, nothing else when the woman waited. The birthday presents had remained on the sideboard, not given to him to deliver, as Timothy had said they probably would be. The two figures stood, hardly moving, at the back door while he hurried across the puddles in the cobbled yard to the car. When he looked back they were no longer there.

'Great,' Eddie said when the woman brought the tea, in a metal pot, cup and saucer and a teaspoon. Milk and sugar were already on the pink patterned oilcloth that covered the table top. 'Thanks,' Eddie said, and when he had finished and had paid he walked through the rain, his headache clearing in the chilly air. In the first jeweller's shop the man said he didn't buy stuff. In the second Eddie was questioned so he said he came from Fardrum, a village he'd driven through. His mother had given him the thing to sell, he explained, the reason being she was sick in bed and needed a dose of medicine. But the jeweller frowned, and the trinket was handed back to him without a further exchange. In a shop that had ornaments and old books in the window Eddie was offered a pound and said he thought the entwined fish were worth more. 'One fifty,' came the offer then, and he accepted it.

It didn't cease to rain. As he drove on through it, Eddie felt better because he'd sold the fish. He felt like stopping in Ballinasloe for another pot of tea but changed his mind. In Galway he dropped the car off in the first car park he came to.

*

Together they cleared away the dishes. Odo found that the gin in the drawing-room had been mostly drunk. Charlotte washed up at the sink. Then Odo discovered that the little ornament was gone from the hall and slowly went to break this news, the first communication between them since their visitor had left.

'These things happen,' Charlotte said, after another silence.

*

The rain was easing when Eddie emerged from a public house in Galway, having been slaking his thirst with 7-Up and watching *Glenroe*. As he walked into the city, it dribbled away to nothing. Watery sunshine slipped through the unsettled clouds, brightening the façades in Eyre Square. He sat on a damp seat there, wondering about picking up a girl, but none passed by so he moved away. He didn't want to think. He wasn't meant to understand, being only what he was. Being able to read Timothy like a book was just a way of putting it, talking big when nobody could hear.

Yet the day still nagged, its images stumbling about, persisting in Eddie's bewilderment. Timothy smiled when he said all he was asking was that a message should be passed on. Eddie's own hand closed over the silver fish. In the dining-room the life drained out of her eyes. Rain splashed the puddles in the cobbled yard and they stood, not moving, in the doorway.

On the quays the breeze from the Atlantic dried the pale stone of the houses and cooled the skin of Eddie's face, freshening it also. People had come out to stroll, an old man with a smooth-haired terrier, a couple speaking a foreign language. Seagulls screeched, swooping and bickering in the air. It had been the natural thing to lift the ornament in the hall since it was there and no one was around: in fairness you could call it payment for scraping the rust off the ballcock valve, easily ten quid that would have cost them. 'A lifetime's celebration,' Timothy said again.

*

'It has actually cleared up,' Odo said at the window, and Charlotte rose from the armchair by the fire and stood there with him, looking out at the drenched garden. They walked in it together when the last drops had fallen.

'Fairly battered the delphiniums,' Odo said.

'Hasn't it just.'

She smiled a little. You had to accept what there was; no point in brooding. They had been hurt, as was intended, punished because one of them continued to be disappointed and repelled. There never is fairness when vengeance is evoked: that had occurred to Charlotte when she was washing up the lunchtime dishes, and to Odo when he tidied the dining-room. 'I'm sorry,' he had said, returning to the kitchen with forks and spoons that had not been used. Not turning round, Charlotte had shaken her head.

They were not bewildered, as their birthday visitor was: they easily understood. Their own way of life was so much debris all around them, but since they were no longer in their prime that hardly mattered. Once it would have, Odo reflected now; Charlotte had known that years ago. Their love of each other had survived the vicissitudes and the struggle there had been; not even the bleakness of the day that had passed could affect it.

They didn't mention their son as they made their rounds of the garden that was now too much for them and was derelict in places. They didn't mention the jealousy their love of each other had bred in him, that had flourished into deviousness and cruelty. The pain the day had brought would not easily pass, both were aware of that. And yet it had to be, since it was part of what there was.

Child's Play

Gerard and Rebecca became brother and sister after a turmoil of distress. Each had witnessed it from a different point of view, Gerard in one house, Rebecca in another. Two years of passionate quarrelling, arguing and agreeing, of beginning again, of failure and reconciliation, of final insults and rejection, constituted the peepshow they viewed.

There were no other children of the two wrecked marriages, and when the final period of acrimonious wrangling came to an end there was an unexpected accord as to the division of the families. This, it was decided, would be more satisfactorily decreed by the principals involved than by the divorce courts. Gerard's father, innocent in what had occurred, agreed that Gerard should live with his mother since that was convenient. Rebecca's mother, innocent also, declared herself unfit to raise the child of a marriage she had come to loathe, and declared as well that she could not bring herself to go on living in the house of the marriage. She claimed that suicidal tendencies had developed in her, aggravated by the familiar surroundings: she would suffer the loss of her child for her child's sake. 'She's trying all this on,' the other woman insisted, but in the end it appeared she wasn't, and so the arrangement was made.

On a warm Wednesday afternoon, the day Quest for Fame won the Derby, Gerard's mother married Rebecca's father. Afterwards all four of them stood, eyes tightened against strong sunlight, while someone took a photograph. The two children were of an age, Gerard ten, Rebecca nine. Gerard was dark-haired, quite noticeably thin, with glasses. Rebecca's reddish hair curved roundly about her rounded cheeks. Her eyes were bright, a deep shade of blue. Gerard's, brown, were solemn.

They were neutrally disposed to one another, with neither fondness nor distaste on either side : they did not know one another well. Gerard was an intruder in the house that had been Rebecca's, but this was far less to bear than the departure from it of her mother.

'They'll settle,' Rebecca's father murmured in a teashop after the wedding.

Watching the two children, silent beside one another, his new wife said she hoped so.

*

They did settle. Thrown together as helpless parties in the stipulations of the peace, they became companions. They missed the past; resentment and deprivation drew them close. They talked about the two people whom they visited on Sundays, and how those two, once at the centre of things, were now defeated and displaced.

At the top of the house, attic space had been reclaimed to form a single, low-roofed room with windows to the ground and a new parquet floor that seemed to stretch for ever. The walls were a shade of washed-out primrose, and shafts of sunlight made the pale ash of the parquet seem almost white. There was no furniture. Two bare electric light-bulbs hung from the long, slanted ceiling. This no-man's-land was where Gerard and Rebecca played their game of marriage and divorce. It became a secret game, words fading on their lips if someone entered, politeness disguising their deceit.

Rebecca recalled her mother weeping at lunch, a sudden collapse into ugly distress while she was spooning peas on to Rebecca's plate. 'Whatever's up ?' Rebecca asked, watching as her mother hurried from the table. Her father did not answer, but instead left the dining-room himself, and a few moments later there were the sounds of a quarrel. 'You've made me hate you,' Rebecca's mother kept screaming so shrilly that Rebecca thought the people in the house next door would hear. 'How could you have made me hate you?'

Gerard entered a room and found his mother nursing the side of her face. His father stood at the window, looking out. Behind his back one hand gripped the other as if in restraint. Gerard was frightened and went away, his brief presence unnoticed.

'Think of that child,' Rebecca's mother pleaded in another mood. 'Stay with us if only for that child.'

'You vicious bitch!' This furious accusation stuttered out of Gerard's father, his voice peculiar, his lips trembling in a grimace he could not control.

Such scenes, seeming like the end of everything that mattered, were later surveyed from the unemotional safety of the new companionship. Regret was exorcized, sore places healed; harshness was the saviour. From information supplied by television a world of sin and romance was put together in the empty attic room. 'Think of that child!' Rebecca mimicked, and Gerard adopted his father's grimace the time he called his mother a vicious bitch. It was fun because the erring couple were so virtuous now.

'I can't think how it happened.' Gerard's version of the guilty husband's voice was not convincing, but it passed whatever muster was required. 'I can't think how I could have been such a fool as to marry her in the first place.'

'Poor thing, it's not her fault.'

'It's that that makes it such an awful guilt.' This came from an old black-and-white film and was used a lot because they liked the sound of it.

When romance was to the fore they spoke in whispers, making a murmuring sound when they didn't know what to say. They tried out dance steps in the attic, pretending they were in a dance-hall they called the Ruby Ballroom or a night-club they called the Nitelite, a title they'd seen in neon somewhere. They called a bar the Bee's Knees, which Rebecca said was a name suitable for a bar, although the original was a stocking shop. They called a hotel the Grand Splendide.

'Some sleazy hotel?' Gerard's father had scornfully put it. 'Some sleazy pay-at-the-door hotel for his sleazy one-night stands?'

'No, actually,' the reply had been. 'It was rather grand.'

Downstairs they watched a television serial in which the wronged ones made the kind of fuss that both Gerard and Rebecca had witnessed. The erring ones met in car parks, or on waste land in the early morning.

'Gosh!' Rebecca exclaimed, softly astonished at what was occurring on the screen. 'He took his tongue out of her mouth. Definitely.'

'She's chewing his lips actually.'

'But his tongue —'

'I know.'

'Horrid great thing, it looked.'

'Look, you be Mrs Edwina, Rebecca.'

They turned the television off and climbed to the top of the house, not saying anything on the way. They closed the door behind them.

'OK,' Rebecca said. 'I'm Mrs Edwina.'

Gerard made his bell-ringing sound.

'Oh, go away!' Staring intently into space, Rebecca went on doing so until the sound occurred again. She sighed, and rose from where she'd been sitting on the floor. Grumbling wordlessly, she ran on the spot, descending stairs.

'Yes, what is it, please?'

'Mrs Edwina?'

'Sure I'm Mrs Edwina.'

'I saw your card in the window of that newsagent's. What's it called? The Good News, is it?'

'What d'you want, please?'

'It says you have a room to let.'

'What of it? I was watching *Dallas*.'

'I'm sorry, Mrs Edwina.'

'D'you want to rent a room?'

'I have a use for a room, yes.'

'You'd best come in.'

'Cold evening, Mrs Edwina.'

'I hope you're not planning a love nest. I don't want no filth in my house.'

'Oh, what a lovely little room!'

'If it's for a love nest it'll be ten pounds more per week. Another ten on top of that if you're into call-girls.'

'I can assure you, Mrs Edwina –'

'You read some terrible tales in the papers these days. *Beauty Queen a Call-girl!* it said the other day. Are you fixing to bring in beauty queens?'

'No, no, nothing like that. A friend and myself have been going to the Grand Splendide but it's not the same.'

'You'd be a married man?'

'Yes.'

'I get the picture.'

Rebecca's mother had demanded to know where the sinning had taken place. Gerard's mother, questioned similarly, had revealed that the forbidden meetings had taken place in different locations – once or twice in her lover's office, after hours; over lunch or five-thirty drinks. A hotel was mentioned, and finally a hired room. 'How sordid!' Rebecca's mother cried, then weeping overcame her and Rebecca crept away. But, elsewhere, Gerard remained. He reported that extraordinary exchanges had followed, that great importance was attached to the room that had been specially acquired, great offence taken.

'I'm tired of this ghastly hole.' Rebecca was good at introducing a whine into her tone, a bad-tempered, spoilt-child sound that years ago she'd once or twice tried on in reality before being sharply told to cease immediately.

'Oh, it's not too bad, darling!'

'It's most unpleasant. It's dirty for a start. Look at the sheets, I've never seen sheets as soiled as that. Then Mrs Edwina is dirty. You can see it on her neck. Filthy dirty that woman is.'

'Oh, she's not too bad.'

'There's a smell of meat in the hall. She never opens a window.'

'Darling –'

'I want to live in a house. I want us to be divorced and married again.'

'I know. I know. But there're the children. And there's the awful guilt I feel.'

'What *I* feel is sick in my bowels. Every time I walk in that door I feel it. Every time I look at that filthy wallpaper I get vomit in my throat.'

'We could paint the place out.'

'Let's go to the Bee's Knees for a cocktail. Let's never come back here.'

'But, angel –'

'Our love's not like it used to be. It's not like it was when we went dancing in the Ruby Ballroom. We haven't been to the Nitelite for a year. Nor the Grand Splendide –'

'You wanted a home-from-home.'

'I don't think you love me any more.'

'Of course I do.'

'Then tell Mrs Edwina what she can do with her horrid old room and let's live in a house.'

'But, dear, the children.'

'Drown the brats in a bucket. Make a present of them to Mrs Edwina for all I care. Cement them into a wall.'

'We'll just get into bed for five minutes –'

'I don't want to get into bed today. Not the way those sheets are.'

'OK. We'll go and have a Babycham.'

'I'd love a Babycham.'

When the house was empty except for themselves it was best. It often was empty in the early afternoon, after the woman who came to clean had gone, when Gerard's mother was out, doing the voluntary work she had recently taken up. They wandered from room to room then, poking into everything. Among other items of interest they found letters, some written by Gerard's mother to Rebecca's father, some by him to her. They were in a dressing-table drawer, in a slim cardboard box, with a rubber band around them. Twice the love affair had broken up. Twice there were fare-wells, twice the admission that one could not live without the other. They could not help themselves. They had to meet again.

'My, my,' Rebecca enthused. 'Hot stuff, this.'

*

After their weekend visits to the two who had been wronged Gerard and Rebecca exchanged reports on Sunday evenings. Gerard's father cooked and used the washing-machine, vacuum-cleaned the house, ironed his own shirts, made his bed and weeded the flowerbeds. Rebecca's mother was in a bedsitting-room, a sorry sight. She ate nuts and chocolate while watching the television, saying it wasn't worth cooking for one, not that she minded in the least. She was keeping her end up, Rebecca's mother insisted. 'You can see,' she confided, 'why I didn't think I should look after you, dear? It wasn't because I didn't want you. You're all that's left to me. You're what I live for, darling.'

Rebecca saw perfectly. The bedsitting-room was uncomfortable.

In one corner the bedclothes of a divan, pulled roughly up in day-time, were lumpy beneath a stained pink bedspread. Possessions Rebecca remembered, though had not known were particularly her mother's – ornaments and a tea set, two pictures of medieval people on horses, a table-lamp, chairs and floor rugs and, in-appropriately, a gong – cluttered the limited space. Her mother's lipstick was carelessly applied. The same clothes she'd worn in the past, smart then, seemed like cast-offs now. She refused to take a penny of alimony, insisting that part of keeping her end up was to stand on her own two feet. She'd found a job in a theatre café and talked a lot about the actors and actresses who bought cups of coffee or tea from her. All this theatrical talk was boring, Rebecca reported on Sunday evenings: her mother had never been boring before.

Gerard's father, hurrying through his household chores so that he could devote himself to entertaining Gerard, was not the same either. He was more serious. He didn't spread himself about in the sitting-room the way he used to, his legs stretched awkwardly out so that people fell over them. Another boy had once shown Gerard how to untie his father's shoe-laces and tie them together while his attention was diverted. His father had never minded being laughed at; Gerard wasn't so sure about that now.

'She said she had three miscarriages,' Rebecca reported. 'I never knew that.'

Gerard wasn't certain what a miscarriage was, and Rebecca, who had been uncertain also, explained that the baby came out too soon, a lot of mush apparently.

'I wonder if I'm adopted,' Gerard mused.

The next weekend he asked his father, and was assured he wasn't. His father said his mother hadn't wanted more than a single child, but from his tone Gerard decided that she hadn't wanted any children at all. 'I'm a mistake,' he said when he and Rebecca were again alone.

Rebecca agreed that this was probably so. She supposed she should be glad she wasn't just a lot of mush. 'You be the detective,' she said.

Gerard rapped with his knuckles on the parquet floor and Rebecca opened and closed the door.

'What do you want?'

'Hotel detective, lady.'

'So what?'

'I'll tell you so what. So what is I have grounds for believing you and your companion are not Mr and Mrs Smith, as per the entry in the register.'

'Of course we're Mr and Mrs Smith.'

'I would appreciate a word with Mr Smith, ma'am.'

'Mr Smith's in the lavatory.'

'Do you categorically state that you are named Mrs Smith, ma'am? Do you categorically state that you and the party in the lavatory are man and wife?'

'Definitely.'

'Do you categorically state you are not in the prostitution business?'

'The very idea!'

'Then what we have here is a case of mistaken identity. Accept my apologies, ma'am. We get all sorts in the Grand Splendide these days.'

'No offence taken, officer. The public has a right to be protected.'

'Time was when only royalty stayed at the Grand Splendide. I knew the King of Greece, you know.'

'Fancy that.'

'Generous to a fault he was. Oh, thank you very much, lady.'

'Fancy a cocktail, officer? Babycham on the rocks OK?'

'Certainly is. Oh, and, ma'am?'

'How can I help you, officer?'

'Feel free to ply your trade, ma'am.'

*

'A little brother,' Gerard's mother informed them. 'Or perhaps a sister.'

Gerard didn't ask if this was another mistake because he could tell from the delight in his mother's eyes that it wasn't. There might even be further babies, Rebecca speculated when they were alone. She didn't care for the idea of other children in the house. 'They'll be the real thing,' she said.

Something else happened: Gerard returned after a weekend to say there had been a black-haired Frenchwoman in his father's house. She strolled about the kitchen in stockinged feet, and did the cooking. One result of this person's advent was to cause Gerard to feel less sympathetically disposed towards his father. He felt his father would be all right now, as his mother and Rebecca's father were all right.

'That'll be nice for you,' Rebecca's mother remarked sourly when Rebecca passed on the information about the expected baby. 'Nice for you and Gerard.'

When Rebecca told her about the Frenchwoman she said that that was nice too. These were the only comments she made, Rebecca told Gerard afterwards. Keeping her end up, her mother engaged in a tedious rigmarole about some famous actor or other, whom Rebecca had never heard of. She also kept saying the rigmarole was funny, a view Rebecca didn't share.

'Let's do the time she caught them,' Rebecca suggested when she'd gone through the rigmarole for Gerard.

'OK.'

Gerard lay down on the parquet and Rebecca went out of the room. Gerard worked his lips in an imaginary embrace. His tongue lolled out.

'This is disgusting!' Rebecca cried, bursting into the room again.

Gerard sat up. He asked her what she was doing here.

'A cleaner let me in. She said I'd find you on the office floor.'

'You'd better go,' Gerard muttered quietly to his pretend companion, pushing himself to his feet.

'I've known for ages.' Real tears spread on Rebecca's rounded cheeks. Quite a gush she managed. She'd always been good at real tears.

'I'm sorry.'

'Sorry, my God!'

'I know.'

'She forgot her panties. She left her panties by the wastepaper basket when she scurried out.'

'Look –'

'She's on the street without her panties. Some man on the tube –'

'Look, don't be bitter.'

'Why not? Why shouldn't I be whatever I want to be? Isn't anything my due? You were down there on the floor with a second-class tart and you expect me to be like the Virgin Mary.'

'I do not expect you to be like anyone.'

'You want me to share you with her, is that it? What a jolliness!'

'Look –'

'Oh, don't keep saying look.'

Rebecca's real tears came in a torrent now, dribbling on to a grey cardigan, reddening her eyes.

'I'd better go after her,' Gerard said, picking up, in pantomime, a garment from the floor.

*

The baby was born, a girl. The black-haired Frenchwoman

moved in with Gerard's father. One Sunday evening Rebecca said:

'She wants me back.'

That day had been spent trailing round flats that were to rent. Each time they entered one Rebecca's mother told whoever was showing them around that she worked in the theatre, and mentioned actresses and actors by name. Afterwards, in the bedsitting-room, she said her new life in the theatre had helped her to pull herself together. She said she felt a strength returning. She intended to take the alimony. She saw it differently now: the alimony was her due.

'So are you, dear,' she said. If there was difficulty, a court of law would put the matter right, no doubt about that: a child goes to the mother if the mother's fit and well.

'What did you say?' Gerard asked.

'Nothing.'

'Not that you'd rather be here?'

'No.'

'*Would* you rather be here, Rebecca?'

'Yes.'

Gerard was silent. He looked away.

'I couldn't say it,' Rebecca said.

'I see you couldn't.'

'She's my mother,' Rebecca said.

'Yes, I know.'

A week ago they had been angry together because unhappiness had made her mother foolish. A week ago Gerard said his father had reverted to something like his old self, his legs stuck out while he read the newspaper. But it was far from being the same as it had been. His father reading the newspaper like that was only a reminder.

Rebecca's real tears began, and when the sound of sobbing ceased there was silence in the room they had made their own.

Gerard wanted to comfort her, as once his father had comforted his mother, saying he forgave her, saying they would try again. But their game wouldn't stretch to that.

They sat on the virgin floor, some distance away from one another, while the white shafts of sunlight faded and the washed-out yellow of the walls dimmed to nothing. Their thoughts were similar and they knew they were. The house that had been Rebecca's would be Gerard's because that was laid down now. Rebecca would come to it at weekends because her father was there, but she would not bring with her her mother's sad tales of the theatre, nor would Gerard relate the latest from his father's new relationship. The easy companionship that had allowed them to sip cocktails and sign the register of the Hotel Grand Splendide had been theirs by chance, a gift thrown out from other people's circumstances. Helplessness was their natural state.

A Bit of Business

On a warm Saturday morning the city was deserted. Its suburbs dozed, its streets had acquired a tranquillity that did not belong to the hour. Shops and cafés were unexpectedly closed. Where there were people, they sat in front of television sets, or listened to transistors.

In Westmoreland Street two youths hurried, their progress marked by a businesslike air. They did not speak until they reached St Stephen's Green. 'No. On ahead,' one said when his companion paused. 'Off to the left in Harcourt Street.' His companion did not argue.

They had been friends since childhood; and today, their purpose being what it was, they knew better than to argue. Argument wasted time, and would distract them. The one who'd given the instruction, the older and taller of the two, was Mangan. The other was a pock-marked, sallow youth known as Lout Gallagher, the sobriquet an expression of scorn on the part of a Christian Brother ten or so years ago. Mangan had gelled short hair, non-descript as to colour, and small eyes that squinted slightly, and a flat, broad nose. 'Here,' he commanded at the end of Harcourt Street, and the two veered off in the direction he indicated.

A marmalade cat sauntered across the street they were in now; no one was about. 'The blue Ford,' Mangan said. Gallagher, within seconds, forced open the driver's door. As swiftly, the bonnet of the car was raised. Work was done with wire; the engine started easily.

*

In the suburb of Rathgar, in Cavendish Road, Mr Livingston watched the red helicopter touch down behind the vesting tents in Phoenix Park. Earlier, at the airport, the Pope's right hand had been raised in blessing, lowered, and then raised again and again, a benign smile accompanying each gesture. In Phoenix Park the crowds knelt in their corrals, and sang 'Holy God, We Praise Thy Name'. Now and again the cameras caught the black dress of clergymen and nuns, but for the most part the crowds were composed of the kind of people Mr Livingston met every day on the streets or noticed going to Mass on a Sunday. The crowds were orderly, awed by the occasion. The yellow and white papal flags fluttered everywhere; occasionally a degree of shoving developed in an effort to gain a better view. Four times already the cameras had shown women fainting – from marvelling, so Mr Livingston was given to understand, rather than heat or congestion. Somewhere in Phoenix Park were the Herlihys, but so far Mr Livingston had failed to identify them. 'I'll wave,' the Herlihy twins had promised, speaking in unison as they always did. Mr Livingston knew they'd forget; in all the excitement they wouldn't even know that a camera had skimmed over them. It was Herlihy himself who would be noticeable, being so big and his red hair easy to pick out. Monica, of course, you could miss.

Mr Livingston, attired now in a dark-blue suit, was a thin man in his sixties, only just beginning to go grey. His lean features, handsome in youth, were affected by wrinkles, his cheeks a little flushed. He had been a widower for a year.

Preceded by Cardinal Ó Fiaich and Archbishop Ryan, the Pope emerged from the papal vesting chamber under the podium. Cheering began in the corrals. Twice the Pope stopped and extended his arms. There was cheering then such as Mr Livingston had never in his life heard before. The Pope approached the altar.

*

Mangan and Gallagher worked quickly, though with no great skill. They pulled open drawers and scattered their contents. They rooted among clothes, and wrenched at the locks of cupboards. Jewellery was not examined, since its worth could not be even roughly estimated. All they found they pocketed, with loose change and notes. A transistor radio was secreted beneath Gallagher's jacket.

'Nothing else,' Mangan said. 'Useless damn place.'

They left the house that they had entered, through a kitchen window. They strolled towards the parked blue Ford, Mangan shaking his head as though, having arrived at the house on legitimate business, they disappointedly failed to find anyone at home. Gallagher drove, slowly in the road where the house was, and then more rapidly. 'Off to the left,' Mangan said, and when the opportunity came Gallagher did as he was bidden. The car drew up again; the two remained seated, both their glances fixed on the driving mirror. 'OK,' Mangan said.

*

Mr Livingston heard a noise and paid it no attention. Although his presence in the Herlihys' house was, officially, to keep an eye on it, he believed that the Herlihys had invited him because he had no television himself. It was their way to invent a reason; their way to want to thank him whenever it was possible for all the baby-sitting he did – not that there wasn't full and adequate payment at the time, the 'going rate' as Monica called it. Earlier that morning, as he'd risen and dressed himself, it had not occurred to him that Herlihy might have been serious when he said it was nice to have someone about the place on a day like this, when the Guards were all out at Phoenix Park. The sound of the television, Herlihy suggested, was as good as a dog.

'A new kind of confrontation,' stated the Pope, 'with values and trends which, up to now, have been unknown and alien to Irish society.'

Mr Livingston nodded in agreement. It would have been nice for Rosie, he thought; she'd have appreciated all this, the way she'd appreciated the royal weddings. When his wife was alive Mr Livingston had hired a television set like everyone else, but later he'd ceased to do so because he found he never watched it on his own. It made him miss her more, sitting there with the same programmes coming on, her voice not commenting any more. They would certainly have watched the whole of the ceremony today, but naturally they wouldn't have attended it in person, being Protestants.

'The sacredness of life,' urged the Pope, 'the indissolubility of marriage, the true sense of human sexuality, the right attitude towards the material goods that progress has to offer.' He advocated the Sacraments, especially the Sacrament of Penance.

Applause broke out, and again Mr Livingston nodded his agreement.

*

Gallagher had wanted to stop, but Mangan said one more house. So they went for the one at the end of the avenue, having noticed that no dog was kept. 'They've left that on,' Mangan whispered in the kitchen when they heard the sound of the television. 'Check it, though, while I'm up there.'

In the Herlihys' main bedroom he slipped the drawers out softly, and eased open anything that was locked. They'd been right to come. This place was the best yet.

Suddenly the sound of the television was louder, and Mangan knew that Gallagher had opened the door of the room it came from. He glanced towards the windows in case he should have to hurry away, but no sound of protest came from downstairs. They'd drive the car to Milltown and get on to the first bus going out of the city. Later on they'd pick up a bus to Bray. It was always worth making the journey to Bray because Cohen gave you better prices.

'Hey,' Gallagher called, not loudly, not panicking in any way whatsoever. At once Mangan knew there was a bit of trouble. He knew, by the sound of the television, that the door Gallagher had opened hadn't been closed again. Once, in a house at night, a young girl had walked across a landing with nothing on her except a sanitary thing. He and Gallagher had been in the shadows, alerted by the flush of a lavatory. She hadn't seen them.

He stuffed a couple of ties into his pockets and closed the bedroom door behind him. On the way downstairs he heard Gallagher's voice before he saw him.

'There's an old fellow here,' Gallagher said, making no effort to speak privately, 'watching His Holiness.'

Gallagher was as cool as a cucumber. You had to admire that in him. The time Mangan had gone with Ossie Power it had been nerves that landed them in it. You couldn't do a job with shaking hands, he'd told Power before they began, but it hadn't been any use. He should have known, of course.

'He's staying quiet,' Gallagher said in a low voice. 'Like I told him, he's keeping his trap tight.'

*

The youth in the doorway was wearing a crushed imitation suede jacket and dark trousers. His white T-shirt was dirty; his chin and cheeks were pitted with the remains of acne. For an instant Mr Livingston received an impression of a second face: a flat, wide nose between two bead-like eyes. Then both intruders stepped back into the hall. Whispering took place but Mr Livingston couldn't hear what was said. On the screen the Popemobile moved slowly through the vast crowd. Hands reached out to touch it.

'Keep your eyes on your man,' a voice commanded, and Mr Livingston knew it belonged to the one he had seen less of because it was gruffer than the other voice. 'Keep company with His Holiness.'

Mr Livingston did not attempt to disobey. Something was placed over his eyes and knotted at the back of his head. The material was rough, like tweed. With something similar his wrists were tied in his lap. Each ankle was tied to a leg of the chair he occupied. His wallet was slipped out of the inside pocket of his jacket.

He had failed the Herlihys; even though it was a pretence, he had agreed to perform a small and simple task; the family would return to disappointment. Mr Livingston had been angry as soon as he realized what was happening, as soon as the first youth appeared. He'd wanted to get up, to look around for something to use as a weapon, but only just in time he'd realized it would be foolish to do that. Helpless in his chair, he felt ashamed.

On the television the cheering continued, and voices described what was happening. 'Ave! Ave!' people sang.

*

'Pull up,' Mangan said in the car. 'Go down that road and pull up at the bottom.'

Lout Gallagher did so, halting the car at the opening to a half-built estate. They had driven further than they'd intended, anxious to move swiftly from the neighbourhood of their morning's work. 'If there's ever a squawk out of you,' Mangan had threatened before they parted from Mr Livingston, 'you'll rue the bloody day, mister.' Taking the third of the ties he'd picked up in the bedroom, he had placed it round the old man's neck. He had crossed the two ends and pulled them tight, watching while Mr Livingston's face and neck became flushed. He released them in good time in case anything went wrong.

'You never know with a geezer like that,' he said now. He turned his head and glanced out of the back window of the car. They were both still edgy. It was the worst thing that could happen, being seen.

'Wouldn't we dump the wagon?' Gallagher said.

'Drive it in on the site.'

They left the car behind the back wall of one of the new houses, and since the place was secluded they counted the money they'd trawled. 'Forty-two pound fifty-four,' Mangan said. As well, there were various pieces of jewellery and the transistor radio. 'You could be caught with that,' Mangan advised, and the transistor was thrown into a cement-mixer.

'He'll issue descriptions,' Mangan said before they turned away from the car. 'He'll squawk his bloody guts out.'

They both knew that. In spite of the ugliness Mangan had injected into his voice, in spite of the old man's face going purple, he would recall the details of the occasion. In the glimpse Mangan had caught of him there was anger in his eyes and his forehead was puckered in a frown.

'I'm going back there,' Mangan said.

'The car's hot.'

Mangan didn't answer, but swore instead, repeatedly and furiously; then they lit cigarettes and both felt calmer. Mangan led the way from the car, through the half-built site and out on to a lane. Within five minutes they reached a main road and came eventually to a public house. High up on the wall above the bar a large television set continued to record the Pope's presence in Ireland. No one took any notice of the two youths who ordered glasses of Smithwick's, and crisps.

*

The people who had been robbed returned to their houses and counted the cost of the Pope's personal blessing. The Herlihys returned and found Mr Livingston tied up with neck-ties, and the television still on. A doctor was summoned, though against Mr Livingston's wishes. The police came later.

That afternoon in Bray, after they'd been to see Cohen, Mangan and Gallagher picked up two girls. 'Jaysus, I could do with a mott,' Lout Gallagher had said the night before, which was how the whole thing began, Mangan realizing he could do with one too. 'Thirty,' Cohen had offered that afternoon, and they'd pushed him up to thirty-five.

They felt better after the few drinks. Today of all days a bit of fecking wouldn't interest the police, with the headaches they'd have when the crowds headed back to the city. 'Why'd they be bothered with an old geezer like that?' Mangan said, and they felt better still.

In the Esplanade Ice-cream Parlour the girls requested a Peach Melba and a sundae. One was called Carmel, the other Marie. They said they were nurses, but in fact they worked in a paper mill.

'Bray's quiet,' Mangan said.

The girls agreed it was. They'd been intending to go to see the Pope themselves, but they'd slept it out. A quarter past twelve it was before Carmel opened her eyes, and Marie was even worse. She wouldn't like to tell you, she said.

'We seen it on the television,' Mangan said. 'Your man's in great form.'

'What line are you in?' Carmel asked.

'Gangsters,' said Mangan, and everyone laughed.

Gallagher wagged his head in admiration. Mangan always gave the same response when asked that question by girls. You might have thought he'd restrain himself today, but that was Mangan all over. Gallagher lit a cigarette, thinking he should have hit the old fellow before he had a chance to turn round. He should have rushed into the room and struck him a blow on the back of the skull with whatever there was to hand, hell take the consequences.

'What's it mean, gangsters?' Marie asked, still giggling, glancing at Carmel and giggling even more.

'Banks,' Mangan said, 'is our business.'

The girls thought of Butch Cassidy and the Sundance Kid and the adventures of Bonnie and Clyde, and laughed again. They knew that if they pressed their question it wouldn't be any good. They knew it was a kind of flirtation, their asking and Mangan teasing with his replies. Mangan was a wag. Both girls were drawn to him.

'Are the ices to our ladyships' satisfaction?' he enquired, causing a further outbreak of giggling.

Gallagher had ordered a banana split. Years ago he used to think that if you filled a room with banana splits he could eat them all. He'd been about five then. He used to think the same thing about fruitcake.

'Are the flicks on today?' Mangan asked, and the girls said on account of the Pope they mightn't be. It might be like Christmas Day, they didn't know.

'We seen what's showing in Bray,' Marie said. 'In any case.'

'We'll go dancing later on,' Mangan promised. He winked at Gallagher, and Gallagher thought the day they made a killing you wouldn't see him for dust. The mail boat and Spain, posh Cockney girls who called you Mr Big. Never lift a finger again.

'Will we sport ourselves on the prom?' Mangan suggested, and the girls laughed again. They said they didn't mind. Each wanted to be Mangan's. He sensed it, so he walked between them on the promenade, linking their arms. Gallagher walked on the outside, linking Carmel.

'Spot of the ozone,' Mangan said. He pressed his forearm against Marie's breast. She was the one, he thought.

'D'you like the nursing?' Gallagher asked, and Carmel said it was all right. A sharp breeze was darting in from the sea, stinging their faces, blowing the girls' hair about. Gallagher saw himself stretched out by a blue swimming-pool, smoking and sipping at a drink. There was a cherry in the drink, and a little stick with an umbrella on the end of it. A girl with one whole side of her bikini open was sharing it with him.

'Bray's a great place,' Mangan said.

'The pits,' Carmel corrected.

You could always tell by the feel of a girl on your arm, Mangan said to himself. Full of sauce the fat one was, no more a nurse than he was. Gallagher wondered if they had a flat, if there'd be anywhere to go when the moment came.

'We could go into the bar of the hotel,' the other one was saying, the way girls did when they wanted to extract their due.

'What hotel's this?' he asked.

'The International.'

'Oh, listen to Miss Ritzy!'

They turned and walked back along the promenade, guided by the girls to the bar in question. Gin and tonic the girls had. Gallagher and Mangan had Smithwick's.

'We could go into town later,' Carmel casually suggested. 'There'll be celebrations on.'

'We'll give the matter thought,' Mangan said.

Another couple of pulls of the tie, Mangan said to himself, and who'd have been the wiser? You get to that age, you'd had your life anyway. As it was, the old geezer had probably conked it on his own, tied up like that. Most likely he was stiffening already.

'Isn't there a disco on in Bray?' he suggested. 'What's wrong with a slap-up meal and then the light fantastic?'

The girls were again amused at his way of putting it. Gallagher was glad to hear the proposal that they should stay where they were. If they went into town the whole opportunity could fall asunder. If you didn't end up near a mott's accommodation you were back where you started.

'You'd die of the pace of it in Bray,' Marie said, and Mangan thought a couple more gins and a dollop of barley wine with their grill and chips. He edged his knee against Marie's. She didn't take hers away.

'Have you a flat or rooms or something?' Gallagher asked, and the girls said they hadn't. They lived at home, they said. They'd give anything for a flat.

A few minutes later, engaged at the urinals in the lavatory, the two youths discussed the implications of that. Mangan had stood up immediately on hearing the news. He'd given a jerk of his head when the girls weren't looking.

'No bloody go,' Gallagher said.

'The fat one's on for it.'

'Where though, man?'

Mangan reminded his companion of other occasions, in car parks and derelict buildings, of the time they propped up the bar of the emergency exit of the Adelphi cinema and went back in afterwards, of the time in the garden shed in Drumcondra.

Gallagher laughed, feeling more optimistic when he remembered all that. He winked to himself, the way he did when he was beginning to feel drunk. He spat into the urinal, another habit at this particular juncture. The seashore was the place; he'd forgotten about the seashore.

'Game ball,' Mangan said.

The memory of the day that had passed seemed rosy now – the empty streets they had hurried through, the quiet houses where their business had been, the red blotchiness in the old man's face and neck, the processions on the television screen. Get a couple more gins into them, Mangan thought again, and then the barley wine. Stretch the fat one out on the soft bloody sand.

'Oh, lovely,' the fat one said when more drinks were offered.

*

Gallagher imagined the wife of a businessman pleading down a telephone, reporting that her captors intended to slice off the tips of her little fingers unless the money was forthcoming. The money was a package in a telephone booth, stashed under the seat. The pictures of Spain began again.

'Hi,' Carmel said.

She'd been to put her lipstick on, but she didn't look any different.

'What d'you do really?' she asked on the promenade.

'Unemployed.'

'You're loaded for an unemployed.' Her tone was suspicious. He watched her trying to focus her eyes. Vaguely, he wondered if she liked him.

'A man's car needed an overhaul,' he said.

Ahead of them, Mangan and Marie were laughing, the sound drifting lightly back above the swish of the sea.

'He's great sport, isn't he?' Carmel said.

'Oh, great all right.'

Mangan turned round before they went down the steps to the shingle. Gallagher imagined his fancy talk and the fat one giggling at it. He wished he was good at talk like that.

'We had plans made to go into town,' Carmel said. 'There'll be great gas in town tonight.'

When they began to cross the shingle she said it hurt her feet, so Gallagher led her back to the concrete wall of the promenade and they sat down with their backs to it. It wasn't quite dark. Cigarette packets and chocolate wrappings were scattered on the sand and pebbles. Gallagher put his arm round Carmel's shoulders. She let him kiss her. She didn't mind when he twisted her sideways so that she no longer had her back to the wall. She felt limp in his arms, and for a moment Gallagher thought she'd passed out, but then she kissed him back. She murmured something and her arms pulled him down on top of her. He realized it didn't matter about the fancy talk.

*

'When then?' Marie whispered, pulling down her clothes. Five minutes ago Mangan had promised they would meet again; he'd sworn there was nothing he wanted more; the sooner the better, he'd said.

'Monday night,' he added now. 'Outside the railway station. Six.' It was where they'd picked the two girls up. Mangan could think of nowhere else and it didn't matter anyway since he had no intention of being anywhere near Bray on Monday night.

'Geez, you're great,' Marie said.

*

On the bus to Dublin they did not say much. Carmel had spewed up a couple of mouthfuls, and in Gallagher's nostrils the sour odour persisted. Marie in the end had been a nag, going on about Monday evening, making sure Mangan wouldn't forget. What both of them were thinking was that Cohen, as usual, had done best out of the bit of business there'd been.

Then the lean features of Mr Livingston were recalled by Mangan, the angry eyes, the frown. They'd made a mess of it, letting him see them, they'd bollocksed the whole thing. That moment in the doorway when the old man's glance had lighted on his face he had hardly been able to control his bowels. 'I'm going back there,' his own voice echoed from a later moment, but he'd known, even as he spoke, that if he returned he would do no more than he had done already.

Beside him, on the inside seat, Gallagher experienced similar recollections. He stared out into the summery night, thinking that if he'd hit the old man on the back of the skull he could have finished him. The thought of that had pleased him when they were with the girls. It made him shiver now.

'God, she was great,' Mangan said, dragging out of himself a single snigger.

His bravado obscured a longing to be still with the girls, ordering gins at the bar and talking fancy. He would have paid what remained in his pocket still to taste her lipstick on the seashore, or to hear her gasp as he touched her for the first time.

Gallagher tried for his dream of Mr Big, but it would not come to him. 'Yeah,' he said, replying to his friend's observation.

The day was over; there was nowhere left to hide from the error that had been made. As they had at the time, they sensed the old man's shame and the hurt to his pride, as animals sense fear or resolution. Privately, each calculated how long it would be before the danger they'd left behind in the house caught up with them.

They stepped off the bus on the quays. The crowds that had celebrated in the city during their absence had dwindled, but people who were on the streets spoke with a continuing excitement about the Pope's presence in Ireland and the great Mass there had been in the sunshine. The two youths walked the way they'd come that morning, both of them wondering if the nerve to kill was something you acquired.

After Rain

In the dining-room of the Pensione Cesarina solitary diners are fitted in around the walls, where space does not permit a table large enough for two. These tables for one are in three of the room's four corners, by the door of the pantry where the jugs of water keep cool, between one family table and another, on either side of the tall casement windows that rattle when they're closed or opened. The dining-room is large, its ceiling high, its plain cream-coloured walls undecorated. It is noisy when the pensione's guests are there, the tables for two that take up all the central space packed close together, edges touching. The solitary diners are well separated from this mass by the passage left for the waitresses, and have a better view of the dining-room's activity and of the food before it's placed in front of them – whether tonight it is *brodo* or pasta, beef or chicken, and what the *dolce* is.

'*Dieci*,' Harriet says, giving the number of her room when she is asked. The table she has occupied for the last eleven evenings has been joined to one that is too small for a party of five: she doesn't know where to go. She stands a few more moments by the door, serving dishes busily going by her, wine bottles grabbed from the marble-topped sideboard by the rust-haired waitress, or the one with a wild look, or the one who is plump and pretty. It is the rust-haired waitress who eventually leads Harriet to the table by the door of the pantry where the water jugs keep cool. '*Da bere?*' she asks and Harriet, still feeling shy although no one glanced in her direction when she stood alone by the door, orders the wine she has ordered on other nights, Santa Cristina.

Wearing a blue dress unadorned except for the shiny blue buckle of its belt, she has earrings that hardly show and a necklace of opaque white beads that isn't valuable. Angular and thin, her dark hair cut short, her long face strikingly like the sharply chiselled faces of Modigliani, a month ago she passed out of her twenties. She is alone in the Pensione Cesarina because a love affair is over.

A holiday was cancelled, there was an empty fortnight. She wanted to be somewhere else then, not in England with time on her hands. '*Io sola,*' she said on the telephone, hoping she had got that right, choosing the Cesarina because she'd known it in childhood, because she thought that being alone would be easier in familiar surroundings.

'*Va bene?*' the rust-haired waitress enquires, proffering the Santa Cristina.

'*Sì, sì.*'

The couples who mostly fill the dining-room are German, the guttural sound of their language drifting to Harriet from the tables that are closest to her. Middle-aged, the women more stylishly dressed than the men, they are enjoying the heat of August and the low-season tariff: demi-pensione at a hundred and ten thousand lire. The heat may be too much of a good thing for some, although it's cooler by dinnertime, when the windows of the dining-room are all open, and the Cesarina is cooler anyway, being in the hills. 'If there's a breeze about,' Harriet's mother used to say, 'it finds the Cesarina.'

Twenty years ago Harriet first came here with her parents, when she was ten and her brother twelve. Before that she had heard about the pensione, how the terracotta floors were oiled every morning before the guests were up, and how the clean smell of oil lingered all day, how breakfast was a roll or two, with tea or coffee on the terrace, how dogs sometimes barked at night, from a farm across the hills. There were photographs of the parched garden and of the stately, ochre-washed exterior, and of the pensione's vineyard, steeply sloping down to two enormous wells. And then she saw for herself, summer after summer in the low season: the vast dining-room at the bottom of a flight of stone steps from the hall, and the three salons where there is Stock or grappa after dinner, with tiny cups of harsh black coffee. In the one with the bookcases there are Giotto reproductions in a volume on the table lectern, and *My Brother Jonathan* and *Rebecca* among the detective novels by George Goodchild on the shelves. The guests spoke in murmurs when Harriet first knew these rooms, English mostly, for it was mostly English who came then. To this day, the Pensione Cesarina does not accept credit cards, but instead will take a Eurocheque for more than the guaranteed amount.

'*Ecco, signora.*' A waitress with glasses, whom Harriet has seen only once or twice before, places a plate of tagliatelle in front of her.

'*Grazie.*'

'*Prego, signora. Buon appetito.*'

If the love affair hadn't ended – and Harriet has always believed that love affairs are going to last – she would now be on the island of Skyros. If the love affair hadn't ended she might one day have come to the Cesarina as her parents had before their children were born, and later might have occupied a family table in the dining-room. There is an American family tonight, and an Italian one, and other couples besides the Germans. A couple, just arrived, spoke what sounded like Dutch upstairs. Another Harriet knows to be Swiss, another she guesses to be Dutch also. A nervous English pair are too far away to allow eavesdropping.

'*Va bene?*' the rust-haired waitress enquires again, lifting away her empty plate.

'*Molto bene. Grazie.*'

Among the other solitary diners is a grey-haired dumpy woman who has several times spoken to Harriet upstairs, an American. A man is noticeable every evening because of his garish shirts, and there's a man who keeps looking about him in a jerky, nervous way, and a woman – stylish in black – who could be French. The man who looks about – small, with delicate, well-tended good features – often glances in this woman's direction, and sometimes in Harriet's. An elderly man whose white linen suit observes the formalities of the past wears a differently striped silk tie each dinnertime.

On the first night of her stay Harriet had *The Small House at Allington* in her handbag, intending to prop it up in front of her in the dining-room, but when the moment came that seemed all wrong. Already, then, she regretted her impulse to come here on her own and wondered why she had. On the journey out the rawness of her pain had in no way softened, if anything had intensified, for the journey on that day should have been different, and not made alone: she had forgotten there would be that.

With the chicken pieces she's offered there are roast potatoes, tomatoes and zucchini, and salad. Then Harriet chooses cheese: pecorino, a little Gorgonzola. Half of the Santa Cristina is left for tomorrow, her room number scribbled on the label. On the envelope provided for her napkin this is more elegantly inscribed, in a sloping hand: *Camera Dieci*. She folds her napkin and tucks it away, and for a moment as she does so the man she has come here to forget pushes through another crowded room, coming towards her in the King of Poland, her name on his lips. 'I love you, Harriet,' he whispers beneath the noise around them. Her eyes close when their caress is shared. 'My darling Harriet,' he says.

Upstairs, in the room where the bookcases are, Harriet wonders if this solitude is how her life will be. Has she returned to this childhood place to seek whatever comfort a happy past can offer? Is that a truer reason than what she told herself at the time? Her thoughts are always a muddle when a love affair ends, the truth befogged; the truth not there at all, it often seems. Love failed her was what she felt when another relationship crumbled into nothing; love has a way of doing that. And since wondering is company for the companionless, she wonders why it should be so. This is the first time that a holiday has been cancelled, that she has come away alone.

'*Mi dispiace*,' a boy in a white jacket apologizes, having spilt some of a liqueur on a German woman's arm. The woman laughs and says in English that it doesn't matter. '*Non importa*,' her husband adds when the boy looks vacant, and the German woman laughs again.

'*Mais oui*, I study the law,' a long-legged girl is saying. 'And Eloise is a stylist.'

These girls are Belgian: the questions of two Englishmen are answered. The Englishmen are young, both of them heavily built, casually turned out, one of them moustached.

'Is stylist right? Is that what you say?'

'Oh, yes.' And both young men nod. When one suggests a liqueur on the terrace Eloise and her friend ask for cherry brandy. The boy in the white jacket goes to pour it in a cupboard off the hall, where the espresso machine is.

'And you?' Eloise enquires as the four pass through the room, through the french windows to the terrace.

'Nev's in business. I go down after wrecks.' The voice that drifts back is slack, accented, confident. English or German or Dutch, these are the people who have made the Pensione Cesarina move with the times, different from the people of Harriet's childhood.

A bearded man is surreptitiously sketching a couple on one of the sofas. The couple, both reading, are unaware. In the hall the American family is much in evidence, the mother with a baby in her arms pacing up and down, the father quietening two other children, a girl and a boy.

'Good evening,' someone interrupts Harriet's observations, and the man in the linen suit asks if the chair next to hers is taken by anyone else. His tie tonight is brown and green, and Harriet notices that his craggy features are freckled with an old man's blotches, that his hair is so scanty that whether it's grey or white doesn't register. What is subtle in his face is the washed-out blue of his eyes.

'You travel alone, too,' he remarks, openly seeking the companionship of the moment when Harriet has indicated that the chair beside her is not taken.

'Yes, I do.'

'I can always pick out the English.'

He offers the theory that this is perhaps something the traveller acquires with age and with the experience of many journeys. 'You'll probably see,' he adds.

The companion of the bearded man who is sketching the couple on the sofa leans forward and smiles over what she sees. In the hall the American father has persuaded his older children to go to bed. The mother still soothes her baby, still pacing up and down. The small man who so agitatedly glanced about the dining-room passes rapidly through the hall, carrying two cups of coffee.

'They certainly feed you,' Harriet's companion remarks, 'these days at the Cesarina.'

'Yes.'

'Quite scanty, the food was once.'

'Yes, I remember.'

'I mean, a longish time ago.'

'The first summer I came here I was ten.'

He calculates, glancing at her face to guess her age. Before his own first time, he says, which was the spring of 1987. He has been coming since, he says, and asks if she has.

'My parents separated.'

'I'm sorry.'

'They'd been coming here all their married lives. They were fond of this place.'

'Some people fall for it. Others not at all.'

'My brother found it boring.'

'A child might easily.'

'I never did.'

'Interesting, those two chaps picking up the girls. I wonder if they'll ever cope with coach tours at the Cesarina.'

He talks. Harriet doesn't listen. This love affair had once, like the other affairs before it, felt like the exorcism of the disappointment that so drearily coloured her life when her parents went their separate ways. There were no quarrels when her parents separated, no bitterness, no drama. They told their children gently, neither blamed the other. Both – for years apparently – had been involved with other people. Both said the separation was a happier outcome than staying together for the sake of the family. They used those words, and Harriet has never forgotten them. Her brother shrugged the disappointment off, but for Harriet it did not begin to go away until the first of her love affairs. And always, when a love affair ended, there had been no exorcism after all.

'I'm off tomorrow,' the old man says.

She nods. In the hall the baby in the American mother's arms is sleeping at last. The mother smiles at someone Harriet can't see and then moves towards the wide stone staircase. The couple on the sofa, still unaware that they've been sketched, stand up and go away. The agitated little man bustles through the hall again.

'Sorry to go,' Harriet's companion finishes something he has been saying, then tells her about his journey: by train because he doesn't care for flying. Lunch in Milan, dinner in Zurich, on neither occasion leaving the railway station. The eleven-o'clock sleeper from Zurich.

'We used to drive out when I came with my parents.'

'I haven't ever done that. And of course won't ever now.'

'I liked it.'

At the time it didn't seem unreal or artificial. Their smiling faces didn't, nor the pleasure they seemed to take in poky French hotels where only the food was good, nor their chattering to one another in the front of the car, their badinage and arguments. Yet retrospect insisted that reality was elsewhere; that reality was surreptitious lunches with two other people, and afternoon rooms, and guile; that reality was a web of lies until one of them found out, it didn't matter which; that reality was when there had to be something better than what the family offered.

'So this time you have come alone?'

He may have said it twice, she isn't sure. Something about his expression suggests he has.

'Yes.'

He speaks of solitude. It offers a quality that is hard to define; much more than the cliché of getting to know yourself. He himself has been on his own for many years and has discovered consolation in that very circumstance, which is an irony of a kind, he supposes.

'I was to go somewhere else.' She doesn't know why she makes this revelation. Politeness, perhaps. On other evenings, after dinner, she has seen this man in conversation with whomever he has chosen to sit beside. He is polite himself. He sounds more interested than inquisitive.

'You changed your mind?'

'A friendship fell apart.'

'Ah.'

'I should be on an island in the sun.'

'And where is that, if I may ask?'

'Skyros it's called. Renowned for its therapies.'

'Therapies?'

'They're a fashion.'

'For the ill, is this? If I may say so, you don't look ill.'

'No, I'm not ill.' Unable to keep the men she loves in love with her. But of course not ill.

'In fact, you look supremely healthy.' He smiles. His teeth are still his own. 'If I may say so.'

'I'm not so sure that I like islands in the sun. But even so I wanted to go there.'

'For the therapies?'

'No, I would have avoided that. Sand therapy, water therapy, sex therapy, image therapy, holistic counselling. I would have steered clear, I think.'

'Being on your own's a therapy too, of course. Although it's nice to have a chat.'

She doesn't listen; he goes on talking. On the island of Skyros tourists beat drums at sunset and welcome the dawn with song. Or they may simply swim and play, or discover the undiscovered self. The Pensione Cesarina – even the pensione transformed by the Germans and the Dutch – offers nothing like it. Nor would it offer enough to her parents any more. Her divided parents travel grandly now.

'I see *The Spanish Farm* is still on the shelves.' The old man has risen and hovers for a moment. 'I doubt that anyone's read it since I did in 1987.'

'No, probably not.'

He says goodnight and changes it to goodbye because he has to make an early start. For a moment, it seems to Harriet, he hesitates, something about his stance suggesting that he'd like to be invited to stay, to be offered a cup of coffee or a drink. Then he goes, without saying anything else. Lonely in old age, she suddenly realizes, wondering why she didn't notice that when he was talking to her. Lonely in spite of all he claims for solitude.

'Goodbye,' she calls after him, but he doesn't hear. They were to come back here the summer of the separation; instead there were cancellations then too, and an empty fortnight.

'*Buona notte.*' The boy in the white jacket smiles tentatively from his cupboard as she passes through the hall. He's new tonight; it was another boy before. She hasn't realized that either.

*

She walks through the heat of the morning on the narrow road to the town, by the graveyard and the abandoned petrol pumps. A few cars pass her, coming from the pensione, for the road leads hardly anywhere else, petering out eventually. It would have been hotter on the island of Skyros.

Clouds have gathered in one part of the sky, behind her as she walks. The shade of clouds might make it cooler, she tells herself, but so far they are not close enough to the sun for that. The road widens and gradually the incline becomes less steep as she approaches the town. There's a park with concrete seats and the first of the churches, its chosen saint Agnese of this town.

There's no one in the park until Harriet sits there beneath the chestnut trees in a corner. Far below her, as the town tails off again, a main road begins to wind through clumps of needle pines and umbrella pines to join, far out of sight, a motorway. 'But weren't we happy?' she hears herself exclaim, a little shrill because she couldn't help it. Yes, they were happy, he agreed at once, anxious to make that clear. Not happy enough was what he meant, and you could tell; something not quite right. She asked him and he didn't know, genuine in his bewilderment.

When she feels cooler she walks on, down shaded, narrow streets to the central piazza of the town, where she rests again, with a cappuccino at a pavement table.

Italians and tourists move slowly in the unevenly paved square, women with shopping bags and dogs, men leaving the barber's, the tourists in their summery clothes. The church of Santa Fabiola dominates the square, grey steps in front, a brick and stone façade. There is another café, across from the one Harriet has chosen, and a line of market stalls beside it. The town's banks are in the square but not its shops. There's a trattoria and a gelateria, their similar decoration connecting them, side by side. 'Yes, they're all one,' her father said.

In this square her father lifted her high above his head and she looked down and saw his laughing, upturned face and she laughed too, because he joked so. Her mother stuttered out her schoolgirl French in the little hotels where they stayed on the journey out, and blushed with shame when no one understood. 'Oh, this is pleasant!' her mother murmured, a table away from where Harriet is now.

A priest comes down the steps of the church, looks about him, does not see whom he thought he might. A skinny dog goes limping by. The bell of Santa Fabiola chimes twelve o'clock and when it ceases another bell, farther away, begins. Clouds have covered the sun, but the air is as hot as ever. There's still no breeze.

It was in the foyer of the Rembrandt Cinema that he said he didn't think their love affair was working. It was then that she exclaimed, 'But weren't we happy?' They didn't quarrel. Not even afterwards, when she asked him why he had told her in a cinema foyer. He didn't know, he said; it just seemed right in that moment, some fragment of a mood they shared. If it hadn't been for their holiday's being quite soon their relationship might have dragged on for a while. Much better that it shouldn't, he said.

The fourteenth of February in London was quite as black, and cold, and as wintersome as it was at Allington, and was, perhaps, somewhat more melancholy in its coldness. She has read that bit before and couldn't settle to it, and cannot now. She takes her dark glasses off: the clouds are not the pretty bundles she noticed before, white cottonwool as decoration is by Raphael or Perugino. The clouds that have come up so quickly are grey as lead, a sombre panoply pegged out against a blue that's almost lost. The first drops fall when Harriet tries the doors of Santa Fabiola and finds them locked. They will remain so, a notice tersely states, until half-past two.

It had been finally arranged that the marriage should take place in London, she reads in the trattoria. *There were certainly many reasons which would have made a marriage from Courcy Castle more convenient. The De Courcy family were all assembled at their country family residence, and could therefore have been present at the ceremony without cost or trouble.* She isn't hungry; she has ordered risotto, hoping it will be small, and mineral water without gas.

'*C'è del pane o della farina nel piatto? Non devo mangiare della farina,*' a woman is saying, and the gaunt-faced waiter carefully listens, not understanding at first and then excitedly nodding. '*Non c'è farina,*' he replies, pointing at items on the menu. The woman is from the pensione. She's with a lanky young man who might be her son, and Harriet can't identify the language they speak to one another.

'Is fine?' the same waiter asks Harriet as he passes, noticing that she has begun to eat her risotto. She nods and smiles and reads again. The rain outside is heavy now.

*

The Annunciation in the church of Santa Fabiola is by an unknown artist, perhaps of the school of Filippo Lippi, no one is certain. The angel kneels, grey wings protruding, his lily half hidden by a pillar. The floor is marble, white and green and ochre. The Virgin looks alarmed, right hand arresting her visitor's advance. Beyond – background to the encounter – there are gracious arches, a balustrade and then the sky and hills. There is a soundlessness about the picture, the silence of a mystery: no words are spoken in this captured moment, what's said between the two has been said already.

Harriet's eye records the details: the green folds of the angel's dress, the red beneath it, the mark in the sky that is a dove, the Virgin's book, the stately pillars and the empty vase, the Virgin's slipper, the bare feet of the angel. The distant landscape is soft, as if no heat has ever touched it. It isn't alarm in the Virgin's eyes, it's wonderment. In another moment there'll be serenity. A few tourists glide about the church, whispering now and again. A man in a black overall is mopping the floor of the central aisle and has roped it off at either end. An elderly woman prays before a statue of the Virgin, each bead of her rosary fingered, lips silently murmuring. Incense is cloying on the air.

Harriet walks slowly past flaring candles and the tomb of a local family, past the relics of the altar, and the story of Santa Fabiola flaking in a side chapel. She has not been in this church before, neither during her present visit nor in the past. Her parents didn't bother much with churches; she might have come here on her own yesterday or on any day of her stay but she didn't bother either. Her parents liked the sun in the garden of the pensione, the walk down to the cafés and drives into the hills or to other little towns, to the swimming-pool at Ponte Nicolo.

The woman who has been praying hobbles to light another candle, then prays again, and hobbles off. Returning to the Annunciation, Harriet sits down in the pew that's nearest it. There is blue as well as grey in the wings of the angel, little flecks of blue you don't notice when you look at first. The Virgin's slipper is a shade of brown, the empty vase is bulb-shaped with a slender stem, the Virgin's book had gold on it but only traces remain.

The rain has stopped when Harriet leaves the church, the air is fresher. Too slick and glib, to use her love affairs to restore her faith in love: that thought is there mysteriously. She has cheated in her love affairs: that comes from nowhere too.

Harriet stands a moment longer, alone on the steps of the church, bewildered by this personal revelation, aware instinctively of its truth. The dust of the piazza paving has been washed into the crevices that separate the stones. At the café where she had her cappuccino the waiter is wiping dry the plastic of the chairs.

*

The sun is still reluctant in the watery sky. On her walk back to the Pensione Cesarina it seems to Harriet that in this respite from the brash smother of heat a different life has crept out of the foliage and stone. A coolness emanates from the road she walks on. Unseen, among the wild geraniums, one bird sings.

Tomorrow, when the sun is again in charge at its time of year, a few midday minutes will wipe away what lingers of this softness. New dust will settle, marble will be warm to touch. Weeks it may be, months perhaps, before rain coaxes out these fragrances that are tender now.

The sun is always pitiless when it returns, harsh in its punishment. In the dried-out garden of the Pensione Cesarina they made her wear a hat she didn't like but they could take the sun themselves, both of them skulking behind dark glasses and high-factor cream. Skyros's sun is its attraction. 'What I need is sun,' he said, and Harriet wonders if he went there after all, if he's there today, not left behind in London, if he even found someone to go with. She sees him in Skyros, windsurfing in Atsitsa Bay, which he has talked about. She sees him with a companion who is un-complicated and happy in Atsitsa Bay, who tries out a therapy just to see what it's like.

The deck-chairs are sodden at the Pensione Cesarina, rose petals glisten. A glass left on a terrace table has gathered an inch of water. The umbrellas in the outer hall have all been used. Windows, closed for a while, are opened; on the vineyard slopes the sprinklers are turned on again.

Not wanting to be inside, Harriet walks in the garden and among the vines, her shoes drenched. From the town comes the chiming of bells: six o'clock at Santa Fabiola, six o'clock a minute

93

later somewhere else. While she stands alone among the dripping vines she cannot make a connection that she knows is there. There is a blankness in her thoughts, a density that feels like muddle also, until she realizes: the Annunciation was painted after rain. Its distant landscape, glimpsed through arches, has the temporary look that she is seeing now. It was after rain that the angel came: those first cool moments were a chosen time.

*

In the dining-room the table where the man with the garish shirts sat has been joined to a family table to allow for a party of seven. There is a different woman where the smart Frenchwoman sat, and no one at the table of the old man. The woman who was explaining in the trattoria that she must not eat food containing flour is given consommé instead of ravioli. New faces are dotted everywhere.

'*Buona sera,*' the rust-haired waitress greets Harriet, and the waitress with glasses brings her salad.

'*Grazie,*' Harriet murmurs.

'*Prego, signora.*'

She pours her wine, breaks off a crust of bread. It's noisy in the dining-room now, dishes clattering, the babble of voices. It felt like noise in the foyer of the Rembrandt Cinema when he told her: the uproar of shock, although in fact it was quite silent there. Bright, harsh colours flashed through her consciousness, as if some rush of blood exploded in a kaleidoscope of distress. For a moment in the foyer of the cinema she closed her eyes, as she had when they told her they weren't to be a family any more.

She might have sent them postcards, but she hasn't. She might have reported that breakfast at the pensione is more than coffee and rolls since the Germans and the Dutch and the Swiss have begun to come: cheese and cold meats, fruit and cereals, fresh sponge cake, a buffet on the terrace. Each morning she has sat there reading *The Small House at Allington*, wondering if they would like to know of the breakfast-time improvement. She wondered today if it would interest them to learn that the abandoned petrol pumps are still there on the road to the town, or that she sat in the deserted park beneath the chestnut trees. She thought of sending him a postcard too, but in the end she didn't. His predecessor it was who encouraged her to bring long novels on holiday, *The Tenant of Wildfell Hall, The Mill on the Floss.*

It's beef tonight, with spinach. And afterwards Harriet has *dolce*, remembering this sodden yellow raisin cake from the past. She won't taste that again; as mysteriously as she knows she has cheated without meaning to in her love affairs, she knows she won't come back, alone or with someone else. Coming back has been done, a private journey that chance suggested. Tomorrow she'll be gone.

In the room with the bookcases and the Giotto reproductions she watches while people drink their grappa or their Stock, or ask the white-jacketed boy for more coffee, or pick up conversations with one another. The Belgian girls have got to know the young Englishman who goes down after wrecks and Nev who's in the business world. All four pass through the room on their way to the terrace, the girls with white cardigans draped on their shoulders because it isn't as warm as it was last night. 'That man drew us!' a voice cries, and the couple who were sketched last night gaze down at their hardly recognizable selves in the pensione's comment book.

He backed away, as others have, when she asked too much of love, when she tried to change the circumstances that are the past by imposing a brighter present, and constancy in the future above all else. She has been the victim of herself: with vivid clarity she knows that now and wonders why she does and why she didn't before. Nothing tells her when she ponders the solitude of her stay in the Pensione Cesarina, and she senses that nothing ever will.

She sees again the brown-and-green striped tie of the old man who talked about being on your own, and the freckles that are blotches on his forehead. She sees herself walking in the morning heat past the graveyard and the rusted petrol pumps. She sees herself seeking the shade of the chestnut trees in the park, and crossing the piazza to the trattoria when the first raindrops fell. She hears the swish of the cleaner's mop in the church of Santa Fabiola, she hears the tourists' whisper. The fingers of the praying woman flutter on her beads, the candles flare. The story of Santa Fabiola is lost in the shadows that were once the people of her life, the family tomb reeks odourlessly of death. Rain has sweetened the breathless air, the angel comes mysteriously also.

Widows

Waking on a warm, bright morning in early October, Catherine found herself a widow. In some moment during the night Matthew had gone peacefully: had there been pain or distress she would have known it. Yet what lay beside her in the bed was less than a photograph now, the fallen jaw harshly distorting a face she'd loved.

Tears ran on Catherine's cheeks and dripped on to her nightdress. She knelt by the bedside, then drew the sheet over the still features. Quiet, gently spoken, given to thought before offering an opinion, her husband had been regarded by Catherine as cleverer and wiser than she was herself, and more charitable in his view of other people. In his business life – the sale of agricultural machinery – he had been known as a man of his word. For miles around – far beyond the town and its immediate neighbourhood – the farm people who had been his customers repaid his honesty and straight dealing with respect. At Christmas there had been gifts of fowls and fish, jars of cream, sacks of potatoes. The funeral would be well attended. 'There'll be a comfort in the memories, Catherine,' Matthew had said more than once, attempting to anticipate the melancholy of their separation: they had known that it was soon to be.

He would have held the memories to him if he'd been the one remaining. 'Whichever is left,' he reminded Catherine as they grew old, 'it's only for the time being.' And in that time-being one of them would manage in what had previously been the other's domain: he ironing his sheets and trousers, working the washing-machine, cooking as he had watched her cook, using the Electrolux; she arranging for someone to undertake the small repairs he had attended to in the house if she or her sister couldn't manage them, paying the household bills and keeping an eye on the bank balance. Matthew had never minded talking about their separation, and had taught her not to mind either.

On her knees by the bedside Catherine prayed, then her tears came again. She reached out for his hand and grasped the cold, stiff fingers beneath the bedclothes. 'Oh, love,' she whispered. 'Oh, love.'

*

The three sons of the marriage came for the funeral, remaining briefly, with their families, in the town where they had spent their childhood. Father Cahill intoned the last words in the cemetery, and soon after that Catherine and her sister Alicia were alone in the house again. Alicia had lived there since her own husband's death, nine years ago; she was the older of the two sisters – fifty-seven, almost fifty-eight.

The house that for Catherine was still haunted by her husband's recent presence was comfortable, with a narrow hall and a kitchen at the back, and bedrooms on two floors. Outside, it was colour-washed blue, with white window-frames and hall-door, the last house of the town, the first on the Dublin road. Opposite was the convent school, behind silver-painted railings, three sides enclosed by the drab concrete of its classrooms and the nuns' house, its play-yard often bustling into noisy excitement. Once upon a time Catherine and Alicia had played there themselves, hardly noticing the house across the road, blue then also.

'You're all right?' Alicia said on the evening of the funeral, when together they cleared up the glasses sherry had been drunk from, and cups and saucers. On the sideboard in the dining-room the stoppers of the decanters had not yet been replaced, crumbs not yet brushed from the dining-table cloth. 'Yes, I'm all right,' Catherine said. In her girlhood she had been pretty – slender and dark, and shyly smiling, dimples in both cheeks. Alicia, taller, dark also, had been considered the beauty of the town. Now, Catherine was greying, and plump about the face, the joints of her fingers a little swollen. Alicia was straight-backed, her beauty still recalled in features that were classically proportioned, her hair greyer than her sister's.

'Good of them all to come,' Catherine said.

'People liked Matthew.'

'Yes.'

For a moment Catherine felt the rising of her tears, the first time since the morning of the death, but stoically she held them in. Their marriage had not gone. Their marriage was still there in children and in grandchildren, in the voices that had spoken well of it, in the bed they had shared, and in remembering. The time-being would not be endless: he had said that too. 'You're managing, Catherine?' people asked, the same words often used, and she tried to convey that strength still came from all there had been.

*

The day after the funeral Fagan from the solicitors' office explained to Catherine the contents of the few papers he brought to the house. It took ten minutes.

'Well, that's that,' he said, and for a moment the finality with which he spoke reminded Catherine of the coffin slipping down, filling the hole that had been dug for it. The papers lay neatly on the well-polished surface of the dining-room table, cleared now of the debris of the day before, and of the cloth that had protected it. Fagan drank a cup of instant coffee and said she had only to pick up the phone if ever there was anything.

'I'll help you,' Alicia said later that same morning when Catherine mentioned Matthew's personal belongings. Clothes and shoes would be accepted gratefully by one of the charities with which Alicia was connected. The signet ring, the watch, the tie-pin, the matching fountain-pen and propelling pencil were earmarked for the family, to be shared among Catherine's sons. Shaving things were thrown away.

Recalling the same sorting out of possessions at the time of her own loss, Alicia was in no way distressed. She had experienced little emotion when her husband's death occurred: for the last nineteen years of her marriage she had not loved him.

'You've been a strength,' Catherine said, for her sister had been that and more, looking after her as she used to, years ago, when they were children.

'Oh no, no,' came Alicia's deprecation.

*

Thomas Pius John Leary was by trade a painter and decorator. He had, for this work, no special qualifications beyond experience; he brought to it no special skill. As a result, he was often accused of poor workmanship, which in turn led to disputes about payment. But he charged less than his competitors and so ensured a reasonably steady demand for his services. When for one reason or another the demand wasn't there he took on any kind of odd job he was offered.

Leary was middle-aged now, married, the father of six children. He was a small, wiry man with tight features and bloodshot eyes, his spareness occasionally reminding people of a hedgerow animal they could not readily name. Sparse grey hair was brushed straight back from the narrow dome of his forehead. Two fore-fingers, thumbs, middle fingers, upper lip and teeth, were stained brown from cigarettes he manufactured with the aid of a small machine. Leary did not wear overalls when at work and was rarely encountered in clothes that did not bear splashes of paint.

It was in this condition, the damp end of a cigarette emerging from a cupped palm, that he presented himself to Catherine and Alicia one afternoon in November, six weeks after the death. He stood on the doorstep, declaring his regrets and his sympathy in a low voice, not meeting Catherine's eye. In the time that had passed, other people had come to the door and said much the same thing, not many, only those who found it difficult to write a letter and considered the use of the telephone to be inappropriate in such circumstances. They'd made a brief statement and then had hurried off. Leary appeared inclined to linger.

'That's very good of you, Mr Leary,' Catherine said.

A few months ago he had repainted the front of the house, the same pale blue. He had renewed the white gloss of the window-frames. 'Poor Leary's desperate for work,' Matthew had said. 'Will we give the rogue a go?' Alicia had been against it, Leary not being a man she'd cared for when he'd done other jobs for them. Catherine, although she didn't much care for Leary either, felt sorry for anyone who was up against it.

'Could I step in for a minute?'

Across the street the convent children were running about in the play-yard before their afternoon classes began. Still watching them, Catherine was aware of checking a frown that had begun to gather. He was looking for more work, she supposed, but there was no question of that. Alicia's misgivings had been justified: there'd been skimping on the amount and quality of the paint used, and inadequate preparation. 'We'll know not to do that again,' Matthew had said. Besides, there wasn't anything else at present.

'Of course.' Catherine stood aside while Leary passed into the long, narrow hall. She led the way down it, to the kitchen because it was warm there. Alicia was polishing the cutlery at the table, a task she undertook once a month.

'Sit down, Mr Leary,' Catherine invited, pulling a chair out for him.

'I was saying I was sorry,' he said to Alicia. 'If there's any way I can assist at all, any little job, I'm always there.'

'It's kind of you, Mr Leary,' Catherine said swiftly, in case her sister responded more tartly.

'I knew him since we were lads. He used be at the Christian Brothers'.'

'Yes.'

'Great old days.'

He seemed embarrassed. He wanted to say something but was having difficulty. One hand went into a pocket of his jacket. Catherine watched it playing with the little contrivance he used for rolling his cigarettes. But the hand came out empty. Nervously, it was rubbed against its partner.

'It's awkward,' Leary said.

'What's awkward, Mr Leary?'

'It isn't easy, how to put it to you. I didn't come before because of your trouble.'

Alicia laid down the cloth with which she had been applying Goddard's Silver Polish to the cutlery and Catherine watched her sister's slow, deliberate movements as she shined the last of the forks and then drew off her pink rubber gloves and placed them one on top of the other beside her. Alicia could sense something; she often had a way of knowing what was coming next.

'I don't know are you aware,' Leary enquired, addressing only Catherine, 'it wasn't paid for?'

'What wasn't?'

'The job I done for you.'

'You don't mean painting the front?'

'I do, ma'am.'

'But of course it was paid for.'

He sighed softly. An outstanding bill was an embarrassment, he said. Because of the death it was an embarrassment.

'My husband paid for the work that was done.'

'Ah no, no.'

The frown Catherine had checked a few moments ago wrinkled her forehead. She knew the bill had been paid. She knew because Matthew had said Leary would want cash, and she had taken the money out of her own Irish Nationwide account since she had easy access to it. 'I'll see you right at the end of the month,' Matthew had promised. It was an arrangement they often had; the building-society account in her name existed for this kind of thing.

'Two hundred and twenty-six pounds is the extent of the damage.' Leary smiled shiftily. 'With the discount for cash.'

She didn't tell him she'd withdrawn the money herself. That wasn't his business. She watched the extreme tip of his tongue licking his upper lip. He wiped his mouth with the back of a paint-stained hand. Softly, Alicia was replacing forks and spoons in the cutlery container.

'It was September the account was sent out. The wife does all that type of thing.'

'The bill was paid promptly. My husband always paid bills promptly.'

She remembered the occasion perfectly. 'I'll bring it down to him now,' Matthew had said, glancing across the kitchen at the clock. Every evening he walked to McKenny's bar and remained there for three-quarters of an hour or so, depending on the company. That evening he'd have gone the long way round, by French Street, in order to call in at the Learys' house in Brady's Lane. Before he left he had taken the notes from the brown Nationwide envelope and counted them, slowly, just as she'd done herself earlier. She'd seen the bill in his hand. 'Chancing his arm with the taxman,' she remembered his remarking lightly, a reference to Leary's preference for cash.

On his return he would have hung his cap on its hook in the scullery passage and settled down at the kitchen table with the

Evening Press, which he bought in Healy's sweetshop on his way back from McKenny's. He went to the public house for conversation as much as anything, and afterwards passed on to Alicia and herself any news he had gleaned. Bottled Smithwick's was his drink.

'D'you remember it?' Catherine appealed to her sister because although she could herself so clearly recall Matthew's departure from the house on that particular September evening, his return eluded her. It lay smothered somewhere beneath the evening routine, nothing making it special, as the banknotes in the envelope had marked the other.

'I remember talk about money,' Alicia recalled, 'earlier that day. If I've got it right, I was out at the Legion of Mary in the evening.'

'A while back the wife noticed the way the bill was unpaid,' Leary went on, having paused politely to hear these recollections. ' "It's the death that's in it," the wife said. She'd have eaten the face off me if I'd bothered you in your trouble.'

'Excuse me,' Catherine said.

She left the kitchen and went to look on the spike in the side-cupboard in the passage, where all receipts were kept. This one should have been close to the top, but it wasn't. It wasn't further down either. It wasn't in the cupboard drawers. She went through the contents of three box-files in case it had been bundled into one in error. Again she didn't find it.

She returned to the kitchen with the next best thing: the Nationwide Building Society account book. She opened it and placed it in front of Leary. She pointed at the entry that recorded the withdrawal of two hundred and twenty-six pounds. She could tell that there had been no conversation in her absence. Leary would have tried to get some kind of talk going, but Alicia wouldn't have responded.

'September the eighth,' Catherine said, emphasizing the printed date with a forefinger. 'A Wednesday it was.'

In silence Leary perused the entry. He shook his head. The tight features of his face tightened even more, bunching together into a knot of bewilderment. Catherine glanced at her sister. He was putting it on, Alicia's expression indicated.

'The money was taken out all right,' Leary said eventually. 'Did he put it to another use in that case?'

'Another use?'

'Did you locate a receipt, missus?'

He spoke softly, not in the cagey, underhand tone of someone attempting to get something for nothing. Catherine was still standing. He turned his head to one side in order to squint up at her. He sounded apologetic, but all that could be put on also.

'I brought the receipt book over with me,' he said.

He handed it to her, a fat greasy notebook with a grey marbled cover that had *The Challenge Receipt Book* printed on it. Blue carbon paper protruded from the dog-eared pages.

'Any receipt that's issued would have a copy left behind here,' he said, speaking now to Alicia, across the table. 'The top copy for the customer, the carbon for ourselves. You couldn't do business without you keep a record of receipts.'

He stood up then. He opened the book and displayed its unused pages, each with the same printed heading: *In account with T. P. Leary*. He showed Catherine how the details of a bill were recorded on the flimsy page beneath the carbon sheet and how, when a bill was paid, acknowledgement was recorded also: *Paid with thanks*, with the date and the careful scrawl of Mrs Leary's signature. He passed the receipt book to Alicia, pointing out these details to her also.

'Anything could have happened to that receipt,' Alicia said. 'In the circumstances.'

'If a receipt was issued, missus, there'd be a record of it here.'

Alicia placed the receipt book beside the much slimmer building-society book on the pale surface of the table. Leary's attention remained with the former, his scrutiny an emphasis of the facts it contained. The evidence offered otherwise was not for him to comment upon: so the steadiness of his gaze insisted.

'My husband counted those notes at this very table,' Catherine said. 'He took them out of the brown envelope that they were put into at the Nationwide.'

'It's a mystery so.'

It wasn't any such thing; there was no mystery whatsoever. The bill had been paid. Both sisters knew that; in their different ways they guessed that Leary – and presumably his wife as well – had planned this dishonesty as soon as they realized death gave them the opportunity. Matthew had obliged them by paying cash so that they could defraud the taxation authorities. He had further obliged them by dying. Catherine said:

'My husband walked out of this house with that envelope in his pocket. Are you telling me he didn't reach you?'

'Was he robbed? Would it be that? You hear terrible things these days.'

'Oh, for heaven's sake!'

Leary wagged his head in his meditative way. It was unlikely certainly, he agreed. Anyone robbed would have gone to the Guards. Anyone robbed would have mentioned it when he came back to the house again.

'The bill was paid, Mr Leary.'

'All the same, we have to go by the receipt. At the heel of the hunt there's the matter of a receipt.'

Alicia shook her head. Either a receipt wasn't issued in the first place, she said, or else it had been mislaid. 'There's a confusion when a person dies,' she said.

If Catherine had been able to produce the receipt Leary would have blamed his wife. He'd have blandly stated that she'd got her wires crossed. He'd have said the first thing that came into his head and then have gone away.

'The only thing is,' he said instead, 'a sum like that is sizeable. I couldn't afford let it go.'

Both Catherine and Alicia had seen Mrs Leary in the shops, red-haired, like a tinker, a bigger woman than her husband, probably the brains of the two. The Learys were liars and worse than liars; the chance had come and the temptation had been too much for them. 'Ah sure, those two have plenty,' the woman would have said. The sisters wondered if the Learys had tricked the bereaved before, and imagined they had. Leary said:

'It's hard on a man that's done work for you.'

Catherine moved towards the kitchen door. Leary ambled after her down the hall. She remembered the evening more clearly even than a while ago: a Wednesday it definitely had been, the day of the Sweetman girl's wedding; and it came back to her, also, Alicia hurrying out on her Legion of Mary business. There'd been talk in McKenny's about the wedding, the unusual choice of midweek, which apparently had something to do with visitors coming from America. She opened the hall-door in silence. Across the street, beyond the silver-coloured railings, the children were still running about in the convent yard. Watery sunlight lightened the unadorned concrete of the classrooms and the nuns' house.

'What'll I do?' Leary asked, wide-eyed, bloodshot, squinting at her.

Catherine said nothing.

*

They talked about it. It could be, Alicia said, that the receipt had remained in one of Matthew's pockets, that a jacket she had disposed of to one of her charities had later found itself in the Learys' hands, having passed through a jumble sale. She could imagine Mrs Leary coming across it, and the temptation being too much. Leary was as weak as water, she said, adding that the tinker wife was a woman who never looked you in the eye. Foxy-faced and furtive, Mrs Leary pushed a ramshackle pram about the streets, her ragged children cowering in her presence. It was she who would have removed the flimsy carbon copy from the soiled receipt book. Leary would have been putty in her hands.

In the kitchen they sat down at the table from which Alicia had cleared away the polished cutlery. Matthew had died as tidily as he'd lived, Alicia said: all his life he'd been meticulous. The Learys had failed to take that into account in any way whatsoever. If it came to a court of law the Learys wouldn't have a leg to stand on, with the written evidence that the precise amount taken out of the building society matched the amount of the bill, and further evidence in Matthew's reputation for promptness about settling debts.

'What I'm wondering is,' Alicia said, 'should we go to the Guards?'

'The Guards?'

'He shouldn't have come here like that.'

That evening there arrived a bill for the amount quoted by Leary, marked *Account rendered*. It was dropped through the letter-box and was discovered the next morning beneath the *Irish Independent* on the hall doormat.

'The little twister!' Alicia furiously exclaimed.

From the road outside the house came the morning commands of the convent girl in charge of the crossing to the school. 'Get ready!' 'Prepare to cross!' 'Cross now!' Impertinence had been added to dishonesty, Alicia declared in outraged tones. It was as though it had never been pointed out to Leary that Matthew had left the house on the evening in question with two hundred and twenty-six pounds in an envelope, that Leary's attention had never been drawn to the clear evidence of the building-society entry.

'It beats me,' Catherine said, and in the hall Alicia turned sharply and said it was as clear as day. Again she mentioned going

to the Guards. A single visit from Sergeant McBride, she maintained, and the Learys would abandon their cheek. From the play-
yard the yells of the girls increased as more girls arrived there, and
then the hand-bell sounded; a moment later there was silence.

'I'm only wondering,' Catherine said, 'if there's some kind of a
mistake.'

'There's no mistake, Catherine.'

Alicia didn't comment further. She led the way to the kitchen
and half filled a saucepan with water for their two boiled eggs.
Catherine cut bread for toast. When she and Alicia had been
girls in that same play-yard she hadn't known of Matthew's existence. Years passed before she even noticed him, at Mass one Saturday night. And it was ages before he first invited her to go out
with him, for a walk the first time, and then for a drive.

'What d'you think happened then?' Alicia asked. 'That
Matthew bet the money on a dog? That he owed it for drink
consumed? Have sense, Catherine.'

Had it been Alicia's own husband whom Leary had charged
with negligence, there would have been no necessary suspension
of disbelief: feckless and a nuisance, involved during his marriage
with at least one other woman in the town, frequenter of race-
courses and dog-tracks and bars, he had ended in an early grave.
This shared thought – that behaviour which was ludicrous
when attached to Matthew had been as natural in Alicia's husband as breathing – was there between the sisters, but was not
mentioned.

'If Father Cahill got Leary on his own,' Alicia began, but Catherine interrupted. She didn't want that, she said; she didn't want
other people brought into this, not even Father Cahill. She didn't
want a fuss about whether or not her husband had paid a bill.

'You'll get more of these,' Alicia warned, laying a finger on the
envelope that had been put through the letter-box. 'They'll keep
on coming.'

'Yes.'

In the night Catherine had lain awake, wondering if Matthew had maybe lost the money on his walk to the Learys' house that evening, if he'd put his hand in his pocket and found it wasn't there and then been too ashamed to say. It wasn't like him; it didn't make much more sense than thinking he had been a secretive man, with private shortcomings all the years she'd been married to him. When Alicia's husband died Matthew had said it was hard to feel sorry, and she'd agreed. Three times Alicia had been left on her own, for periods that varied in length, and on each occasion they'd thought the man was gone for good; but he returned and Alicia always took him back. Of course Matthew hadn't lost the money; it was as silly to think that as to wonder if he'd been a gambler.

'In case they'd try it on anyone else,' Alicia was saying, 'isn't it better they should be shown up? Is a man who'd get up to that kind of game safe to be left in people's houses the way a workman is?'

That morning they didn't mention the matter again. They washed up the breakfast dishes and then Catherine went out to the shops, which was always her chore, while Alicia cleaned the stairs and the hall, the day being a Thursday. As Catherine made her way through the familiar streets, and then while Mr Deegan sliced bacon for her and Gilligan greeted her in the hardware, she thought about the journey her husband had made that Wednesday evening in September. Involuntarily, she glanced into Healy's, where he had bought the *Evening Press*, and into McKenny's bar. Every evening except Sunday he had brought back the news, bits of gossip, anything he'd heard. It was at this time, too, that he went to Confession, on such occasions leaving the house half an hour earlier.

In French Street a countrywoman opened her car door without looking and knocked a cyclist over. 'Ah, no harm done,' the youth on the bicycle said, the delivery boy for Lawless the West Street butcher, the last delivery boy in the town. 'Sure, I never saw him at all,' the countrywoman protested to Catherine as she went by. The car door was dinged, but the woman said what did it matter if the lad was all right?

Culliney, the traveller from Limerick Shirts, was in town that day. Matthew had always bought his shirts direct from Culliney, the same striped pattern, the stripe blue or brown. Culliney had his measurements, the way he had the measurements of men all over Munster and Connacht, which was his area. Catherine could tell when she saw Culliney coming towards her that he didn't know about the death, and she braced herself to tell him. When she did so he put a hand on her arm and spoke in a whisper, saying that Matthew had been a good man. If there was anything he could ever do, he said, if there was any way he could help. More people said that than didn't.

It was then that Catherine saw Mrs Leary. The house-painter's wife was pushing her pram, a child holding on to it as she advanced. Catherine crossed the street, wondering if the woman had seen her and suspecting she had. In Jerety's she selected a pan loaf from the yesterday's rack, since neither she nor Alicia liked fresh bread and yesterday's was always reduced. When she emerged, Mrs Leary was not to be seen.

'Nothing only a woman knocked young Nallen off his bike,' she reported to Alicia when she returned to the house. '*Is* he a Nallen, that boy of Lawless's?'

'Or a Keane, is he? Big head on him?'

'I don't think he's a Keane. Someone told me a Nallen. Whoever he is, there's no harm done.' She didn't say she'd seen Mrs Leary because she didn't want to raise the subject of what had occurred again. She knew that Alicia was right: the bill would keep coming unless she did something about it. Once they'd set out on the course they'd chosen, why should the Learys give up? Alicia didn't refer to the Learys either but that evening, when they had switched off the television and were preparing to go to bed, Catherine said:

'I think I'll pay them. Simplest, that would be.'

With her right hand on the newel of the banister, about to ascend the stairs, Alicia stared in disbelief at her sister. When Catherine nodded and continued on her way to the kitchen she followed her.

'But you can't.' Alicia stood in the doorway while Catherine washed and rinsed the cups they'd drunk their bedtime tea from. 'You can't just pay them what isn't owing.'

Catherine turned the tap off at the sink and set the cups to drain, slipping the accompanying saucers between the plastic bars of the drainer. Tomorrow she would withdraw the same sum from the building-society account and take it herself to the Learys in Brady's Lane. She would stand there while a receipt was issued.

'Catherine, you can't hand out more than two hundred pounds.'

'I'd rather.'

As she spoke, she changed her mind about the detail of the payment. Matthew had been obliging Leary by paying cash, but there was no need to oblige him any more. She would arrange for the Irish Nationwide to draw a cheque payable to T. P. Leary. She would bring it round to the Learys instead of a wad of notes.

'They've taken you for a fool,' Alicia said.

'I know they have.'

'Leary should go behind bars. You're aiding and abetting him. Have sense, woman.'

A disappointment rose in Alicia, bewildering and muddled. The death of her own husband had brought an end, and her expectation had been that widowhood for her sister would be the same. Her expectation had been that in their shared state they would be as once they were, now that marriage was over, packed away with their similar mourning clothes. Yet almost palpable in the kitchen was Catherine's resolve that what still remained for her should not be damaged by a fuss of protest over a confidence trick. The Guards investigating clothes sold at a jumble sale, strangers asked if a house-painter's wife had bought this garment or that, private intimacies made public: Catherine was paying money in case, somehow, the memory of her husband should be accidentally tarnished. And knowing her sister well, Alicia knew that this resolve would become more stubborn as more time passed. It would mark and influence her sister; it would breed new eccentricities in her. If Leary had not come that day there would have been something else.

'You'd have the man back, I suppose?' Alicia said, trying to hurt and knowing she succeeded. 'You'd have him back in to paint again, to lift the bits and pieces from your dressing-table?'

'It's not to do with Leary.'

'What's it to do with then?'

'Let's leave it.'

Hanging up a tea-towel, Catherine noticed that her fingers were trembling. They never quarrelled; even in childhood they hadn't. In all the years Alicia had lived in the house she had never spoken in this unpleasant way, her voice rudely raised.

'They're walking all over you, Catherine.'

'Yes.'

They did not speak again, not even to say goodnight. Alicia closed her bedroom door, telling herself crossly that her expectation had not been a greedy one. She had been unhappy in her foolish marriage, and after it she had been beholden in this house. Although it ran against her nature to do so, she had borne her lot without complaint; why should she not fairly have hoped that in widowhood they would again be sisters first of all?

*

In her bedroom Catherine undressed and for a moment caught a glimpse of her nakedness in her dressing-table looking-glass. She missed his warmth in bed, a hand holding hers before they slept, that last embrace, and sometimes in the night his voice saying he loved her. She pulled her nightdress on, then knelt to pray before she turned the light out.

Some instinct, vague and imprecise, drew her in the darkness on to the territory of Alicia's disappointment. In the family photographs – some clearly defined, some drained of detail, affected by the sun – they were the sisters they had been: Alicia beautiful, confidently smiling; Catherine in her care. Catherine's first memory was of a yellow flower, and sunlight, and a white cloth hat put on her head. That flower was a cowslip, Alicia told her afterwards, and told her that they'd gone with their mother to the ruins by the river that day, that it was she who found the cowslip. 'Look, Catherine,' she'd said. 'A lovely flower.' Catherine had watched in admiration when Alicia paraded in her First Communion dress, and later when boys paid her attention. Alicia was the important one, responsible, reliable, right about things, offered the deference that was an older sister's due. She'd been a strength, Catherine said after the funeral, and Alicia was pleased, even though she shook her head.

Catherine dropped into sleep after half an hour of wakefulness. She woke up a few times in the night, on each occasion to find her thoughts full of the decision she had made and of her sister's outraged face, the two tiny patches of red that had come into it, high up on her cheeks, the snap of disdain in her eyes. 'A laughing-stock,' Alicia said in a dream. 'No more than a laughing-stock, Catherine.'

As Catherine lay there she imagined the silent breakfast there would be, and saw herself walking to Brady's Lane, and Leary fiddling with his cigarette-making gadget, and Mrs Leary in fluffy pink slippers, her stockingless legs mottled from being too close to the fire. Tea would be offered, but Catherine would refuse it. 'A decenter man never stood in a pair of shoes,' Leary could be counted upon to state.

She did not sleep again. She watched the darkness lighten, heard the first cars of the day pass on the road outside the house. By chance, a petty dishonesty had made death a potency for her sister, as it had not been when she was widowed herself. Alicia had cheated it of its due; it took from her now, as it had not then.

Catherine knew this intuition was no trick of her tired mind. While they were widows in her house Alicia's jealousy would be the truth they shared, tonight's few moments of its presence lingering insistently. Widows were widows first. Catherine would mourn, and feel in solitude the warmth of love. For Alicia there was the memory of her beauty.

Gilbert's Mother

On November 20th 1989, a Monday, in an area of South London not previously notable for acts of violence, Carol Dickson, a nineteen-year-old shop assistant, was bludgeoned to death between the hours of ten-fifteen and midnight. At approximately nine-fifty she had said goodnight to her friend Lindsayanne Trotter, with whom she had been watching *Coronation Street*, *Brookside* and *Boon*. She set out to walk the seven hundred yards to her parents' house on the Ralelands estate, but did not arrive. Her parents, imagining that she and Lindsayanne had gone to a disco – notwithstanding that the night was Monday – went to bed at eleven o'clock, their normal practice whether their daughter had returned to the house or not. Carol Dickson's body was discovered by a window-cleaner the following morning, lying on fallen leaves and woody straggles of cotoneaster, more than a mile and a half away, in Old Engine Way. Not wishing to become involved in what he described as 'obviously something tacky', the window-cleaner remounted his bicycle and rode on; an hour later schoolchildren reported a dead body in the bushes in Old Engine Way. Since the window-cleaner – Ronald Craig Thomas – was known to take this route along Old Engine Way every weekday morning, he was later interrupted in his work and questioned by the police. At midday on that same day, in broadcasting news of the tragedy, a radio announcer drew attention to this fact, stating that a man was helping the police with their enquiries. He also stated that Carol Dickson had been raped before her death, which was either a misinterpretation of information passed on to him or speculation on his part. It was not true.

*

Rosalie Mannion, fifty a month ago, peeled potatoes at the sink in her kitchen, listening to *The Archers*. Middle age suited her features; her round, pretty face had taken charge of what wrinkles had come, by chance distributing them favourably. Still a slight figure, she had in no way run to fat; the grey in her hair lent it a distinction that had not been there before. Her brown eyes had lost only a little of the luminosity that had been distinctive in Rosalie's childhood.

'Hullo,' she called out, hearing her son's footsteps on the stairs. She didn't catch Gilbert's reply because of the chatter of voices on the radio, but she knew he would have made one because he always did. *The Archers'* music came on, and then there was talk about irradiated food.

At the time of her divorce it was decided that Rosalie should have the house. That was sixteen years ago, in 1973. There hadn't been a quarrel about the house, nor even an argument. It was Gilbert's home; it was only fair that Gilbert's life should be disrupted as slightly as possible. So 21 Blenheim Avenue, SW15, was made over to her, while the man she'd been married to joined another woman in a Tudor-style property near Virginia Water. Rosalie returned to the botanical research she'd been engaged in before her marriage but after three years she found herself so affected by tiredness that she gave it up. She worked part-time now, in a shop that sold furniture fabrics.

At the back of Rosalie's mind was the comforting feeling that 21 Blenheim Avenue would one day become Gilbert's livelihood. She planned to convert the attics and the first floor, making them into self-contained flats. She and Gilbert would easily find room to spread themselves on the ground floor, which would of course retain the garden, and after her death that pattern would continue, and there would be an income from what Gilbert's father had invested on his behalf. Gilbert, she knew, would never marry. At present he worked in an architect's office – filing drawings, having photocopies made, taking the correspondence to be franked at the post office, delivering packages or collecting them, making tea and coffee, tidying. In the evenings Rosalie heard about the inspirations Gilbert had had about rearranging the contents of the drawings' cabinets or heard that Kall Kwik were cheaper than Instant Action by twopence a sheet. 'Oh, great,' was all anyone at the office ever said apparently; but his mother listened to the details.

'Was everything all right today?' she asked when he came downstairs again on the evening of November 21st. He rooted in the kitchen drawers for knives and forks and table-mats.

'Mega,' he said, telling her about his day while he made the mustard.

He assembled the cutlery and the table-mats with the galleons on them, and took a tray into the dining-room, where he set the table and turned the television on. They always ate watching the television, but not with plates on their knees, which both of them disliked. They sat side by side at the table and when they'd finished Gilbert helped to wash up and then usually went out, walking to the Arab Boy or the Devonshire Arms, sometimes driving over to the Bull or the Market Gardener. Rosalie had often listened while he explained that he liked to relax in this way after his day's work; that he liked having people around him, while being alone himself; that he liked the sound of voices, and music if someone played the juke-box. He didn't drink much; cider because he didn't care for beer, a couple of half pints in the course of an evening. He often told her that also. He told her everything, Gilbert said, looking at her steadily, his tone of voice indicating that this was not true.

*

The window-cleaner, Ron, had been reprimanded by the police inspector in charge of the case, and later by a sergeant and by a woman constable. The body in the cotoneaster could have been still alive, he was told; it hadn't been, but it easily could have. It was the duty of any citizen to report something of that nature, instead of which he'd callously ridden off.

Ron, who happened to be the same age as Gilbert Mannion – twenty-five – replied that he had a contract: the shop windows in Disraeli Street and Lower Street had to be washed by nine o'clock; if he delayed, either in the work itself or on his journey to it, that deadline would not be met. As well as which, he had been unnerved by the sight of a half-dressed girl lying all twisted up like that, her two eyes staring at him; no one like that could be alive, he maintained.

For five hours the police had worried about Ron Thomas. He had previous convictions, for petty larceny and damage to property. But there was still nothing to connect him with the crime that had been committed, beyond the fact that he'd failed to report it. In reprimanding him on that count, the inspector, the sergeant and the woman constable managed to assuage their impatience and frustration. The night before, between the hours of ten-fifteen and midnight, Ron Thomas's whereabouts were firmly accounted for. 'You appear to be a brute, Thomas,' the inspector pronounced in a take-it-or-leave-it voice, and turned his attention to a silver-coloured Vauxhall that had been noticed in the vicinity.

A woman called Mathers had seen it, as had a couple who'd been kissing in a doorway. The car drove down Old Engine Way earlier in the evening, nine or so it would have been, then turned into a cul-de-sac – Stables Lane – where it remained parked for half an hour, although no one had emerged. Mrs Mathers, who lived in Stables Lane, heard the engine of a car and went to the window to look. The headlights had been switched off; Mrs Mathers had the feeling that whoever was in the vehicle was up to no good and remarked as much to her sister. The couple in the doorway said that when the headlights came on again the car turned very slowly in the cul-de-sac; as it emerged into Old Engine Way, they were dazzled by its lights for a moment; they couldn't see its occupant.

'Occupants more like,' the inspector wearily corrected when the couple had left. 'Some slag on the game.'

Even so, a description of the Vauxhall was put together, its bodywork scraped and rusty, its radio aerial twisted into a knot: within minutes, calls came in from all over London, of silver-coloured Vauxhalls with such distinguishing features. Some of the calls were malicious – the opportunity seized to settle old scores against the owners of such vehicles; others led nowhere. But a woman, phoning from a call-box, said that a friend of hers had been driven to Stables Lane the night before, at the time in question. The woman gave neither her name nor her profession, only adding that her friend had been driven to Stables Lane because there was a family matter to be discussed in the car and Stables Lane was quiet. It was assumed that this was the prostitute or part-time prostitute suggested by the inspector; as with Ron Thomas, interest in the silver-coloured Vauxhall was abandoned.

*

Gilbert was dark-haired, five foot eight tall, sparely made. His features were neat, a neat mouth and nose, brown eyes very like his mother's, high cheekbones. Everything about Gilbert went together; even his voice – soft and unemphatic – belonged to a whole. The most distinctive thing about him was that – for no apparent reason, and even when he was not being loquacious – his presence in a room could not be overlooked; and often his presence lingered after he had left.

When Gilbert was two there had been an intensity in his gaze that Rosalie considered strange. Staring at the leg of a chair or at his own foot, he managed not to blink for minutes on end. He made no sound, and it was this she found unnerving. He took to examining, very closely, the palms of his hands. He splayed his fingers the way an old man might, and still in silence appeared to search the skin for flaws. Then, as abruptly as it all began, the staring ceased. But when he was five certain small objects from the kitchen disappeared – teaspoons, egg-cups, a potato-peeler. They were never found.

When he was nine Gilbert underwent psychiatric attention. The immediate reason for this was because one day he did not return from school. He should have returned on the bus, travelling with a handful of other children who lived in the same neighbourhood. Later that afternoon the police were informed, but Gilbert wasn't found and there were no reports of his having been seen anywhere. At half-past seven the next morning he rang the bell of 21 Blenheim Avenue, having spent the night in the basement of a block of flats. He gave his mother no explanation. Silence replaced his normal eagerness to communicate, as it had when he had first begun to examine his hands and when the kitchen objects disappeared.

Soon after that Gilbert refused to do the homework he was set and took to sitting, silent and still, in the classroom, refusing to open his books or even to take them out of his satchel. When asked, he again offered no explanation. The doggedness that was to characterize Gilbert in adult life began then: a psychiatrist declared that the child believed he was being deprived of certain rights, and a psychoanalyst – some time later – read the trouble similarly, while presenting it with his own professional variation and an adjustment of jargon. Gilbert, fourteen in 1978, spent that year in a centre devoted to the observation of erratic behavioural tendencies. 'Gilbert'll be encouraged to share his difficulties with us,' a man with a beard told Rosalie, adding vaguely: 'And of course there'll be regular counselling.' But when Gilbert returned to 21 Blenheim Avenue he was the same as he'd been before except that he'd grown almost two inches and possessed a notice-able fuzz of down on his upper lip and chin. Since the time he'd refused to co-operate in school he had successfully taught himself mathematics, Latin, geography, French and rudimentary German. He read voraciously, mainly history and historical biographies; in correctly spelt, grammatical prose he wrote long essays and talked to Rosalie about Cavour and Charlemagne and various treaties and land settlements. In 1984, when he was twenty, he disap-peared for a week. At the end of the following year he disappeared for longer, but sent Rosalie picture postcards from a number of South Coast seaside resorts, saying he was OK, working in hotels. Later he didn't elaborate on that, and the next time he disap-peared there were cards from the same area; when he returned he had acquired a Skoda. His mother never discovered when and where he had learnt to drive, or in what manner he had obtained the licence she discovered in one of his dressing-table drawers. He worked for a while in the potting department of a jam factory before moving to the architect's office, which he said was a more interesting place to be. A social worker – a conscientious woman who had known Gilbert during his time in the behavioural centre – still occasionally visited him, coming to the house on Saturday mornings, when he didn't have to go to work. *Talks excessively about photocopying*, she noted once, and felt it was too harsh to add that Gilbert's loquaciousness was very boring to listen to. In the end, remarking to Rosalie that her son did not appear to be benefiting from her counselling and had settled well into his employment, she ceased her Saturday-morning visits. *Seems satisfactory*, she noted. *Gives no trouble.*

Rosalie did not share that sanguine view. She did not believe her son was satisfactory. She had not believed it for a long time, and was aware that the afternoon he had failed to return from school was a single bead in the chain of unease that was beginning to form. When he had been taken into the behavioural centre her hope was that he would remain there indefinitely. 'Now, let's try to discover why you wish that, Mrs Mannion,' one of the staff had pressed her, his manner loftily clinical. But when she said it was simply something she felt, she was brought up sharply. It was pointed out to her that the centre was for observation and study, and the accumulation of case histories: in that respect it was doing well by Gilbert, but it stood to reason he could not remain there. Her son was fortunate to have her, she was informed. She had a role, that same lofty manner insisted, without words. She was, after all, the mother.

*

On the evening of Tuesday, November 21st Gilbert helped with the washing-up as usual, and then said he intended to drive over to the Bull public house. He reminded his mother where it was, as he often did: at the corner of Upper Richmond Road and Sheen Lane.

'I'll not stay long,' he said.

On the nine o'clock television News a picture was shown of the straggling cotoneaster and the dead leaves where Carol Dickson's body had lain. Carol's mother, appealing for witnesses to come forward, broke down in the middle of what she was saying; the camera lingered on her distress.

Rosalie turned the television off, not moving from where she sat, using the remote control. For the moment she couldn't even remember if Gilbert had gone out last night, then she remembered that he had and had come back earlier than usual. It was always the News, on the radio or the television, that prompted her dread. When a fire was said to have been started deliberately, or a child enticed, or broken glass discovered in baby-food jars in a supermarket, the dread began at once – the hasty calculations, the relief if time and geography ruled out involvement. More than once, before she became used to it, she had gone to lie trembling on her bed, struggling to control the frenzy that threatened. The second time he sent his picture postcards, her mocking little screen had shown a burnt-out dance hall, fourteen fatalities obscured by blankets in a Brighton car park. There had been a fire – deliberately started also, so the News suspected – on a cross-channel ferry four days after Gilbert had announced, 'I'll just take the Skoda here and there.' He had been away when a branch of the Halifax Building Society was held up by a gun-man who left his weapon on the counter, a water-pistol as it was afterwards discovered. He had been away when an old woman was tied to a chair in her council flat and only an alarm clock stolen from her, which reminded Rosalie of the teaspoons and egg-cups and the potato-peeler. She was certain a kind of daring came into it, even if the chances he took were loaded in his favour: he did not place himself in danger, he had a right to survive his chosen acts of recklessness, he had a right to silence. He would not be caught.

Last night he had come back earlier than usual: again, unable to help herself, she established that. But the recollection hardly made a difference. As soon as she'd seen the place where the body had been and noted the tired bewilderment in the police inspec-tor's eyes, she knew there was a mystery; that weeks, or months, would pass without progress, that the chances were the crime would remain unsolved. She knew, as well, that if she went to Gil-bert's room she'd find not a single leaf of cotoneaster, no titbit taken from the girl's clothing. There wouldn't be a scratch any-where on Gilbert, nor a tear in his clothes, nor a speck of blood in his Skoda.

It had never been said that Rosalie's marriage failed because of Gilbert, but often during the sixteen years that had passed since the divorce she wondered if somehow this could be so. Had she, even then – when Gilbert was only nine – been half destroyed by the nagging of her fears, made unattractive, made limp, wrung out by an obsession that spread insidiously? None of that was said: the other woman was the reason and the cause. An irresistible love was what was spoken of.

Rosalie had often since considered that the irresistible love had picked up the fragments that were already there. Hidden at the time – like something beneath a familiar stone, something that had arrived without being noticed as a danger – was the reason and the cause. This view was strengthened by subsequent events. Since the divorce there had been kindness from men who liked her, theatre visits and tête-à-tête dinners, hints of romance. But there had always been a fizzling-out, caution creeping in. She tried on all such occasions not to talk about her son, but she knew that he was somehow there anyway, and dread is hard to hide. It intensified her solitude, spread nerviness and was exhausting. In the fabrics shop, when voices all around her were saying what a terrible thing, it wasn't easy to keep her hands from shaking.

*

'I've brought you back the *Evening Standard*,' Gilbert said, smiling at her. It was a habit of his to pick up newspapers in public houses. He played a game sometimes, watching the people who were reading them, trying to guess which one would be left behind. He never bought a newspaper himself.

'Thank you, dear,' she said, returning his smile. *I believe Gilbert has stolen a car*, she had written to his father, who phoned as soon as he received the letter, listening without interrupting to everything she said. But he'd pointed out, quite gently, that she was merely guessing, that it was suspicion, nothing more.

'Cake?' Gilbert said. 'A Mr Kipling's, have we?'

She said there was a cake in the kitchen, in the Quality Street tin.

'Tea?' he offered.

She shook her head. 'No, not tonight, dear.'

He didn't leave the room, telling her instead about his visit to the public house. He had drunk half a pint of cider and watched the other drinkers. Two girls were crawling all over a man with a moustache, a man who was much older than they were. The girls were drunk, shrill when they laughed or spoke. The red, white-spotted skirt of one of them had ridden up so far that Gilbert could see her panties. Blue the panties were.

'Funny, that,' Gilbert said. 'The way she didn't mind.'

On the front of the *Evening Standard* she could see a half-page photograph of Carol Dickson, not a particularly pretty girl, her mouth clenched tight in a grin, bright blonde hair. She might have guessed he'd bring in the *Evening Standard*; she would have if she'd thought about it. 'You're an imaginative woman,' one of the experts she'd pleaded with had stated, fingering papers on his desk. 'Better, really, to be down to earth in a case like this.'

In the public house an old man had bothered him, he said. 'Busy tonight, ' the old man had remarked.

Gilbert had agreed, moving slightly so that he could watch the girls, but the old man was still in his way.

'Fag, dear?' the old man offered, holding out a packet of Benson & Hedges.

She could always guess, Rosalie sometimes thought: what would happen next, how he wouldn't refer to the girl on the front of the *Evening Standard*, how the panic would softly gather inside her and harden without warning into a knot, how the dryness in her mouth would make speech difficult.

'Afterwards I flagged down a police car,' Gilbert said. ' "That old poufta's out again tonight," I told them. Well, I had to.'

He'd noticed the police car crawling along, he said, so he drew in in front of it and made a hand signal. 'I told them he'd still be there if they went along immediately. They wrote down what he'd said to me, tone of voice and everything. When I put it to them they agreed an obscene way of talking is against the law. Quite nice they were. I thought I'd better report it, I explained to them, in case the next time it was some young boy. They said quite right. They'll have him on their books now. Even if they decide not to take him in tonight they'll have him on their books. They can give a man like that a warning or they can take him in if there are charges preferred. I'd always be ready to prefer charges because of the harm that could be done to an innocent boy. I said that. I said this was the eighth or ninth time he'd addressed me in that tone of voice. They quite agreed that people should be allowed to have a drink in peace.'

'You didn't go out again last night, did you, dear?'

'*Last* night? It was tonight the poufta –'

'No, I meant last night. You were back quite early, weren't you?'

Headachy for no particular reason, she'd gone to bed after supper. But she'd heard him coming in, no later than a quarter-past nine, certainly no later than half-past. She'd fallen asleep about ten; she thought she remembered the sound of the television just before she dropped off.

'*The Big Sleep* last night,' he said. 'But you can't re-set a thing like that in England. It doesn't make sense. A girl in the Kall Kwik was saying it was great, but I said I thought it was pathetic. I said it didn't make any sense, interfering with an original like that. Silly of them to go interfering, I said.'

'Yes.'

'West Indian the girl was.'

Rosalie smiled and nodded.

'Funny, saying it was great. Funny kind of view.'

'Perhaps she didn't know there'd been an original.'

'I said. I explained about it. But she just kept saying it was great. They're like that, the West Indian girls.'

Sometimes, when he went on talking, she felt like the shadow of a person who was not there. Ordinary-sounding statements he made exhausted her. Was it a deliberate act, that tonight he'd had a conversation with the police? Was it all part of being daring, of challenging the world that would take his rights from him? Often it seemed to her that his purposeless life was full of purpose.

'I'll make us tea,' he said. 'Really cold it is tonight.'

'Not tea for me, dear.'

'Chap in the Kall Kwik was saying the anti-freeze on his windscreen froze. If you can believe him, of course. Whopper Toms they call him. Says he likes the taste of paper. Eats paper bags, cardboard, anything like that. *If* you can believe him. Means no harm, though.'

'No, I'm sure he doesn't.'

'Congenital. Pity, really. I mean, I've seen him chewing, always chewing he is. It's just that it could be gum. Could be a toffee, come to that.'

Impassive she sat, staring at the grey empty screen of the television set when he went to make his tea. His father had found it impossible to love him, long before the marriage had collapsed. That had not been said either, but she knew it was true. For some reason he did not inspire love, even in a father. Yet it had broken her heart to say he should be retained in the centre where they'd studied him. It had broken her heart each time she'd begged that he should be put somewhere else, when they'd said the centre wasn't suitable. Vigilance was his due, a vigilance she was herself unable, adequately, to supply. All she could do was listen to his rigmaroles, and care that he couldn't bear wool next to his skin. The policemen he'd flagged down would have said he had a screw loose. In the Kall Kwik they would say the same.

'You saw it to the end?' she asked when he returned with a tray. 'You saw that film to the end even though it was so silly?'

'What film's that?'

'*The Big Sleep.*'

'Really grotty it was.'

He turned the television on. Politicians discussed Romania. His features, coloured by the highlights from the screen, displayed no emotion, neither elation nor melancholy. He was meticulous about taking the drugs prescribed. 'There is nothing to fear,' she had been assured, 'if the medication is taken. Nothing whatsoever.'

The time of the dance-hall fire she'd thought she'd never see him again. She'd thought he wouldn't come back and that eventually there'd be questions, two and two put together. She had imagined waiting, and nothing happening, day after day; and then, in some unexpected place, his apprehension. Instead he returned.

'Mr Kipling's Fancies,' he said, offering her the iced cakes, still in their cardboard carton. When she shook her head he poured his tea.

'Bet you it's gum he chews,' he said. 'Bet you.'

If he'd gone out again last night she'd have heard the car starting. The car would have woken her. She'd have sat up, worrying. She'd have turned her bedside light on and waited to hear the car returning. Even if he'd left the house again almost as soon as he'd entered it he would have to have driven very fast to reach that part of London by five to ten, which was the time they gave; five to ten at the latest, since the girl had said goodnight to her friend at nine-fifty and only had seven hundred yards to walk. There was nothing unusual about his bringing back the *Evening Standard*. He'd mentioned the old homosexual who bothered him before: it just happened that tonight there was a police car prowling.

'This is lousy stuff,' he said, and changed the television channel. His hands were thin – delicate hands, not much larger than her own. He was not given to violence. 'No! No!' he used to cry, still sometimes did, when she swatted a fly. In all his acts of bravado there had never been violence – when he refused to open his schoolbooks, when he spent a night in a basement, when he acquired a motor-car without money. No one would deny his cleverness, cunningly concealed beneath his tedious chatter. No one would deny being baffled by him, but there was never violence.

'Hey, look at that,' he suddenly exclaimed, drawing her attention to overweight people at a holiday camp for the obese. He laughed, and she remembered his infant's face when first they showed it to her. People didn't want him. His father and a whole army of medical people, the social worker, people he tried to make friends with: all of them deserted him too soon. He was on sufferance in the architect's office; wherever he went he was on sufferance.

'Awful,' he said, 'as fat as that.'

Then the News was on again, on Channel 3, and he sat silent – that awful silence that closed him down. On the screen the face of Carol Dickson was just as it was in the newspaper. Her mother broke down, the police inspector gave out his facts: all of it was repetition.

She watched him staring at the screen intently, as if mesmerized. He listened carefully. When the News was over he crossed the room and picked up the *Evening Standard*. He read it, his tea and cakes forgotten. She turned the television off.

'Goodnight, Gilbert,' she said when he rose to go to bed. He did not answer.

The newspaper was on the floor beside his chair, the face of Carol Dickson spread out for her, the right way up. She remembered how he'd stood when he'd come back after his first disappearance, how he leaned against the kitchen door-frame, following her with his eyes, silent. When he'd come back with the Skoda she'd thought of going to the police. She'd thought of trying to explain to some kindly older man in a uniform, asking for help. But of course she hadn't.

She might dial 999 now. Or she might go tomorrow to a police station, apologizing even before she began, hoping for reassurance.

But even as these thoughts occurred she knew they were pretence. Before his birth she had possessed him. She had felt the tug of his lips on her breasts, a helpless creature then, growing into the one who controlled her now, who made her isolation total. Her fear made him a person, enriching him with power. He had sensed it when he had first idly examined the palms of his hands, and felt her mother's instinct disturbed. He had sensed it when he had hidden the kitchen objects where they could not be found, when he had not come back from school, when he had talked to the social worker about photocopying. He knew about the jaded thoughts recurring, the worry coursing round and round at its slow, familiar pace. The Skoda had been stolen; parked outside the house, it was always a reminder.

All night, she knew, she would sit there, the muzzy image of Carol Dickson where he had left it, a yard away. She did not want to sleep because sleeping meant waking up and there would be the moment when reality began to haunt again. Her role was only to accept: he had a screw loose, she had willed him to be born. No one would ever understand the mystery of his existence, or the unshed tears they shared.

The Potato Dealer

Mulreavy would marry her if they paid him, Ellie's uncle said: she couldn't bring a fatherless child into the world. He didn't care what was done nowadays; he didn't care what the fashion was; he wouldn't tolerate the talk there'd be. 'Mulreavy,' her uncle repeated. 'D'you know who I mean by Mulreavy?'

She hardly did. An image came into her mind of a big face that had a squareness about it, and black hair, and a cigarette butt adhering to the lower lip while a slow voice agreed or disagreed, and eyes that were small, and sharp as splinters. Mulreavy was a potato dealer. Once a year he came to the farm, his old lorry rattling into the yard, then backed up to where the sacks stood ready for him. Sometimes he shook his head when he examined the potatoes, saying they were too small. He tried that on, Ellie's uncle maintained. Cagey, her uncle said.

'I'll tell you one thing, girl,' her uncle said when she found the strength to protest at what was being proposed. 'I'll tell you this: you can't stay here without there's something along lines like I'm saying. Nowadays is nothing, girl. There's still the talk.'

He was known locally as Mr Larrissey, rarely by his Christian name, which was Joseph. Ellie didn't call him 'Uncle Joseph', never had; 'uncle' sometimes, though not often, for even in that there seemed to be an intimacy that did not belong in their relationship. She thought of him as Mr Larrissey.

'It's one thing or the other, girl.'

Her mother – her uncle's sister – didn't say anything. Her mother hadn't opened her mouth on the subject of Mulreavy, but

Ellie knew that she shared the sentiments that were being expressed, and would accept, in time, the solution that had been offered. She had let her mother down; she had embittered her; why should her mother care what happened now? All of it was a mess. In the kitchen of the farmhouse her mother and her uncle were thinking the same thing.

Her uncle – a worn, tired man, not used to trouble like this – didn't forgive her and never would: so he had said, and Ellie knew it was true. Since the death of her father she and her mother had lived with him on the farm on sufferance: that was always in his eyes, even though her mother did all the cooking and the cleaning of the house, even though Ellie, since she was eleven, had helped in summer in the fields, had collected and washed the eggs and nourished the pigs. Her uncle had never married; if she and her mother hadn't moved on to the farm in 1978, when Ellie was five, he'd still be on his own, managing as best he could.

'You have the choice, girl,' he said now, the repetition heavy in the farmhouse kitchen. He was set in his ways, Ellie's mother often said; lifelong bachelors sometimes were.

He'd said at first – a fortnight ago – that his niece should get herself seen to, even though it was against religion. Her mother said no, but later wondered if it wasn't the only way out, the trip across the water that other girls had gone on, what else was there? They could go away and have it quietly done, they could be visiting the Galway cousins, no one would be the wiser. But Ellie, with what spirit was left in her, though she was in disgrace and crying, would not agree. In the fortnight that passed she many times, tearfully, repeated her resolve to let the child be born.

Loving the father, Ellie already loved the child. If they turned her out, if she had to walk the roads, or find work in Moyleglass or some other town, she would. But Ellie didn't want to do that; she didn't want to find herself penniless because it would endanger the birth. She would never do that was the decision she had privately reached the moment she was certain she was to have a child.

'Mulreavy,' her uncle said again.

'I know who he is.'

Her mother sat staring down at the lines of grain that years of scrubbing had raised on the surface of the kitchen table. Her mother had said everything she intended to say: disgrace, shame, a dirtiness occurring when people's backs were turned, all the thanks you get for what you give, for sacrifices made. 'Who'd want you now?' her mother had asked her, more than once.

'Mind you, I'm not saying Mulreavy'll bite,' Ellie's uncle said. 'I'm not saying he'd take the thing on.'

Ellie didn't say anything. She left the kitchen and walked out into the yard, where the turkeys screeched and ran towards her, imagining she carried meal to scatter, as often she did. She passed them by, and let herself through the black iron gate that led to the sloping three-cornered field beyond the outbuildings, the worst two acres of her uncle's property. Ragweed and gorse grew in profusion, speckled rock-surfaces erupted. It was her favourite field, perhaps because she had always heard it cursed and as a child had felt sorry for it. 'Oh, now, that's nice!' the father of her unborn baby said when she told him she felt sorry for the three-cornered field. It was then that he'd said he wished he'd known her as a child, and made her describe herself as she had been.

*

When it was put to Mulreavy he pretended offence. He didn't expostulate, for that was not his way. But as if in melancholy consideration of a personal affront he let the two ends of his mouth droop, as he sometimes did when he held a potato in his palm, shaking his head over its unsatisfactory size or shape. Ash from his cigarette dribbled down his shirt-front, the buttons of a fawn cardigan open because the day was warm, his shirt-collar open also and revealing a line of grime where it had been most closely in contact with the skin of his neck.

'Well, that's a quare one,' Mulreavy said, his simulated distaste slipping easily from him, replaced by an attempt at outraged humour.

'There's a fairish sum,' Mr Larrissey said, but didn't say what he had in mind and Mulreavy didn't ask. Nor did he ask who the father was. He said in a by-the-way voice that he was going out with a woman from Ballina who'd come to live in Moyleglass, a dressmaker's assistant; but the information was ignored.

'I only thought it was something would interest you,' Mr Larrissey said.

Their two vehicles were drawn up on the road, a rusting Ford Cortina and Mulreavy's lorry, the driving-side windows of both wound down. Mulreavy offered a cigarette. Mr Larrissey took it. As if about to drive away, he had put his hand on the gear when he said he'd only thought the proposition might be of interest.

'What's the sum?' Mulreavy asked when the cigarettes were lit, and a horn hooted because the vehicles were blocking the road. Neither man took any notice: they were of the neighbourhood, local people, the road was more theirs than strangers'.

When the extent of the money offered was revealed Mulreavy knew better than to react, favourably or otherwise. It would be necessary to give the matter thought, he said, and further considerations were put to him, so that at leisure he could dwell on those also.

*

Ellie's mother knew how it was, and how it would be: her brother would profit from the episode. The payment would be made by her: the accumulated pension, the compensation from the time of the accident in 1978. Her brother saw something for himself in the arrangement he hoped for with the potato dealer; the moment he had mentioned Mulreavy's name he'd been aware of a profit to be made. Recognizing at first, as she had herself, only shame and folly in the fact that his niece was pregnant, he had none the less explored the situation meticulously: that was his way. She had long been aware of her brother's hope that one day Ellie would marry some suitable young fellow who would join them in the farmhouse and could be put to work, easing the burden in the fields: that was how the debt of taking in a sister and a niece might at last be paid. But with a disaster such as there had been, there would be no young fellow now. Instead there was the prospect of Mulreavy, and what her brother had established in his mind was that Mulreavy could ease the burden too. A middle-aged potato dealer wasn't ideal for the purpose, but he was better than nothing.

Ellie's mother, resembling her brother in appearance, lean-faced and with his tired look, often recalled the childhood he and she had shared in this same house. More so than their neighbours, they were known to be a religious family, never missing Mass, going all together in the trap on Sundays and later by car, complimented for the faith they kept by Father Hanlon and his successor. The Larrisseys were respected people, known for the family virtues of hard work and disdain for ostentation, never seeming to be above themselves. She and her brother had all their lives been part of that, had never rebelled against these laid-down *mores* during the years of their upbringing.

Now, out of the cruel blue, there was this; and as far as brother and sister could remember, in the farmhouse there had never been anything as dispiriting. The struggle in bad seasons to keep two ends together, to make something of the rock-studded land even in the best of times, had never been lowering. Adversity of that kind was expected, the lot the family had been born into.

It had been expected also, when the accident occurred to the man she'd married, that Ellie's mother would return to the house that had become her brother's. She was forty-one then; her brother forty-four, left alone two years before when their parents had died within the same six months. He hadn't invited her to return, and though it seemed, in the circumstances, a natural consequence to both of them, she knew her brother had always since considered her beholden. As a child, he'd been like that about the few toys they shared, insisting that some were more his than hers.

'I saw Mulreavy,' he said on the day of the meeting on the road, his unsmiling, serious features already claiming a successful outcome.

*

Mulreavy's lorry had reached the end of its days and still was not fully paid for: within six months or so he would find himself unable to continue trading. This was the consideration that had crept into his mind when the proposition was put to him, and it remained there afterwards. There was a lorry he'd seen in McHugh Bros. with thirty-one thousand on the clock and at an asking price that would be reduced, the times being what they were. Mulreavy hadn't entirely invented the dressmaker from Ballina in whom he had claimed an interest: she was a wall-eyed woman he had recently seen about the place, who had arrived in Moyleglass to assist Mrs Toomey in her cutting and stitching. Mulreavy had wondered if she had money, if she'd bought her way into Mrs Toomey's business, as he'd heard it said. He'd never spoken to her or addressed her in any way, but after his conversation with Mr Larrissey he made further enquiries, only to discover that rumour now suggested the woman was employed by Mrs Toomey at a small wage. So Mulreavy examined in finer detail the pros and cons of marrying into the Larrisseys.

'There'd be space for you in the house,' was how it had been put to him. 'Maybe better than if you took her out of it. And storage enough for the potatoes in the big barn.'

A considerable saving of day-to-day expenses would result, Mulreavy had reflected, closing his eyes against the smoke from his cigarette when those words were spoken. He made no comment, waiting for further enticements, which came in time. Mr Larrissey said:

'Another thing is, the day will come when the land'll be too much for me. Then again, the day will come when there'll be an end to me altogether.'

Mr Larrissey had crossed himself. He had said no more, allowing the references to land and his own demise to dangle in the silence. Soon after that he jerked his head in a farewell gesture and drove away.

He'd marry the girl, Mulreavy's thoughts were later, after he'd heard the news about the dressmaker; he'd vacate his property, holding on to it until the price looked right and then disposing of it, no hurry whatsoever since he'd already be in the Larrisseys' farmhouse, with storage facilities and a good lorry. If he attended a bit to the land, the understanding was that he'd inherit it when the day came. It could be done in writing; it could be drawn up by Blaney in Moyleglass.

Eight days after their conversation on the road the two men shook hands, as they did when potatoes were bought and sold. Three weeks went by and then there was the wedding.

*

The private view of Ellie's mother – shared with neither her daughter nor her brother – was that the presence of Mulreavy in the farmhouse was a punishment for the brazen sin that had occurred. When the accident that had made a widow of her occurred, when she'd looked down at the broken body lying there, knowing it was lifeless, she had not felt that there was punishment in that, either directed at her or at the man she'd married. He had done little wrong in his life; indeed, had often sought to do good. Neither had she transgressed, herself, except in little ways. But what had led to the marriage of her daughter and the potato dealer was deserving of this harsh reprimand, which was something that must now be lived with.

*

 Mulreavy was given a bedroom that was furnished with a bed and a cupboard. He was not offered, and did not demand, his conjugal rights. He didn't mind; that side of things didn't interest him; it hadn't been mentioned; it wasn't part of the arrangement. Instead, daily, he surveyed the land that was to be his inheritance. He walked it, lovingly, at first when no one was looking, and later to identify the weed that had to be sprayed and to trace the drains. He visualized a time when he no longer travelled about as a middle-man, buying potatoes cheaply and selling at a profit, when the lorry he had acquired with the dowry would no longer be necessary. On these same poor acres sufficient potatoes could be grown to allow him to trade without buying in. Mulreavy wasn't afraid of work when there was money to be made.

*

The midwife called down the farmhouse stairs a few moments after Mulreavy heard the first cry. Mr Larrissey poured out a little of the whiskey that was kept in the wall-cupboard in case there was toothache in the house. His sister was at the upstairs bedside. The midwife said a girl had been born.

A year ago, it was Mr Larrissey, not his sister, who had first known about the summer priest who was the father of this child. On his way back from burning stubble he had seen his niece in the company of the man and had known from the way they walked that there was some kind of intimacy between them. When his niece's condition was revealed he had not, beneath the anger he displayed, been much surprised.

Mulreavy, clenching his whiskey glass, his lips touched with a smile, had not known he would experience a moment of happiness when the birth occurred; nor had he guessed that the dourness of Mr Larrissey would be affected, that whiskey would be offered. The thing would happen, he had thought, maybe when he was out in the fields. He would walk into the kitchen and they would tell him. Yet in the kitchen, now, there was almost an air of celebration, a satisfaction that the arrangement lived up to its promise.

Above where the two men sat, Ellie's mother did as the midwife directed in the matter of the afterbirth's disposal. She watched the baby being taken from its mother's arms and placed, sleeping now, in the cradle by the bedside. She watched her daughter struggling for a moment against the exhaustion that possessed her, before her eyes closed too.

*

The child was christened Mary Josephine – these family names chosen by Ellie's mother, and Ellie had not demurred. Mulreavy played his part, cradling the infant in his big arms for a moment at the font, a suit bought specially for the occasion. It wasn't doubted that he was the father, although the assumption also was that the conception had come first, the marriage later, as sometimes happened. There'd been some surprise at the marriage, not much.

Ellie accepted with equanimity what there was. She lived a little in the past, in the summer of her love affair, expecting of the future only what she knew of the present. The summer curate who had loved her, and whom she loved still, would not miraculously return. He did not even know that she had given life to his child. 'It can't be,' he'd said when they lay in the meadow that was now a potato field. 'It can't ever be, Ellie.' She knew it couldn't be : a priest was a priest. There would never, he promised, as if in compensation, be another love like this in all his life. 'Nor for me,' she swore as eagerly, although he did not ask for that, in fact said no, that she must live her normal life. 'No, not for me,' she repeated. 'I feel it too.' It was like a gift when she knew her child was to be born, a fulfilment, a forgiveness almost for their summer sin.

As months and then years went by, the child walked and spoke and suffered childhood ills, developed preferences, acquired characteristics that slipped away again or stubbornly remained. Ellie watched her mother and her uncle ageing, while they in turn were reminded by the child's presence of their own uneasy companionship in the farmhouse when they were as young as the child was now. Mulreavy, who did not go in for nostalgia or observing changes in other people, increased his potato yield. Like Mr Larrissey, he would have preferred the child who had been born to be a boy since a boy, later on, would be more useful, but he did not ever complain on this count. Mr Larrissey himself worked less, in winter often spending days sitting in the kitchen, warm by the Esse stove. For Ellie's mother, passing time did not alter her belief that the bought husband was her daughter's reprimand on earth.

All that was how things were on the farm and in the farmhouse. A net of compromise and acceptance and making the best of things held the household together. Only the child was aware of nothing, neither that a man had been bought to be her father nor that her great-uncle had benefited by the circumstances, nor that her grandmother had come to terms with a punishment, nor that her mother still kept faith with an improper summer love. The child's world when she was ten had more to do with reading whole pages more swiftly than she had a year ago, and knowing where Heligoland was, and reciting by heart *The Wreck of the Hesperus*.

But, without warning, the household was disturbed. Ellie was aware only of some inner restlessness, its source not identified, which she assumed would pass. But it did not pass, and instead acquired the intensity of unease: what had been satisfactory for the first ten years of her child's life was strangely not so now. In search of illumination, she pondered all that had occurred. She had been right not to wish to walk the roads with her fatherless infant, she had been right to agree to the proposal put to her: looking back, she could not see that she should, in any way whatsoever, have done otherwise. A secret had been kept; there were no regrets. It was an emotion quite unlike regret that assailed her. Her child smiled back at her from a child's innocence, and she remembered those same features, less sure and less defined, when they were newly in the farmhouse, and wondered how they would be when another ten years had passed. Not knowing now, her child would never know. She would never know that her birth had been accompanied by money changing hands. She would never know that, somewhere else, her father forgave the sins of other people, and offered Our Saviour's blood and flesh in solemn expiation.

'Can you manage them?' Ellie's husband asked when she was loading sacks on to the weighing scales, for she had paused in the work as if to rest.

'I'm all right.'

'Take care you don't strain yourself.'

He was often kind in practical ways. She was strong, but the work was not a woman's work and, although it was never said, he was aware of this. In the years of their marriage they had never quarrelled or even disagreed, not being close enough for that, and in this way their relationship reflected that of the brother and sister they shared the house with.

'They're a good size, the Kerrs,' he said, referring to the produce they worked with. 'We hit it right this year.'

'They're nice all right.'

She had loved her child's father for every day of their child's life and before it. She had falsified her confessions and a holy baptism. Black, ugly lies were there when their child smiled from her innocence, nails in another cross. It hadn't mattered at first, when their child wouldn't have understood.

'I'll stop now,' Ellie said, recording in the scales book the number of sacks that were ready to be sealed. 'I have the tea to get.'

Her mother was unwell, confined to her bedroom. It was usually her mother who attended to the meals.

'Go on so, Ellie,' he said. He still smoked forty cigarettes a day, his life's indulgence, a way to spend a fraction of the money he accumulated. He had bought no clothes since his purchase of the christening suit except for a couple of shirts, and he questioned the necessity of the clothes Ellie acquired herself or for her child. Meanness was a quality he was known for; commercially, it had assisted him.

'Oh, I got up,' Ellie's mother said in the kitchen, the table laid and the meal in the process of preparation. 'I couldn't lie there.'

'You're better?'

'I'd say I was getting that way.'

Mr Larrissey was washing traces of fertilizer from his hands at the sink, roughly rubbing in soap. From the yard came the cries of the child, addressing the man she took to be her father as she returned from her evening task of ensuring that the bullocks still had grass to eat.

*

All the love there had been, all the love there still was – love that might have nourished Ellie's child, that might have warmed her – was the deprivation the child suffered. Ellie remembered the gentle, pale hands of the lover who had given her the gift of her child, and heard again the whisper of his voice, and his lips lingered softly on hers. She saw him as she always now imagined him, in his cassock and his surplice, the embroidered cross that marked his calling repeated again in the gestures of his blessing. His eyes were still a shade of slate, his features retained their delicacy. Why should a child not have some vision of him too? Why should there be falsity?

'You've spoken to them, have you?' her husband asked when she said what she intended.

'No, only you.'

'I wouldn't want the girl told.'

He turned away in the potato shed, to heft a sack on to the lorry. She felt uneasy in herself, she said, the way things were, and felt that more and more. That feeling wasn't there without a reason. It was a feeling she was aware of most at Mass and when she prayed at night.

Mulreavy didn't reply. He had never known the identity of the father. Some runaway fellow, he had been told at the time by Mr Larrissey, who had always considered the shame greater because a priest was involved. 'No need Mulreavy should know that,' Ellie had been instructed by her mother, and had abided by this wish.

'It was never agreed,' Mulreavy maintained, not pausing in his loading. 'It wasn't agreed the girl would know.'

Ellie spoke of a priest then; her husband said nothing. He finished with the potato sacks and lit a cigarette. That was a shocking thing, he eventually remarked, and lumbered out of the barn.

'Are you mad, girl?' Her mother rounded on her in the kitchen, turning from the draining-board, where she was shredding cabbage. Mr Larrissey, who was present also, told her not to be a fool. What good in the world would it do to tell a child the like of that?

'Have sense, for God's sake,' he crossly urged, his voice thick with the bluster that obscured his confusion.

'You've done enough damage, Ellie,' her mother said, all the colour gone from her thin face. 'You've brought enough on us.'

When Mulreavy came into the kitchen an hour later he guessed at what had been said, but he did not add anything himself. He sat down to wait for his food to be placed in front of him. It was the first time since the arrangement had been agreed upon that any reference to it had been made in the household.

'That's the end of it,' Ellie's mother laid down, the statement made as much for Mulreavy's benefit as for Ellie's. 'We'll hear no more of this.'

Ellie did not reply. That evening she told her child.

*

People knew, and talked about it now. What had occurred ten years ago suddenly had an excitement about it that did not fail to please. Minds were cast back, memories ransacked in a search for the name and appearance of the summer priest who had been and gone. Father Mooney, who had succeeded old Father Hanlon, spoke privately to Ellie, deploring the exposure she had 'so lightly' been responsible for.

With God's grace, he pointed out, a rough and ready solution had been found and disgrace averted ten years ago. There should have been gratitude for that, not what had happened now. Ellie explained that every time she looked at her child she felt a stab of guilt because a deception of such magnitude had been perpetrated. 'Her life was no more than a lie,' Ellie said, but Father Mooney snappishly replied that that was not for her to say.

'You flew in the face of things once,' he fulminated, 'and now you've done it again.' When he glared at her, it showed in his expression that he considered her an unfit person to be in his parish. He ordered Hail Marys to be repeated, and penitence practised, with humility and further prayer.

But Ellie felt that a weight had been lifted from her, and she explained to her child that even if nothing was easy now, a time would come when the difficulties of the moment would all be gone.

*

Mulreavy suffered. His small possession of pride was bruised; he hardly had to think to know what people said. He went about his work in the fields, planting and harvesting, spreading muck and fertilizer, folding away cheques until he had a stack ready for lodgement in Moyleglass. The sour atmosphere in the farmhouse affected him, and he wondered if people knew, on top of everything else, that he occupied a bedroom on his own and always had, that he had never so much as embraced his wayward young bride. Grown heavier over the years, he became even heavier after her divulgence, eating more in his despondency.

He liked the child; he always had. The knowledge that a summer priest had fathered her caused him to like her no less, for the affection was rooted in him. And the child did not change in her attitude to him, but still ran to him at once when she returned from school, with tales of how the nuns had been that day, which one bad-tempered, which one sweet. He listened as he always had, always pausing in his work to throw in a word or two. He continued to tell brief stories of his past experiences on the road: he had traded in potatoes since he was hardly more than a child himself, fifteen when he first assisted his father.

But in the farmhouse Mulreavy became silent. In his morose mood he blamed not just the wife he'd married but her elders too. They had deceived him. And knowing more than he did about these things, they should have foreseen more than they had. The child bore his name. 'Mrs Mulreavy' they called his wife. He was a laughing-stock.

*

'I don't remember that man,' he said when almost a year had passed, a September morning. He had crossed the furrows to where she was picking potatoes from the clay he'd turned, the plough drawn by the tractor. 'I don't know did I ever see him.'

Ellie looked up at the dark-jowelled features, above the rough, thick neck. She knew which man he meant. She knew, as well, that it had required an effort to step down from his tractor and cross to where she was, to stand unloved in front of her. She said at once:

'He was here only a summer.'

'That would be it so. I was always travelling then.'

She gave the curate's name and he nodded slowly over it, then shook his head. He'd never heard that name, he said.

The sun was hot on her shoulders and her arms. She might have pointed across the ploughed clay to the field that was next to the one they were in. It was there, below the slope, that the conception had taken place. She wanted to say so, but she didn't. She said:

'I had to tell her.'

He turned to go away, then changed his mind, and again looked down at her.

'Yes,' he said.

She watched him slowly returning to where he'd left the tractor. His movements were always slow, his gait suggesting an economy of energy, his arms loose at his sides. She mended his clothes, she kept them clean. She assisted him in the fields, she made his bed. In all the time she'd known him she had never wondered about him.

The tractor started. He looked behind to see that the plough was as he wanted it. He lit another cigarette before he set off on his next brief journey.

Lost Ground

On the afternoon of September 14th 1989, a Thursday, Milton Leeson was addressed by a woman in his father's upper orchard. He was surprised. If the woman had been stealing the apples she could easily have dodged out of sight around the slope of the hill when she heard his footfall. Instead, she came forward to greet him, a lean-faced woman with straight black hair that seemed too young for her wasted features. Milton had never seen her before.

Afterwards he remembered that her coat, which did not seem entirely clean, was a shade of dark blue, even black. At her throat there was a scarf of some kind. She wasn't carrying anything. If she'd been stealing the apples she might have left whatever contained her takings behind the upper orchard's single growth of brambles, only yards from where she stood.

The woman came close to Milton, smiling at him with her eyes and parted lips. He asked her what she wanted; he asked her what she was doing in the orchard, but she didn't reply. In spite of her benign expression he thought for a moment she was mad and intended to attack him. Instead, the smile on her lips increased and she raised her arms as if inviting him to step into her embrace. When Milton did not do so the woman came closer still. Her hands were slender, her fingers as frail as twigs. She kissed him and then turned and walked away.

Afterwards Milton recalled very thin calves beneath the hem of her dark coat, and narrow shoulders, and the luxuriant black hair that seemed more than ever not to belong. When she'd kissed him her lips hadn't been moist like his mother's. They'd been dry as a bone, the touch of them so light he had scarcely felt it.

*

'Well?' Mr Leeson enquired that evening in the farmhouse kitchen.

Milton shook his head. In the upper orchard the Cox's were always the first to ripen. Nobody expected them to be ready as soon as this, but just occasionally, after a sunny summer, the first of the crop could catch you out. Due to his encounter with the stranger, he had forgotten to see if an apple came off easily when he twisted it on the branch. But he had noticed that not many had fallen, and guessed he was safe in intimating that the crop was better left for a while yet. Shyness prevented him from reporting that there'd been a woman in the orchard; if she hadn't come close to him, if she hadn't touched his lips with hers, it would have been different.

Milton was not yet sixteen. He was chunky, like his father and his brothers, one of them much older, the other still a child. The good looks of the family had gone into the two girls, which Mrs Leeson privately gave thanks for, believing that otherwise neither would have married well.

'They look laden from the lane,' Mr Leeson said, smearing butter on half a slice of bread cut from the loaf. Mr Leeson had small eyes and a square face that gave an impression of determination. Sparse grey hair relieved the tanned dome of his head, more abundant in a closely cropped growth around his ears and the back of his neck.

'They're laden all right,' Milton said.

The Leesons' kitchen was low-ceilinged, with a flagged floor and pale blue walls. It was a rambling, rectangular room, an illusion of greater spaciousness created by the removal of the doors from two wall-cupboards on either side of a recess that for almost fifty years had held the same badly stained Esse cooker. Sink and draining-boards, with further cupboards, lined the wall opposite, beneath narrow windows. An oak table, matching the proportions of the room, dominated its centre. There was a television set on a corner shelf, to the right of the Esse. Beside the door that led to the yard a wooden settee with cushions on it, and a high-backed chair, were placed to take advantage of the heat from the Esse while viewing the television screen. Five unpainted chairs were arranged around the table, four of them now occupied by the Leesons.

Generations of the family had sat in this kitchen, ever since 1809, when a Leeson had married into a household without sons. The house, four-square and slated, with a porch that added little to its appeal, had been rebuilt in 1931, when its walls were discovered to be defective. The services of a reputable local builder being considered adequate for the modifications, no architect had been employed. Nearly sixty years later, with a ragged front garden separating it from a lane that was used mainly by the Leesons, the house still stood white and slated, no tendrils of creeper softening its spare usefulness. At the back, farm buildings with red corrugated roofs and breeze-block walls were clustered around a concrete yard; fields and orchards were on either side of the lane. For three-quarters of a mile in any direction this was Leeson territory, a tiny fraction of County Armagh. The yard was well kept, the land well tended, both reflecting the hard-working Protestant family the Leesons were.

'There's more, Milton.'

His mother offered him salad and another slice of cold bacon. She had fried the remains of the champ they'd had in the middle of the day: potatoes mashed with butter and spring onions now had a crispy brown crust. She dolloped a spoonful on to Milton's plate beside the bacon and passed the plate back to him.

'Thanks,' Milton said, for gratitude was always expressed around this table. He watched his mother cutting up a slice of bacon for his younger brother, Stewart, who was the only other child of the family still at home. Milton's sister Addy had married the Reverend Herbert Cutcheon a year ago; his other sister was in Leicester, married also. His brother Garfield was a butcher's assistant in Belfast.

'Finish it up.' Mrs Leeson scooped the remains of the champ and spooned it on to her husband's plate. She was a small, delicately made woman with sharp blue eyes and naturally wavy hair that retained in places the reddish-brown of her girlhood. The good looks of her daughters had once been hers also and were not yet entirely dispelled.

Having paused while the others were served – that, too, being a tradition in the family – Milton began to eat again. He liked the champ best when it was fried. You could warm it in the oven or in a saucepan, but it wasn't the same. He liked crispness in his food – fingers of a soda farl fried, the spicy skin of a milk pudding, fried champ. His mother always remembered that. Milton sometimes thought his mother knew everything about him, and he didn't mind: it made him fond of her that she bothered. He felt affection for her when she sat by the Esse on winter's evenings or by the open back door in summer, sewing and darning. She never read the paper and only glanced up at the television occasionally. His father read the paper from cover to cover and never missed the television News. When Milton was younger he'd been afraid of his father, although he'd since realized that you knew where you were with him, which came from the experience of working with him in the fields and the orchards. 'He's fair,' Mrs Leeson used to repeat when Milton was younger. 'Always remember that.'

Milton was the family's hope, now that Garfield had gone to Belfast. Questioned by his father three years ago, Garfield had revealed that if he inherited the farm and the orchards he would sell them. Garfield was urban by inclination; his ambition during his growing-up was to find his feet in Belfast and to remain there. Stewart was a mongol.

'We'll fix a day for the upper orchard,' his father said. 'I'll fix with Gladdy about the boxes.'

*

That night Milton dreamed it was Esme Dunshea who had come to the upper orchard. Slowly she took off her dark coat, and then a green dress. She stood beneath an apple tree, skimpy underclothes revealing skin as white as flour. Once he and Billie Carew had followed his sisters and Esme Dunshea when they went to bathe in the stream that ran along the bottom of the orchards. In his dream Esme Dunshea turned and walked away, but to Milton's disappointment she was fully dressed again.

*

The next morning that dream quickly faded to nothing, but the encounter with the stranger remained with Milton, and was as vivid as the reality had been. Every detail of the woman's appearance clung tightly to some part of his consciousness – the black hair, the frail fingers outstretched, her coat and her scarf.

On the evening of that day, during the meal at the kitchen table, Milton's father asked him to cut the bramble patch in the upper orchard. He meant the next morning, but Milton went at once. He stood among the trees in the twilight, knowing he was not there at his father's behest but because he knew the woman would arrive. She entered the upper orchard by the gate that led to the lane and called down to where he was. He could hear her perfectly, although her voice was no more than a whisper.

'I am St Rosa,' the woman said.

She walked down the slope toward him, and he saw that she was dressed in the same clothes. She came close to him and placed her lips on his.

'That is holy,' she whispered.

She moved away. She turned to face him again before she left the orchard, pausing by the gate to the lane.

'Don't be afraid,' she said, 'when the moment comes. There is too much fear.'

Milton had the distinct impression that the woman wasn't alive.

*

Milton's sister Hazel wrote every December, folding the pages of the year's news inside her Christmas card. Two children whom their grandparents had never seen had been born to her in Leicester. Not once since her wedding had Hazel been back to County Armagh.

We drove to Avignon the first day even though it meant being up half the night. The children couldn't have been better, I think the excitement exhausted them.

On the third Sunday in December the letter was on the mantelpiece of what the household had always called the back room, a room used only on Sundays in winter, when the rest of the year's stuffiness was disguised by the smoke from a coal fire. Milton's sister Addy and Herbert Cutcheon were present on the third Sunday in December, and Garfield was visiting for the weekend. Stewart sat on his own Sunday chair, grimacing to himself. Four o'clock tea with sandwiches, apple-pie and cakes, was taken on winter Sundays, a meal otherwise dispensed with.

'They went travelling to France,' Mr Leeson stated flatly, his tone betraying the disappointment he felt concerning his older daughter's annual holiday.

'*France?*' Narrow-jawed and beaky, head cocked out inquisitively, the Reverend Herbert Cutcheon dutifully imbued his repetition of the word with a note of surprised disdain. It was he who had conducted Hazel's wedding, who had delivered a private homily to the bride and bridegroom three days before the ceremony, who had said that at any time they could turn to him.

'See for yourself.' Mr Leeson inclined his tanned pate toward the mantelpiece. 'Have you read Hazel's letter, Addy?'

Addy said she had, not adding that she'd been envious of the journey to Avignon. Once a year she and Herbert and the children went for a week to Portrush, to a boarding-house with reduced rates for clergy.

'France,' her husband repeated. 'You'd wonder at that.'

'Aye, you would,' her father agreed.

Milton's eyes moved from face to face as each person spoke. There was fatigue in Addy's prettiness now, a tiredness in the skin even, although she was only twenty-seven. His father's features were impassive, nothing reflecting the shadow of resentment in his voice. A thought glittered in Herbert Cutcheon's pale brown eyes and was accompanied by a private nod: Milton guessed he was saying to himself it was his duty to write to Hazel on this matter. The clergyman had written to Hazel before: Milton had heard Addy saying so in the kitchen.

'I think Hazel explained in the letter,' Mrs Leeson put in. 'They'll come one of these years,' she added, although she, more than anyone, knew they wouldn't. Hazel had washed her hands of the place.

'Sure, they will,' Garfield said.

Garfield was drunk. Milton watched him risking his observation, his lips drawn loosely back in a thick smile. Specks of foam lingered on the top of the beer can he held, around the triangular opening. He'd been drinking Heineken all afternoon. Mr Leeson drank only once a year, on the occasion of the July celebration; Herbert Cutcheon was teetotal. But neither disapproved of Garfield's tippling when he came back for the weekend, because that was Garfield's way and if you raised an objection you wouldn't see him for dust.

Catching Milton's eye on him, Garfield winked. He was not entirely the reason why Hazel would not return, but he contributed to it. For in Belfast Garfield was more than just a butcher's assistant. Garfield had a role among the Protestant paramilitaries, being what he himself called a 'hard-man volunteer' in an organization intent on avenging the atrocities of the other side. The tit-for-tat murders spawned by that same hard-man mentality, the endless celebration of a glorious past on one side and the picking over of ancient rights on the other, the reluctance to forgive: all this was what Hazel had run away from. 'Only talk,' Mrs Leeson confidently dismissed Garfield's reports of his activities as, recalling that he had always been a boaster. Mr Leeson did not comment.

'Hi!' Stewart suddenly exclaimed in the back room, the way he often did. 'Hi! Hi!' he shouted, his head bent sideways to his shoulder, his mouth flopping open, eyes beginning to roll.

'Behave yourself, Stewart,' Mrs Leeson sternly commanded. 'Stop it now.'

Stewart took no notice. He completed his effort at communication, his fat body becoming awkward on the chair. Then the tension left him and he was quiet. *Give Stewart a hug from all of us*, Hazel's letter said.

Addy collected her husband's cup and her father's. More tea was poured. Mrs Leeson cut more cake.

'Now, pet.' She broke a slice into portions for Stewart. 'Good boy now.'

Milton wondered what they'd say if he mentioned the woman in the orchard, if he casually said that on the fourteenth of September, and again on the fifteenth, a woman who called herself St Rosa had appeared to him among the apple trees of the upper orchard. It wouldn't have been necessary to say he'd dreamed about her also; the dream was just an ordinary thing, a dream he might have had about any woman or girl. 'Her hair was strange,' he might have said.

But Milton, who had kept the whole matter to himself,

continued to do so. Later that evening, alone in the back room with Garfield, he listened while his brother hinted at his city exploits, which he always did when he'd been drinking. Milton watched the damp lips sloppily opening and closing, the thick smile flashing between statements about punishment meted out and premises raided, youths taken in for questioning, warnings issued. There was always a way to complete the picture, Garfield liked to repeat, and would tell about some Catholic going home in the rain and being given a lift he didn't want to accept. Disposal completed the picture, you could call it that: you could say he was in the disposal business. When the phone rang in the middle of the night he always knew at once. No different from dealing with the side of a cow, a professional activity. Garfield always stopped before he came to the end of his tales; even when he'd had a few he left things to the imagination.

*

Every summer Mr Leeson gave the six-acre field for the July celebration – a loyal honouring, yet again renewed, of King William's famous victory over Papist James in 1690. Bowler-hatted and sashed, the men assembled there on the twelfth of the month, their drums and flutes echoing over the Leeson lands. At midday there was the long march to the village, Mr Leeson himself prominent among the marchers. He kept a dark serge suit specially for Sundays and the July celebration, as his father and his grandfather had. Before Garfield had gone to Belfast he'd marched also, the best on the flute for miles around. Milton marched, but didn't play an instrument because he was tone-deaf.

Men who had not met each other since the celebration last year came to the six-acre field in July. Mr Leeson's elderly Uncle Willie came, and Leeson cousins and relatives by marriage. Milton and his friend Billie Carew were among the younger contingent. It pleased Mr Leeson and the other men of his age that boys made up the numbers, that there was no falling away, new faces every year. The Reverend Cutcheon gave an address before the celebration began.

With the drums booming and the flutes skilfully establishing the familiar tunes, the marchers swung off through the iron gate of the field, out on to the lane, later turning into the narrow main road. Their stride was jaunty, even that of Mr Leeson's Uncle Willie and that of Old Knipe, who was eighty-four. Chins were raised, umbrellas carried as rifles might be. Pride was everywhere on these faces; in the measured step and the music's beat, in the swing of the arms and the firm grip of the umbrellas. No shoe was unpolished, no dark suit unironed. The men of this neighbourhood, by long tradition, renewed their Protestant loyalty and belief through sartorial display.

Milton's salt-and-pepper jacket and trousers had been let down at the cuffs. This showed, but only on close scrutiny – a band of lighter cloth and a second band, less noticeable because it had faded, where the cuffs had been extended in the past. His mother had said, only this morning, that that was that, what material remained could not be further adjusted. But she doubted that Milton would grow any more, so the suit as it was should last for many years yet. While she spoke Milton felt guilty, as many times he had during the ten months that had passed since his experience in the upper orchard. It seemed wrong that his mother, who knew everything about him, even that he wouldn't grow any more, shouldn't have been confided in, yet he hadn't been able to do it. Some instinct assured him that the woman would not return. There was no need for her to return, Milton's feeling was, although he did not know where the feeling came from: he would have found it awkward, explaining all that to his mother. Each of the seasons that had passed since September had been suffused by the memory of the woman. That autumn had been warm, its shortening days mellow with sunshine until the rain came in

November. She had been with him in the sunshine and the rain, and in the bitter cold that came with January. On a day when the frost remained, to be frozen again at nightfall, he had walked along the slope of the upper orchard and looked back at the long line of his footsteps on the whitened grass, for a moment surprised that hers weren't there, miraculously, also. When the first primroses decorated the dry, warm banks of the orchards he found himself thinking that these familiar flowers were different this year because he was different himself and saw them in some different way. When summer came the memory of the woman was more intense.

'They'll draw in,' a man near the head of the march predicted as two cars advanced upon the marchers. Obediently the cars pressed into a gateway to make room, their engines turned off, honouring the music. Women and children in the cars waved and saluted; a baby was held up, its small paw waggled in greeting. 'Does your heart good, that,' one of the men remarked.

The day was warm. White clouds were stationary, as if pasted on to the vast dome of blue. It was nearly always fine for the July celebration, a fact that did not pass unnoticed in the neighbourhood, taken to be a sign. Milton associated the day with sweat on his back and in his armpits and on his thighs, his shirt stuck to him in patches that later became damply cold. As he marched now the sun was hot on the back of his neck. 'I wonder will we see the Kissane girl?' Billie Carew speculated beside him.

The Kissane girl lived in one of the houses they passed. She and her two younger sisters usually came out to watch. Her father and her uncles and her brother George were on the march. She was the best-looking girl in the neighbourhood now that Milton's sisters were getting on a bit. She had glasses, which she took off when she went dancing at the Cuchulainn Inn. She had her hair done regularly and took pains to get her eyeshadow right; she matched the shade of her lipstick to her dress. There wasn't a better pair of legs in Ulster, Billie Carew claimed.

'Oh, God!' he muttered when the marchers rounded a bend and there she was with her two young sisters. She had taken her glasses off and was wearing a dress that was mainly pink, flowers like roses on it. When they drew nearer, her white sandals could be seen. 'Oh, God!' Billie Carew exclaimed again, and Milton guessed he was undressing the Kissane girl, the way they used to undress girls in church. One of the girl's sisters had a Union Jack, which she waved.

Milton experienced no excitement. Last year he, too, had undressed the Kissane girl, which hadn't been much different from undressing Esme Dunshea in church. The Kissane girl was older than Esme Dunshea, and older than himself and Billie Carew by five or six years. She worked in the chicken factory.

'D'you know who she looks like?' Billie Carew said. 'Ingrid Bergman.'

'Ingrid Bergman's dead.'

Busy with his thoughts, Billie Carew didn't reply. He had a thing about Ingrid Bergman. Whenever *Casablanca* was shown on the television nothing would get him out of the house. For the purpose he put her to it didn't matter that she was dead.

'God, man!' Billie Carew muttered, and Milton could tell from the urgency of his intonation that the last of the Kissane girl's garments had been removed.

At ten to one the marchers reached the green corrugated-iron sheds of McCourt's Hardware and Agricultural Supplies. They passed a roadside water pump and the first four cottages of the village. They were in Catholic country now: no one was about, no face appeared at a window. The village was a single wide street, at one end Vogan's stores and public house, at the other Tiernan's grocery and filling station, where newspapers could be obtained. Next door was O'Hanlon's public house and then the road widened, so that cars could turn in front of the Church of the Holy Rosary and the school. The houses of the village were colour-washed different colours, green and pink and blue. They were modest houses, none of more than two storeys.

As the marchers melodiously advanced upon the blank stare of so many windows, the stride of the men acquired an extra fervour. Arms were swung with fresh intent, jaws were more firmly set. The men passed the Church of the Holy Rosary, then halted abruptly. There was a moment of natural disarray as ranks were broken so that the march might be reversed. The Reverend Herbert Cutcheon's voice briefly intoned, a few glances were directed at, and over, the nearby church. Then the march returned the way it had come, the music different, as though a variation were the hidden villagers' due. At the corrugated sheds of McCourt's Hardware and Agricultural Supplies the men swung off to the left, marching back to Mr Leeson's field by another route.

*

The picnic was the reward for duty done, faith kept. Bottles appeared. There were sandwiches, chicken legs, sliced beef and ham, potato crisps and tomatoes. The men urinated in twos, against a hedge that never suffered from its annual acidic dousing – this, too, was said to be a sign. Jackets were thrown off, bowler hats thrown down, sashes temporarily laid aside. News was exchanged; the details of a funeral or a wedding passed on; prices for livestock deplored. The Reverend Herbert Cutcheon passed among the men who sat easily on the grass, greeting those from outside his parish whom he hadn't managed to greet already, enquiring after womenfolk. By five o'clock necks and faces were redder than they had earlier been, hair less tidy, beads of perspiration catching the slanting sunlight. There was euphoria in the field, some drunkenness, and an occasional awareness of the presence of God.

'Are you sick?' Billie Carew asked Milton. 'What's up with you?'

Milton didn't answer. He was maybe sick, he thought. He was sick or going round the bend. Since he had woken up this morning she had been there, but not as before, not as a tranquil presence. Since he'd woken she had been agitating and nagging at him.

'I'm OK,' he said.

He couldn't tell Billie Carew any more than he could tell his mother, or anyone in the family, yet all the time on the march he had felt himself being pressed to tell, all the time in the deadened village while the music played, when they turned and marched back again and the tune was different. Now, at the picnic, he felt himself being pressed more than ever.

'You're bloody not OK,' Billie Carew said.

Milton looked at him and found himself thinking that Billie Carew would be eating food in this field when he was as old as Old Knipe. Billie Carew with his acne and his teeth would be satisfied for life when he got the Kissane girl's knickers off. 'Here,' Billie Carew said, offering him his half-bottle of Bushmills.

'I want to tell you something,' Milton said, finding the Reverend Herbert Cutcheon at the hedge where the urinating took place.

'Tell away, Milton.' The clergyman's edgy face was warm with the pleasure the day had brought. He adjusted his trousers. Another day to remember, he said.

'I was out in the orchards a while back,' Milton said. 'September it was. I was seeing how the apples were doing when a woman came in the top gate.'

'A woman?'

'The next day she was there again. She said she was St Rosa.'

'What d'you mean, St Rosa, Milton?'

The Reverend Cutcheon had halted in his stroll back to the assembled men. He stood still, frowning at the grass by his feet. Then he lifted his head and Milton saw bewilderment, and astonishment, in his opaque brown eyes.

'What d'you mean, St Rosa?' he repeated.

Milton told him, and then confessed that the woman had kissed him twice on the lips, a holy kiss, as she'd called it.

'No kiss is holy, boy. Now, listen to me, Milton. Listen to this carefully, boy.'

A young fellow would have certain thoughts, the Reverend Cutcheon explained. It was the way of things that a young fellow could become confused, owing to the age he was and the changes that had taken place in his body. He reminded Milton that he'd left school, that he was on the way to manhood. The journey to manhood could have a stumble or two in it, he explained, and it wasn't without temptation. One day Milton would inherit the farm and the orchards, since Garfield had surrendered all claim to them. That was something he needed to prepare himself for. Milton's mother was goodness itself, his father would do anything for you. If a neighbour had a broken fence while he was laid up in bed, his father would be the first to see to it. His mother had brought up four fine children, and it was God's way that the fifth was afflicted. God's grace could turn affliction into a gift: poor Stewart, you might say, but you only had to look at him to realize you were glad Stewart had been given life.

'We had a great day today, Milton, we had an enjoyable day. We stood up for the people we are. That's what you have to think of.'

In a companionable way the clergyman's arm was placed around Milton's shoulders. He'd put the thing neatly, the gesture suggested. He'd been taken aback but had risen to the occasion.

'She won't leave me alone,' Milton said.

Just beginning to move forward, the Reverend Cutcheon halted again. His arm slipped from Milton's shoulders. In a low voice he said:

'She keeps bothering you in the orchards, does she?'

Milton explained. He said the woman had been agitating him

all day, since the moment he awoke. It was because of that that he'd had to tell someone, because she was pressing him to.

'Don't tell anyone else, Milton. Don't tell a single soul. It's said now between the two of us and it's safe with myself. Not even Addy will hear the like of this.'

Milton nodded. The Reverend Cutcheon said:

'Don't distress your mother and your father, son, with talk of a woman who was on about holiness and the saints.' He paused, then spoke with emphasis, and quietly. 'Your mother and father wouldn't rest easy for the balance of their days.' He paused again. 'There are no better people than your mother and father, Milton.'

'Who was St Rosa?'

Again the Reverend Cutcheon checked his desire to rejoin the men who were picnicking on the grass. Again he lowered his voice.

'Did she ask you for money? After she touched you did she ask you for money?'

'Money?'

'There are women like that, boy.'

Milton knew what he meant. He and Billie Carew had many a time talked about them. You saw them on television, flamboyantly dressed on city streets. Billie Carew said they hung about railway stations, that your best bet was a railway station if you were after one. Milton's mother, once catching a glimpse of these street-traders on the television, designated them 'Catholic strumpets'. Billie Carew said you'd have to go careful with them in case you'd catch a disease. Milton had never heard of such women in the neighbourhood.

'She wasn't like that,' he said.

'You'd get a travelling woman going by and maybe she'd be thinking you had a coin or two on you. Do you understand what I'm saying to you, Milton?'

'Yes.'

'Get rid of the episode. Put it out of your mind.'

'I was only wondering about what she said in relation to a saint.'

'It's typical she'd say a thing like that.'

Milton hesitated. 'I thought she wasn't alive,' he said.

*

Mr Leeson's Uncle Willie used to preach. He had preached in the towns until he was too old for it, until he began to lose the thread of what he was saying. Milton had heard him. He and Garfield and his sisters had been brought to hear Uncle Willie in his heyday, a bible clenched in his right hand, gesturing with it and quoting from it. Sometimes he spoke of what happened in Rome, facts he knew to be true: how the Pope drank himself into a stupor and had to have the sheets of his bed changed twice in a night, how the Pope's own mother was among the women who came and went in the papal ante-rooms.

Men still preached in the towns, at street corners or anywhere that might attract a crowd, but the preachers were fewer than they had been in the heyday of Mr Leeson's Uncle Willie because the popularity of television kept people in at nights, and because people were in more of a hurry. But during the days that followed the July celebration Milton remembered his great-uncle's eloquence. He remembered the words he had used and the way he could bring in a quotation, and the way he was so certain. Often he had laid down that a form of cleansing was called for, that vileness could be exorcized by withering it out of existence.

The Reverend Cutcheon had been more temperate in his advice, even if what he'd said amounted to much the same thing: if you ignored what happened it wouldn't be there any more. But on the days that followed the July celebration Milton found it increasingly impossible to do so. With a certainty that reminded him of his great-uncle's he became convinced beyond all doubt that he was not meant to be silent. Somewhere in him there was the uncontrollable urge that he should not be. He asked his mother why the old man had begun to preach, and she replied that it was because he had to.

*

Father Mulhall didn't know what to say.

To begin with, he couldn't remember who St Rosa had been, even if he ever knew. Added to which, there was the fact that it wasn't always plain what the Protestant boy was trying to tell him. The boy stammered rapidly through his account, beginning sentences again because he realized his meaning had slipped away, speaking more slowly the second time but softening his voice to a pitch that made it almost inaudible. The whole thing didn't make sense.

'Wait now till we have a look,' Father Mulhall was obliged to offer in the end. He'd said at first that he would make some investigations about this saint, but the boy didn't seem satisfied with that. 'Sit down,' he invited in his living-room, and went to look for *Butler's Lives of the Saints*.

Father Mulhall was fifty-nine, a tall, wiry man, prematurely white-haired. Two sheepdogs accompanied him when he went to find the relevant volume. They settled down again, at his feet, when he returned. The room was cold, hardly furnished at all, the carpet so thin you could feel the boards.

'There's the Blessed Roseline of Villeneuve,' Father Mulhall said, turning over the pages. 'And the Blessed Rose Venerini. Or there's St Rose of Lima. Or St Rosalia. Or Rose of Viterbo.'

'I think it's that one. Only she definitely said Rosa.'

'Could you have fallen asleep? Was it a hot day?'

'It wasn't a dream I had.'

'Was it late in the day? Could you have been confused by the shadows?'

'It was late the second time. The first time it was the afternoon.'

'Why did you come to me?'

'Because you'd know about a saint.'

Father Mulhall heard how the woman who'd called herself St Rosa wouldn't let the boy alone, how she'd come on stronger and stronger as the day of the July celebration approached, and so strong on the day itself that he knew he wasn't meant to be silent, the boy said.

'About what though?'

'About her giving me the holy kiss.'

The explanation could be that the boy was touched. There was another boy in that family who wasn't the full shilling either.

'Wouldn't you try getting advice from your own clergyman? Isn't Mr Cutcheon your brother-in-law?'

'He told me to pretend it hadn't happened.'

The priest didn't say anything. He listened while he was told how the presence of the saint was something clinging to you, how neither her features nor the clothes she'd worn had faded in any way whatsoever. When the boy closed his eyes he could apparently see her more clearly than he could see any member of his family, or anyone he could think of.

'I only wanted to know who she was. Is that place in France?'

'Viterbo is in Italy actually.'

One of the sheepdogs had crept on to the priest's feet and settled down to sleep. The other was asleep already. Father Mulhall said:

'Do you feel all right in yourself otherwise?'

'She said not to be afraid. She was on about fear.' Milton paused. 'I can still feel her saying things.'

'I would talk to your own clergyman, son. Have a word with your brother-in-law.'

'She wasn't alive, that woman.'

Father Mulhall did not respond to that. He led Milton to the hall-door of his house. He had been affronted by the visit, but he didn't let it show. Why should a saint of his Church appear to a Protestant boy in a neighbourhood that was overwhelmingly Catholic, when there were so many Catholics to choose from? Was it not enough that that march should occur every twelfth of July, that farmers from miles away should bang their way through the village just to show what was what, strutting in their get-up? Was that not enough without claiming the saints as well? On the twelfth of July they closed the village down, they kept people inside. Their noisy presence was a reminder that beyond this small, immediate neighbourhood there was a strength from which they drew their own. This boy's father would give you the time of day if he met you on the road, he'd even lean on a gate and talk to you, but once your back was turned he'd come out with his statements. The son who'd gone to Belfast would salute you and maybe afterwards laugh because he'd saluted a priest. It was widely repeated that Garfield Leeson belonged in the ganglands of the Protestant back streets, that his butcher's skills came in handy when a job had to be done.

'I thought she might be foreign,' Milton said. 'I don't know how I'd know that.'

Two scarlet dots appeared in Father Mulhall's scrawny cheeks. His anger was more difficult to disguise now; he didn't trust himself to speak. In silence Milton was shown out of the house.

When he returned to his living-room Father Mulhall turned on the television and sat watching it with a glass of whiskey, his sheepdogs settling down to sleep again. 'Now, that's amazing!' a chat-show host exclaimed, leading the applause for a performer who balanced a woman on the end of his finger. Father Mulhall wondered how it was done, his absorption greater than it would have been had he not been visited by the Protestant boy.

*

Mr Leeson finished rubbing his plate clean with a fragment of loaf bread, soaking into it what remained of bacon fat and small pieces of black pudding. Milton said:

'She walked in off the lane.'

Not fully comprehending, Mr Leeson said the odd person came after the apples. Not often, but you knew what they were like. You couldn't put an orchard under lock and key.

'Don't worry about it, son.'

Mrs Leeson shook her head. It wasn't like that, she explained; that wasn't what Milton was saying. The colour had gone from Mrs Leeson's face. What Milton was saying was that a Papist saint had spoken to him in the orchards.

'An apparition,' she said.

Mr Leeson's small eyes regarded his son evenly. Stewart put his side plate on top of the plate he'd eaten his fry from, with his knife and fork on top of that, the way he had been taught. He made his belching noise and to his surprise was not reprimanded.

'I asked Father Mulhall who St Rosa was.'

Mrs Leeson's hand flew to her mouth. For a moment she thought she'd scream. Mr Leeson said:

'What are you on about, boy?'

'I have to tell people.'

Stewart tried to speak, gurgling out a request to carry his two plates and his knife and fork to the sink. He'd been taught that also, and was always obedient. But tonight no one heeded him.

'Are you saying you went to the priest?' Mr Leeson asked.

'You didn't go into his house, Milton?'

Mrs Leeson watched, incredulous, while Milton nodded. He said Herbert Cutcheon had told him to keep silent, but in the end he couldn't. He explained that on the day of the march he had told his brother-in-law when they were both standing at the hedge, and later he had gone into Father Mulhall's house. He'd sat down while the priest looked the saint up in a book.

'Does anyone know you went into the priest's house, Milton?' Mrs Leeson leaned across the table, staring at him with widened eyes that didn't blink. 'Did anyone see you?'

'I don't know.'

Mr Leeson pointed to where Milton should stand, then rose from the table and struck him on the side of the face with his open palm. He did it again. Stewart whimpered, and became agitated.

'Put them in the sink, Stewart,' Mrs Leeson said.

The dishes clattered into the sink, and the tap was turned on as Stewart washed his hands. The side of Milton's face was inflamed, a trickle of blood came from his nose.

*

Herbert Cutcheon's assurance that what he'd heard in his father-in-law's field would not be passed on to his wife was duly honoured. But when he was approached on the same subject a second time he realized that continued suppression was pointless. After a Sunday-afternoon visit to his in-laws' farmhouse, when Mr Leeson had gone off to see to the milking and Addy and her mother were reaching down pots of last year's plum jam for Addy to take back to the rectory, Milton had followed him to the yard. As he drove the four miles back to the rectory, the clergyman repeated to Addy the conversation that had taken place.

'You mean he wants to *preach*?' Frowning in astonishment, Addy half shook her head, her disbelief undisguised.

He nodded. Milton had mentioned Mr Leeson's Uncle Willie. He'd said he wouldn't have texts or scriptures, nothing like that.

'It's not Milton,' Addy protested, this time shaking her head more firmly.

'I know it's not.'

He told her then about her brother's revelations on the day of

the July celebration. He explained he hadn't done so before because he considered he had made her brother see sense, and these
matters were better not referred to.

'Heavens above!' Addy cried, her lower jaw slackened in fresh
amazement. The man she had married was not given to the kind
of crack that involved lighthearted deception, or indeed any kind
of crack at all. Herbert's virtues lay in other directions, well
beyond the realm of jest. Even so, Addy emphasized her bewilderment by stirring doubt into her disbelief. 'You're not serious
surely?'

He nodded without taking his eyes from the road. Neither of
them knew of the visit to the priest or of the scene in the kitchen
that had ended in a moment of violence. Addy's parents, in turn
believing that Milton had been made to see sense by his father's
spirited response, and sharing Herbert Cutcheon's view that such
matters were best left unaired, had remained silent also.

'Is Milton away in the head?' Addy whispered.

'He's not himself certainly. No way he's himself.'

'He never showed an interest in preaching.'

'D'you know what he said to me just now in the yard?'

But Addy was still thinking about the woman her brother
claimed to have conversed with. Her imagination had stuck there,
on the slope of her father's upper orchard, a Catholic woman
standing among the trees.

'Dudgeon McDavie,' Herbert Cutcheon went on. 'He mentioned that man.'

Nonplussed all over again, Addy frowned. Dudgeon McDavie
was a man who'd been found shot dead by the roadside near
Loughgall. Addy remembered her father coming into the kitchen
and saying they'd shot poor Dudgeon. She'd been seven at the
time; Garfield had been four, Hazel a year older; Milton and
Stewart hadn't been born. 'Did he ever do a minute's harm?' she
remembered her father saying. 'Did he ever so much as raise his

voice?' Her father and Dudgeon McDavie had been schooled together; they'd marched together many a time. Then Dudgeon
McDavie had moved out of the neighbourhood, to take up a position as a quantity surveyor. Addy couldn't remember ever having
seen him, although from the conversation that had ensued between her mother and her father at the time of his death it was apparent that he had been to the farmhouse many a time. 'Blew half
poor Dudgeon's skull off': her father's voice, leaden and grey,
echoed as she remembered. 'Poor Dudgeon's brains all over the
tarmac.' Her father had attended the funeral, full honours because Dudgeon McDavie had had a hand in keeping law and
order, part-time in the UDR. A few weeks later two youths from
Loughgall were set upon and punished, although they vehemently
declared their innocence.

'Dudgeon McDavie's only hearsay for Milton,' Addy pointed
out, and her husband said he realized that.

Drawing up in front of the rectory, a low brick building with
metal-framed windows, he said he had wondered about going in
search of Mr Leeson when Milton had come out with all that in
the yard. But Milton had hung about by the car, making the whole
thing even more difficult.

'Did the woman refer to Dudgeon McDavie?' Addy asked. 'Is
that it?'

'I don't know if she did. To tell you the truth, Addy, you
wouldn't know where you were once Milton gets on to this stuff.
For one thing, he said to me the woman wasn't alive.'

In the rectory Addy telephoned. 'I'll ring you back,' her mother
said and did so twenty minutes later, when Milton was not within
earshot. In the ensuing conversation what information they
possessed was shared: the revelations made on the day of the
July celebration, what had later been said in the kitchen and an
hour ago in the yard.

'Dudgeon McDavie,' Mrs Leeson reported quietly to her

husband as soon as she replaced the receiver. 'The latest thing is he's on to Herbert about Dudgeon McDavie.'

*

Milton rode his bicycle one Saturday afternoon to the first of the towns in which he wished to preach. In a car park two small girls, sucking sweets, listened to him. He explained about St Rosa of Viterbo. He felt he was a listener too, that his voice came from somewhere outside himself – from St Rosa, he explained to the two small girls. He heard himself saying that his sister Hazel refused to return to the province. He heard himself describing the silent village, and the drums and the flutes that brought music to it, and the suit his father wore on the day of the celebration. St Rosa could mourn Dudgeon McDavie, he explained, a Protestant man from Loughgall who'd been murdered ages ago. St Rosa could forgive the brutish soldiers and their masked adversaries, one or other of them responsible for the shattered motor-cars and shrouded bodies that came and went on the television screen. Father Mulhall had been furious, Milton said in the car park, you could see it in his eyes: he'd been furious because a Protestant boy was sitting down in his house. St Rosa of Viterbo had given him her holy kiss, he said: you could tell that Father Mulhall considered that impossible.

The following Saturday Milton cycled to another town, a little further away, and on the subsequent Saturday he preached in a third town. He did not think of it as preaching, more just telling people about his experience. It was what he had to do, he explained, and he noticed that when people began to listen they usually didn't go away. Shoppers paused, old men out for a walk passed the time in his company, leaning against a shop window or the wall of a public lavatory. Once or twice in an afternoon someone was abusive.

On the fourth Saturday Mr Leeson and Herbert Cutcheon

arrived in Mr Leeson's Ford Granada and hustled Milton into it. No one spoke a word on the journey back.

'Shame?' Milton said when his mother employed the word.

'On all of us, Milton.'

In church people regarded him suspiciously, and he noticed that Addy sometimes couldn't stop staring at him. When he smiled at Esme Dunshea she didn't smile back; Billie Carew avoided him. His father insisted that in no circumstances whatsoever should he ever again preach about a woman in the orchards. Milton began to explain that he must, that he had been given the task.

'No,' his father said.

'That's the end of it, Milton,' his mother said. She hated it even more than his father did, a woman kissing him on the lips.

The next Saturday afternoon they locked him into the bedroom he shared with Stewart, releasing him at six o'clock. But on Sunday morning he rode away again, and had again to be searched for on the streets of towns. After that, greater care was taken. Stewart was moved out of the bedroom and the following weekend Milton remained under duress there, the door unlocked so that he could go to the lavatory, his meals carried up to him by his mother, who said nothing when she placed the tray on a chest of drawers. Milton expected that on Monday morning everything would be normal again, that his punishment would then have run its course. But this was not so. He was released to work beside his father, clearing out a ditch, and all day there were never more than a couple of yards between them. In the evening he was returned to the bedroom. The door was again secured, and so it always was after that.

On winter Sundays when his sister Addy and the Reverend Cutcheon came to sit in the back room he remained upstairs. He no longer accompanied the family to church. When Garfield came from Belfast at a weekend he refused to carry food to the bedroom, although Milton often heard their mother requesting him to. For a long time now Garfield had not addressed him or sought his company.

When Milton did the milking his father didn't keep so close to him. He put a padlock on the yard gate and busied himself with some task or other in one of the sheds, or else kept an eye on the yard from the kitchen. On two Saturday afternoons Milton climbed out of the bedroom window and set off on his bicycle, later to be pursued. Then one day when he returned from the orchards with his father he found that Jimmy Logan had been to the farmhouse to put bars on his bedroom window. His bicycle was no longer in the turf shed; he caught a glimpse of it tied on to the boot of the Ford Granada and deduced that it was being taken to be sold. His mother unearthed an old folding card-table, since it was a better height for eating off than the chest of drawers. Milton knew that people had been told he had become affected in the head, but he could tell from his mother's demeanour that not even this could exorcize the shame he had brought on the family.

When the day of the July celebration came again Milton remained in his bedroom. Before he left the house his father led him to the lavatory and waited outside it in order to lead him back again. His father didn't say anything. He didn't say it was the day of the July celebration, but Milton could tell it was, because he was wearing his special suit. Milton watched the car drawing out of the yard and then heard his mother chatting to Stewart in the kitchen, saying something about sitting in the sun. He imagined the men gathering in the field, the clergyman's blessing, the drums strapped on, ranks formed. As usual, the day was fine; from his bedroom window he could see there wasn't a cloud in the sky.

It wasn't easy to pass the time. Milton had never been much of a one for reading, had never read a book from cover to cover. Sometimes when his mother brought his food she left him the weekly newspaper and he read about the towns it gave news of, and the different rural neighbourhoods, one of which was his own. He listened to his transistor. His mother collected all the jigsaw puzzles she could find, some of which had been in the farmhouse since Hazel and Garfield were children, others of a simple nature bought specially for Stewart. She left him a pack of cards, with only the three of diamonds missing, and a cardboard box containing scraps of wool and a spool with tacks in it that had been Addy's French-knitting outfit.

On the day of the celebration he couldn't face, yet again, completing the jigsaw of Windsor Castle or the Battle of Britain, or playing patience with the three of diamonds drawn on the back of an envelope, or listening all day to cheery disc-jockeys. He practised preaching, all the time seeing the woman in the orchard instead of the sallow features of Jesus or a cantankerous-looking God, white-haired and bearded, frowning through the clouds.

From time to time he looked at his watch and on each occasion established the point the march had reached. The Kissane girl and her sisters waved. Cars drew courteously in to allow the celebration to pass by. McCourt's Hardware and Agricultural Supplies was closed, the village street was empty. Beyond the school and the Church of the Holy Rosary the march halted, then returned the way it had come, only making a change when it reached McCourt's again, swinging off to the left.

Mrs Leeson unlocked the door and handed in a tray, and Milton imagined the chicken legs and the sandwiches in the field, bottles coming out, the men standing in a row by the hedge. 'No doubt about it,' his father said. 'Dr Gibney's seen cases like it before.' A nutcase, his father intimated without employing the term, but when he was out of hearing one of the men muttered that he knew for a fact Dr Gibney hadn't been asked for an opinion. In the field the shame that was spoken about spread from his father to the men themselves.

Milton tumbled out on the card-table the jigsaw pieces of a jungle scene and slowly turned them right side up. He didn't know any more what would happen if they opened the door and freed him. He didn't know if he would try to walk to the towns, if he'd feel again the pressure to do so or if everything was over, if he'd been cleansed, as his father's old uncle would have said. Slowly he found the shape of a chimpanzee among the branches of a tree. He wished he were in the field, taking the half-bottle from Billie Carew. He wished he could feel the sun on his face and feel the ache going out of his legs after the march.

He completed the top left-hand corner of the jungle scene, adding brightly coloured birds to the tree with the chimpanzees in it. The voices of his mother and Stewart floated up to him from the yard, the incoherent growling of his brother, his mother soothing. From where he sat he saw them when they moved into view, Stewart lumbering, his mother holding his hand. They passed out of the yard, through the gate that was padlocked when he did the milking. Often they walked down to the stream on a warm afternoon.

Again he practised preaching. He spoke of his father ashamed in the field, and the silent windows of the village. He explained that he had been called to go among people, bearing witness on a Saturday afternoon. He spoke of fear. It was that that was most important of all. Fear was the weapon of the gunmen and the soldiers, fear quietened the village. In fear his sister had abandoned the province that was her home. Fearful, his brother disposed of the unwanted dead.

Later Milton found the two back legs of an elephant and slipped the piece that contained them into place. He wondered if he would finish the jigsaw or if it would remain on the mildewed baize of the card-table with most of its middle part missing. He hadn't understood why the story of Dudgeon McDavie had oc-curred to him as a story he must tell. It had always been there; he'd heard it dozens of times; yet it seemed a different kind of story when he thought about the woman in the orchard, when over and over again he watched her coming towards him, and when she spoke about fear.

He found another piece of the elephant's grey bulk. In the distance he could hear the sound of a car. He paid it no attention, not even when the engine throbbed with a different tone, indicating that the car had drawn up by the yard gate. The gate rattled in a familiar way, and Milton went to his window then. A yellow Vauxhall moved into the yard.

He watched while a door opened and a man he had never seen before stepped out from the driver's seat. The engine was switched off. The man stretched himself. Then Garfield stepped out too.

*

'It took a death to get you back,' her father said.

On the drive from the airport Hazel did not reply. She was twenty-six, two years younger than Addy, small and dark-haired, as Addy was, too. Ever since the day she had married, since her exile had begun, the truth had not existed between her and these people she had left behind. The present occasion was not a time for prevarication, not a time for pretence, yet already she could feel both all around her. Another death in a procession of deaths had occurred; this time close to all of them. Each death that came was close to someone, within some family: she'd said that years ago, saying it only once, not arguing because none of them wanted to have a conversation like that.

Mr Leeson slowed as they approached the village of Glenavy, then halted to allow two elderly women to cross the street. They waved their thanks, and he waved back. Eventually he said:

'Herbert's been good.'

Again Hazel did not respond. 'God took him for a purpose,' she imagined Herbert Cutcheon comforting her mother. 'God has a job for him.'

'How's Addy?'

Her sister was naturally distressed also, she was told. The shock was still there, still raw in all of them.

'That stands to reason.'

They slid into a thin stream of traffic on the motorway, Mr Leeson not accelerating much. He said:

'I have to tell you what it was with Milton before we get home.'

'Was it the Provos? Was Milton involved in some way?'

'Don't call them the Provos, Hazel. Don't give them any kind of title. They're not worthy of a title.'

'You have to call them something.'

'It wasn't them. There was no reason why it should have been.'

Hazel, who had only been told that her brother had died violently – shot by intruders when he was alone in the house – heard how Milton had insisted he'd received a supernatural visitation from a woman. She heard how he had believed the woman was the ghost of a Catholic saint, how he had gone to the priest for information, how he had begun street-corner preaching.

'He said things people didn't like?' she suggested, ignoring the more incredible aspect of this information.

'We had to keep him in. I kept him by me when we worked, Garfield wouldn't address him.'

'You kept him in?'

'Poor Milton was away in the head, Hazel. He'd be all right for a while, maybe for weeks, longer even. Then suddenly he'd start about the woman in the orchard. He wanted to travel the six counties preaching about her. He told me that. He wanted to stand up in every town he came to and tell his tale. He brought poor Dudgeon McDavie into it.'

'What d'you mean, you kept him in?'

'We sometimes had to lock his bedroom door. Milton didn't know what he was doing, girl. We had to get rid of his bicycle, but even so he'd have walked. A couple of times on a Saturday he set off to walk, and myself and Herbert had to get him back.'

'My God!'

'You can't put stuff like that in a letter. You can't blame anyone for not writing that down for you. Your mother didn't want to. "What've you said to Hazel?" I asked her one time and she said, "Nothing," so we left it.'

'Milton went mad and no one told me?'

'Poor Milton did, Hazel.'

Hazel endeavoured to order the confusion of her thoughts. Pictures formed: of the key turned in the bedroom door; of the household as it had apparently become, her parents' two remaining children a double burden – Stewart's mongol blankness, Milton's gibberish. 'Milton's been shot,' she had said to her husband after the telephone call, shocked that Milton had apparently become involved, as Garfield was, drawn into it no doubt by Garfield. Ever since, that assumption had remained.

They left the motorway, bypassed Craigavon, then again made their way on smaller roads. This is home, Hazel found herself reflecting in that familiar landscape, the reminder seeming alien among thoughts that were less tranquil. Yet in spite of the reason for her visit, in spite of the upsetting muddle of facts she'd been presented with on this journey, she wanted to indulge the moment, to close her eyes and let herself believe that it was a pleasure of some kind to be back where she belonged. Soon they would come to Drumfin, then Anderson's Crossroads. They would pass the Cuchulainn Inn, and turn before reaching the village. Everything would be familiar then, every house and cottage, trees and gateways, her father's orchards.

'Take it easy with your mother,' he said. 'She cries a lot.'

'Who was it shot Milton?'

'There's no one has claimed who it was. The main concern's your mother.'

Hazel didn't say anything, but when her father began to speak again she interrupted him.

'What about the police?'

'Finmoth's keeping an open mind.'

The car passed the Kissanes' house, pink and respectable, delphiniums in its small front garden. Next came the ruined cowshed in the middle of Malone's field, three of its stone walls standing, the fourth tumbled down, its disintegrating roof mellow with rust. Then came the orchards, and the tarred gate through which you could see the stream, steeply below.

Her father turned the car into the yard of the farmhouse. One of the dogs barked, scampering back and forth, wagging his tail as he always did when the car returned.

'Well, there we are.' With an effort Mr Leeson endeavoured to extend a welcome. 'You'd recognize the old place still!'

In the kitchen her mother embraced her. Her mother had a shrunken look; a hollowness about her eyes, and shallow cheeks that exposed the shape of bones beneath the flesh. A hand grasped at one of Hazel's and clutched it tightly, as if in a plea for protection. Mr Leeson carried Hazel's suitcase upstairs.

'Sit down.' With her free hand Hazel pulled a chair out from the table and gently eased her mother toward it. Her brother grinned across the kitchen at her.

'Oh, Stewart!'

She kissed him, hugging his awkward body. Pimples disfigured his big forehead, his spiky short hair tore uncomfortably at her cheek.

'We should have seen,' Mrs Leeson whispered. 'We should have known.'

'You couldn't. Of course you couldn't.'

'He had a dream or something. That's all he was on about.'

Hazel remembered the dreams she'd had herself at Milton's age, half-dreams because sometimes she was awake – close your eyes and you could make Mick Jagger smile at you, or hear the music of U2 or The Damage. 'Paul Hogan had his arms round me,' Addy giggled once. Then you began going out with someone and everything was different.

'Yet how would he know about a saint?' her mother whispered. 'Where'd he get the name from?'

Hazel didn't know. It would have come into his head, she said to herself, but didn't repeat the observation aloud. In spite of what she said, her mother didn't want to think about it. Maybe it was easier for her mother, too, to believe her son had been away in the head, or maybe it made it worse. You wouldn't know that, you couldn't tell from her voice or from her face.

'Don't let it weigh on you,' she begged. 'Don't make it worse for yourself.'

Later Addy and Herbert Cutcheon were in the kitchen. Addy made tea and tumbled biscuits on to a plate. Herbert Cutcheon was solemn, Addy subdued. Like her father, Hazel sensed, both of them were worried about her mother. Being worried about her mother was the practical aspect of the grief that was shared, an avenue of escape from it, a distraction that was permitted. Oblivious to all emotion, Stewart reached out for a biscuit with pink marshmallow in it, his squat fingers and bitten nails ugly for an instant against the soft prettiness.

'He'll get the best funeral the Church can give him,' Herbert Cutcheon promised.

*

Garfield stood a little away from them, with a black tie in place and his shoes black also, not the trainers he normally wore. Looking at him across the open grave, Hazel suddenly knew. In ignorance she had greeted him an hour ago in the farmhouse; they had stood together in the church; she had watched while he stepped forward to bear the coffin. Now, in the bleak churchyard, those images were illuminated differently. The shame had been exorcized, silence silently agreed upon.

'*I will keep my mouth as it were with a bridle,*' Herbert Cutcheon proclaimed, his voice heavy with the churchiness that was discarded as soon as his professional duties ceased, never apparent on a Sunday afternoon in the back room of the farmhouse. 'Forasmuch as it hath pleased Almighty God.'

Earth was thrown on to the coffin. '*Our Father, who art in heaven,*' Herbert Cutcheon suitably declared, and Hazel watched Garfield's lips, in unison with Addy's and their parents'. Stewart was there too, now and again making a noise. Mrs Leeson held a handkerchief to her face, clinging on to her husband in sudden bright sunshine. '*And forgive us our trespasses.*' Garfield mouthed the words too.

With bitter calmness, Hazel allowed the facts to settle into place. Milton had been told not to. He had been told, even by Garfield himself, that you had fancies when you were fifteen. He had been told that talk about a Catholic saint was like the Catholics claiming one of their idolatrous statues had been seen to move. But in spite of all that was said to him Milton had disobeyed. 'Your bodies a living sacrifice,' Hazel's Great-Uncle Willie used to thunder, steadfast in his certainty. Prominent among the mourners, the old man's granite features displayed no emotion now.

'Amen,' Herbert Cutcheon prompted, and the mourners murmured and Mrs Leeson sobbed. Hazel moved closer to her, as Addy did, receiving her from their father's care. All of them knew, Hazel's thoughts ran on: her father knew, and her mother, and Addy, and Herbert Cutcheon. It was known in every house in the neighbourhood; it was known in certain Belfast bars and clubs, where Garfield's hard-man reputation had been threatened, and then enhanced.

'It's all right, Mother,' Addy whispered as the three women turned from the grave, but Hazel did not attempt to soothe her mother's distress because she knew she could not. Her mother would go to her own grave with the scalding agony of what had happened still alive within her; her father would be reminded of the day of the occurrence on all the July marches remaining to him. The family would not ever talk about the day, but through their pain they would tell themselves that Milton's death was the way things were, the way things had to be: that was their single consolation. Lost ground had been regained.

A Day

In the night Mrs Lethwes wakes from time to time, turns and murmurs in her blue-quilted twin bed, is aware of fleeting thoughts and fragments of memory that dissipate swiftly. Within her stomach, food recently consumed is uneasily digested. Briefly, she suffers a moment of cramp.

Mrs Lethwes dreams: a child again, she remains in the car while her brother, Charlie, visits the Indian family who run the supermarket. Kittens creep from beneath inverted flowerpots in the Bunches' back yard, and she is there, in the yard too, looking for Charlie because he is visiting the Bunches now. 'You mustn't go bothering the Bunches,' their mother upbraids him. 'People are busy.' There are rivers to cross, and the streets aren't there any more; there is a seashore, and tents.

In her garden, while Mrs Lethwes still sleeps, the scent of night-stock fades with the cool of night. Dew forms on roses and geraniums, on the petals of the cosmos and the yellow spikes of broom. Slugs creep towards lettuce plants, avoiding a line of virulent bait; a silent cat, far outside its own domain, waits for the emergence of the rockery mice.

It is July. Dawn comes early, casting a pale twilight on the brick of the house, on the Virginia creeper that covers half a wall, setting off white-painted window-frames and decorative wrought-iron. This house and garden, in a tranquil wooded neighbourhood, constitute one part of the achievement of Mrs Lethwes's husband, are a symbol of professional advancement conducted over twenty years, which happens also to be the length of this marriage.

Abruptly, Mrs Lethwes is fully awake and knows her night's sleep is over. Hunched beneath the bedclothes in the other bed, her husband does not stir when she rises and crosses the room they share to the window. Drawing aside the edge of a curtain, she glances down into the early-morning garden and almost at once drops the curtain back into place. In bed again, she lies on her side, facing her husband because, being fond of him, she likes to watch him sleeping. She feels blurred and headachy, as she always does at this time, the worst moment of her day, Mrs Lethwes considers.

Is Elspeth awake too? She wonders that. Does Elspeth, in her city precinct, share the same pale shade of dawn? Is there, as well, the orange glow of a street lamp and now, beginning in the distance somewhere, the soft swish of a milk dray, a car door banging, a church bell chiming five? Mrs Lethwes doesn't know where Elspeth lives precisely, or in any way what she looks like, but imagines short black hair and elfin features, a small, thin body, fragile fingers. An hour and three-quarters later – still conducting this morning ritual – she hears bath-water running; and later still there is music. Vivaldi, Mrs Lethwes thinks.

Her husband wakes. His eyes remember, becoming troubled, and then the trouble lifts from them when he notices, without surprise, that she's not asleep. In another of her dreams during the night that has passed he carried her, and his voice spoke softly, soothing her. Or was it quite a dream, or only something like one? She tries to smile; she says she's sorry, knowing now.

*

At ten, when the cleaning woman comes, Mrs Lethwes goes out to shop. She parks her small, white Peugeot in the Waitrose car park, and in a leisurely manner gathers vegetables and fruit, and tins and jars, pork chops for this evening, vermouth and Gordon's gin, Edam, and Normandy butter because she has noticed the butter is getting low, Comfort and the cereal her husband favours, the one called Common Sense. Afterwards, with everything in the boot, she makes her way to the Trompe-L'Oeil for coffee. Her make-up is in place, her hair drawn up, the way she has taken to wearing it lately. She smiles at people she knows by sight, the waitress and other women who are having coffee, at the cashier when she pays her bill. There is some conversation, about the weather.

In her garden, later, the sound of the Hoover reaches her from the open windows of the house as the cleaning woman, Marietta, moves from room to room. The day is warm, Mrs Lethwes's legs are bare, her blue dress light on her body, her Italian sandals comfortable yet elegant. Marietta claims to be Italian also, having had an Italian mother, but her voice and manner are Cockney and Mrs Lethwes doubts that she has ever been in Italy, even though she regularly gives the impression that she knows Venice well.

Mrs Lethwes likes to be occupied when Marietta comes. When it's fine she finds something to do in the garden, and when the weather doesn't permit that she lingers for longer in the Trompe-L'Oeil and there's the pretence of letter-writing or tidying drawers. She likes to keep a closed door between herself and Marietta, to avoid as best she can the latest about Marietta's daughter Ange, and Liam, whom Ange has been contemplating marriage with for almost five years, and the latest about the people in the house next door, who keep Alsatians.

In the garden Mrs Lethwes weeds a flowerbed, wishing that Marietta didn't have to come to the house three times a week, but knowing that of course she must. She hopes the little heart-leafed things she's clearing from among the delphiniums are not the germination of seeds that Mr Yatt has sown, a misfortune that occurred last year with his Welsh poppies. Unlike Marietta, Mr Yatt is dour and rarely speaks, but he has a way of slowly raising his head and staring, which Mrs Lethwes finds disconcerting.

When he's in the garden – Mondays only, all day – she keeps out of it herself.

Not Vivaldi now, perhaps a Telemann minuet, run Mrs Lethwes's thoughts in her garden. Once, curious about the music a flautist plays, she read the information that accompanied half a dozen compact discs in a music shop. She didn't buy the discs but, curious again, she borrowed some from the music section of the library and played them all one morning. Thirty-six, or just a little younger, she sees Elspeth as, unmarried of course and longing to bear the child of the man she loves: Mrs Lethwes is certain of that, since she has experienced this same longing herself. In the flat she imagines, there's a smell of freshly made coffee. The fragile fingers cease their movement. The instrument is laid aside, the coffee poured.

It was in France, in the Hôtel St-Georges during their September holiday seven years ago, that Mrs Lethwes found out about her husband's other woman. There was a letter, round feminine handwriting on an air-mail envelope, an English stamp: she knew at once. The letter had been placed in some-one else's key-box by mistake, and was later handed to her with a palaver of apologies when her husband was swimming in the Mediterranean. 'Ah, *merci*,' she thanked the smooth-haired girl receptionist and said the error didn't matter in the very least. She knew at once: the instinct of a barren wife, she after-wards called it to herself. So this was why he made a point of being down before her every morning, why he had always done so during their September holiday in France; she'd never won-dered about it before. On the terrace she examined the post-mark. It was indecipherable, but again the handwriting told a lot, and only a woman with whom a man had an association would write to him on holiday. From the letter itself, which she read and then destroyed, she learned all there was otherwise to know.

There are too many of the heart-leafed plants, and when she looks in other areas of the border and in other beds she finds they're not in evidence there. Clearly, it's the tragedy of the Welsh poppies all over again. Mrs Lethwes begins to put back what she has taken out, knowing as she does so that this isn't going to work.

*

'"Silly girl," I said, straight to her face. "Silly girl, Ange, no way you're not."'

Marietta has established herself at the kitchen table, her shapeless bulk straining the seams of a pink overall, her feet temporarily removed from the carpet slippers she brings with her because they're comfortable to work in.

'No, not for me, thanks,' Mrs Lethwes says, which is what she always says when she is offered instant coffee at midday. Real coffee doesn't agree with Marietta, never has. Toxic in Marietta's view.

'All she give's a giggle. That's Ange all over, that. Always has been.'

This woman has watched Ange's puppy-fat go, has seen her through childhood illnesses. And Bernardo, too. This woman could have had a dozen children, borne them and nursed them, loved them and been loved herself. 'Well, I drew a halt at two, dear. Drew the line, know what I mean? He said have another go, but I couldn't agree.'

Five goes, Mrs Lethwes has had herself: five failures, in bed for every day the third and fourth time, told she mustn't try again, but she did. The same age she was then as she imagines her husband's other woman to be: thirty-six when she finally accepted she was a childless wife.

'Decent a bloke as ever walked a street is little Liam, but Ange don't see it. One day she'll look up and he'll be gone and away. Talking to a wall you are.'

'Is Ange in love, though?'

'Call it how you like, dear. Mention it to Ange and all she give's a giggle. Well, Liam's small. A little fellow, but then where's the harm in small?'

Washing traces of soil from her hands at the sink, Mrs Lethwes says there is no harm in a person being small. Hardly five foot, she has many times heard Liam is. But strong as a horse.

'I said it to her straight, dear. Wait for some bruiser and you'll build your life on regrets. No good to no one, regrets.'

'No good at all.'

Of course was what she'd thought on the terrace of the Hôtel St-Georges: a childless marriage was a disappointment for any man. She'd failed him, although naturally it had never been said; he wasn't in the least like that. But she had failed and had compounded her failure by turning away from talk of adoption. She had no feeling for the idea; she wasn't the kind to take on other people's kids. Their own particular children were the children she wanted, an expression of their love, an expression of their marriage: more and more, she'd got that into her head. When the letter arrived at the Hôtel St-Georges she'd been reconciled for years to her barren state; they lived with it, or so she thought. The letter changed everything. The letter frightened her; she should have known.

'We need the window-cleaners one of them days,' Marietta says, dipping a biscuit into her coffee. 'Shocking, the upstairs panes is.'

'I'll ring them.'

'Didn't mind me mentioning it, dear? Only with the build-up it works out twice the price. No saving really.'

'Actually, I forget. I wasn't trying to –'

'Best done regular I always say.'

'I'll ring them this afternoon.'

Mrs Lethwes said nothing in the Hôtel St-Georges and she

hasn't since. He doesn't know she knows; she hopes that nothing ever shows. She sat for an hour on the terrace of the hotel, working it out. Say something, she thought, and as soon as she does it'll be in the open. The next thing is he'll be putting it gently to her that nothing is as it should be. Gently because he always has been gentle, especially about her barren state; sorry for her, dutiful in their plight, tied to her. He'd have had an Eastern child, any little slit-eyed thing, but when she hadn't been able to see it he'd been good about that too.

'Sets the place off when the windows is done, I always say.'

'Yes, of course.'

He came back from his swim; and the letter from a woman who played an instrument in an orchestra was already torn into little pieces and in a waste-bin in the car park, the most distant one she could find. 'Awfully good, this,' she said when he came and sat beside her. *Some Do Not* was the book she laid aside. He said he had read it at school.

'I'll do the window-sills when they've been. Shocking with flies, July is. Filthy really.'

'I'll see if I can get them next week.'

There hadn't been an address, just a date: September 4th. No need for an address because of course he knew it, and from the letter's tone he had for ages. She wondered what that meant and couldn't think of a time when a change had begun in his manner towards her. There hadn't been one; and in other ways, too, he was as he always had been: unhurried in his movements and his speech, his square healthy features the same terracotta shade, the grey in his hair in no way diminishing his physical attractiveness. It was hardly surprising that someone else found him attractive too. Driving up through France, and back again in England, she became used to pretending in his company that the person called Elspeth did not exist, while endlessly conjecturing when she was alone.

'I'll do the stairs down,' Marietta says, 'and then I'll scoot, dear.'

'Yes, you run along whenever you're ready.'

'I'll put in the extra Friday, dear. Three-quarters of an hour I owe all told.'

'Oh, please don't worry –'

'Fair's fair, dear. Only I'd like to catch the twenty-past today, with Bernardo anxious for his dinner.'

'Yes, of course you must.'

*

The house is silent when Marietta has left, and Mrs Lethwes feels free again. The day is hers now, until the evening. She can go from room to room in stockinged feet, and let the telephone ring unanswered. She can watch, if the mood takes her, some old black-and-white film on the television, an English one, for she likes those best, pretty girls' voices from the 1940s, Michael Wilding young again, Ann Todd.

She doesn't have much lunch. She never does during the week: a bit of cheese on the Ritz biscuits she has a weakness for, gin and dry Martini twice. In her spacious sitting-room Mrs Lethwes slips her shoes off and stretches out on one of the room's two sofas. Then the first sharp tang of the Martini causes her, for a moment, to close her eyes with pleasure.

Silver-framed, a reminder of her wedding day stands on a round inlaid surface among other photographs near by. August 26th 1974: the date floats through her midday thoughts. 'I *know* this'll work out,' her mother – given to speaking openly – had remarked the evening before, when she met for the first time the parents of her daughter's fiancé. The remark had caused a silence, then someone laughed.

She reaches for a Ritz. The soft brown hair that's hardly visible beneath the bridal veil is blonded now and longer than it was, which is why she wears it gathered up, suitable in middle age. She was pretty then and is handsome now; still loose-limbed, she has put on only a little weight. Her teeth are still white and sound; only her light-blue eyes, once brilliantly clear, are blurred, like eyes caught out of focus. Afterwards her mother's remark on the night before the wedding became a joke, because of course the marriage had worked out. A devoted couple; a perfect marriage, people said – and still say, perhaps – except for the pity of there being no children. It's most unlikely, Mrs Lethwes believes, that anyone much knows about his other woman. He wouldn't want that; he wouldn't want his wife humiliated, that never was his style.

Mrs Lethwes, who smokes one cigarette a day, smokes it now as she lies on the sofa, not yet pouring her second drink. On later September holidays there had been no letters, of that she was certain. Some alarm had been raised by the one that didn't find its intended destination: dreadful, he would have considered it, a liaison discovered by chance, and would have felt afraid. 'Please understand. I'm awfully sorry,' he would have said, and Elspeth would naturally have honoured his wishes, even though writing to him when he was away was precious.

'No more. That's all.' On her feet again to pour her second drink, Mrs Lethwes firmly makes this resolution, speaking aloud since there is no one to be surprised by that. But a little later she finds herself rooting beneath underclothes in a bedroom drawer, and finding there another bottle of Gordon's and pouring some and adding water from a bathroom tap. The bottle is returned, the fresh drink carried downstairs, the Ritz packet put away, the glass she drank her two cocktails from washed and dried and returned to where the glasses are kept. Opaque, blue to match the bathroom paint, the container she drinks from now is a toothbrush beaker, and holds more than the sedate cocktail glass, three times as much almost. The taste is different, the plastic beaker feels different in her grasp, not stemmed and cool as the glass was,

warmer on her lips. The morning that has passed seems far away
as the afternoon advances, as the afternoon connects with the
afternoon of yesterday and of the day before, a repetition that
must have a beginning somewhere but now is lost.

He is with her now. They are together in the flat she shares
with no one, being an independent girl. At three o'clock, that is
Mrs Lethwes's thought. Excuses are not difficult; in his position in
the office, he would not even have to make them. Lunch with the
kind of business people he often refers to, lunch in the Milano or
the Petit Escargot, and then a taxi to the flat that is a second
home. 'Surprise!' he says on the doorstep intercom, and takes his
jacket off while she makes tea. 'I'll not be back this afternoon,' is
all he has said on the phone to his bespectacled and devoted
secretary.

They sit by the french windows that open on to a small balcony
and are open now. It is a favourite place in summer, geraniums
blooming in the balcony's two ornamental containers, the passers-
by on the street below viewed through the metal scrolls that
decorate the balustrade, the drawn-back curtains undisturbed by
breezes. The teacups are a shade of pink. The talk is about the
orchestra, where it is going next, how long she'll be away, the dates
precisely given because that's important. In winter the imagined
scene is similar, except that they sit by the gas fire beneath the re-
production of *Field of Poppies,* the curtains drawn because it's
darkening outside even as early as this. In winter there's Mahler
on the CD player, instead of the passers-by to watch.

Why couldn't it be? Mrs Lethwes wonders at ten past five when
a film featuring George Formby comes to an end. Why couldn't it
be that he would come back this evening and confess there has
been a miscalculation? 'She is to have a child': why shouldn't it be
that he might say simply that? And how could Elspeth, busy with
her orchestra, travelling to Cleveland and Chicago and San Fran-
cisco, to Rome and Seville and Nice and Berlin, possibly be a

mother? And yet, of course, Elspeth would want his child, women do when they're in love.

Vividly, Mrs Lethwes sees this child, a tiny girl on a rug in the garden, a sunshade propped up, Mr Yatt bent among the dwarf sweetpeas. And Marietta saying in the kitchen, 'My, my, there's looks for you!' The child is his, Mrs Lethwes reflects, pouring again; at least what has happened is halfway there to what might have been if the child was hers also. Beggars can't be choosers.

*

At fifteen minutes past five, fear sets in, the same fear there was on the terrace of the Hôtel St-Georges when the letter was still be-' tween her fingers. He will go from her; it is pity that keeps him with a barren woman; he will find the courage, and with it will come the hardness of heart that is not naturally his. Then he will go.

Once, not long ago – or maybe it was a year or so ago, hard to be accurate now – she said on an impulse that she had been wrong to resist the adoption of an unwanted child, wrong to say a child for them must only be his and hers. In response he shook his head. Adoption would not be easy now, he said, in their middle age, and that was that. Some other day, on the television, there was a woman who took an infant from a pram, and she felt sympathy for that woman then, though no one else did. Whenever she saw a baby in a pram she thought of the woman taking it, and at other times she thought of that girl who walked away with the baby she was meant to be looking after, and the woman who took one from a hospital ward. When she told him she felt sympathy he put his arms around her and wiped away her tears. This after-noon, the fear lasts for half an hour; then, at a quarter to six, it is so much nonsense. Never in a thousand years would he develop that hardness of heart.

'I have to go now,' he says in his friend's flat. They cease their observation of the passers-by below. Again they embrace and then he goes. The touch of her lips goes with him, her regretful smile, her fragile fingers where for so long that afternoon they rested in his hand. He drives through traffic, perfectly knowing the way, not having to think. And in the flat she plays her music, and finds in it a consolation. It is his due to have his other woman: on the hotel terrace she decided that. In the hour she sat there with the letter not yet destroyed everything fell into place. She knew she must never say she had discovered what she had. She knew she didn't want him ever not to be there.

Lovers quarrel. Love affairs end. What life is it for Elspeth, scraps from a marriage he won't let go of? Why shouldn't she tire of waiting? 'No,' he says when Elspeth cheats, allowing her pregnancy to occur in order to force his hand. Still he says he can't, and all there is is a mess where once there was romance. He turns to his discarded wife and there between them is his confession. 'She travels, you see. She has to travel, she won't give up her music.' How quickly should there be forgiveness? Should there be some pretence of anger? Should there be tears? His friend set a trap for him, his voice goes on, a tender trap, as in the song: that is where his weakness has landed him. His voice apologizes and asks for understanding and for mercy. His other woman has played her part although she never knew it; without his other woman there could not be a happy ending.

She sets the table for their dinner, the tweed mats, the cutlery, the pepper-mill, the German mustard, glasses for wine because he deserves a little wine after his day, Châteauneuf-du-Pape. The bottle's on the table, opened earlier because she knows to do that from experience: it's difficult later on to open wine with all the rush of cooking. And the wine should breathe: years ago he taught her that.

In the kitchen she begins to cut the fat off the pork chops she bought that morning, a long time ago it seems now. Marietta's recipe she's intending to do: pork chops in tomato sauce, onions and peppers. On the mottled working surface the blue toothbrush beaker is almost full again, reached out for often. The meat slides about although, in actual fact, it doesn't move. It is necessary to be careful with the knife; her little finger is wrapped in a band-aid from a week ago. On the radio Humphrey Lyttelton asks his teams to announce the Late Arrivals at the Undertakers Ball.

'Of course,' Mrs Lethwes says aloud. 'Of course, we'll offer it a home.'

*

At five to seven, acting instinctively as she does every evening at about this time, Mrs Lethwes washes the blue plastic beaker and replaces it in the bathroom. Twice, before she hears the car wheels on the tarmac, she raises the gin bottle directly to her lips, then pours herself, conventionally, a cocktail of Gordon's and Martini. She knows it will happen tonight. She knows he will enter with a worry in his features and stand by the door, not coming forward for a moment, that then he'll pour himself a drink, too, and sit down slowly and begin to tell her. 'I'm sorry,' is probably how he'll put it, and she'll stop him, telling him she can guess. And after he has spoken for twenty minutes, covering all the ground that has been lost, she'll say, of course: 'The child must come here.'

The noisy up-and-over garage door falls into place. In a hurry Mrs Lethwes raises the green bottle to her lips because suddenly she feels the need of it. She does so again before there is the darkness that sometimes comes, arriving suddenly today just as she is whispering to herself that tomorrow, all day long, she'll not take anything at all and thinking also that, for tonight, the open wine will be enough, and if it isn't there's always more that can be broached. For, after all, tonight is a time for celebration. A schoolgirl on a summer's day, just like the one that has passed, occupies the upper room where only visitors sleep. She comes downstairs and chatters on, about her friends, her teachers, a worry she has, not understanding a poem, and together at the kitchen table they read it through. Oh, I do love you, Mrs Lethwes thinks, while there is imagery and words rhyme.

*

On the mottled worktop in the kitchen the meat is where Mrs Lethwes left it, the fat partly cut away, the knife still separating it from one of the chops. The potatoes she scraped earlier in the day are in a saucepan of cold water, the peas she shelled in another. Often, in the evenings, it is like that in the kitchen when her husband returns to their house. He is gentle when he carries her, as he always is.

Marrying Damian

'I'm going to marry Damian,' Joanna said.

Claire wasn't paying attention. She smiled and nodded, intent on unravelling a ball of garden twine that had become tangled. I said:

'Well, that's nice, of course. But Damian's married already.'

It didn't matter, Joanna said, and repeated her resolve. Joanna was five at the time.

*

Twenty-two years later Damian stood on the wild grass, among the cornflowers and the echiums and the lavatera, under the cricket-bat willow that had been a two-foot shrub when Joanna made her announcement. He was wearing blue sunglasses and a powder-blue suit that looked new. In contrast, his tie – its maroon and gold stripes seeming to indicate membership of some club to which almost certainly Damian did not belong – was lank, and the collar of his shirt was frayed. We hadn't been expecting him; we hadn't heard from Damian for years. Since the spring of 1985, Claire later calculated, the year of his second divorce, from an American widow in upstate New York. After that there was an Englishwoman who lived in Venice, about whom we were never told very much. When Joanna had declared her childhood intention Damian had been still married to the only one of his three wives Claire and I actually knew: a slender, pretty girl, the daughter of the Bishop of Killaloe. We had known her since the wedding; I'd been Damian's best man.

I was actually asleep when Damian walked into our garden all those years later, and I think Claire was too. We were lolling in deck-chairs, Claire's spaniels stretched out under hers, avoiding the afternoon sun.

'Yes,' Damian said. 'It's Damian.'

We were surprised, but perhaps not much: turning up out of the blue had always been his habit. He never telephoned first or intimated his intention by letter or on a postcard. Over the years he had arrived in all seasons and at varying times of day, once rousing us at two o'clock in the morning. Invariably he brought with him details of a personal disaster which had left him with the need to borrow a little money. These loans were not paid back; even as he accepted them he made no pretence that they would be.

'Damian.' Claire hugged him, laughing, playfully demanding to know what he was doing in that awful suit. I asked him where he'd been and he said oh, a lot of places – Vancouver, Oregon, Spain. Claire made him sit down, saying she was going to make some tea, inviting him to stay a while. He was the tonic we needed, Claire said, for she's always afraid that we'll slump into dullness unless we're careful. A woman, somewhere, had given him the suit: we both guessed that.

'I wasn't all that well in Spain,' Damian said. 'Some kind of sunstroke.'

We are the same age, Damian and I, not young any more; that day, as we sat together in the garden, we were sixty and a bit, Claire five years younger. She's tall and slim, and I can't believe she'll ever be anything but elegant, but of course I know I may be wrong. When we married she came to live in the country town I've always known, acquiring an extra identity as the doctor's wife and the receptionist at the practice, as the mother of a daughter and a son, the organizer of a playgroup, the woman who first taught the illiterate of the town to read.

Damian, at the first opportunity, fled this neighbourhood. On his return to it the time before this one he had carried – clearly an affectation – a silver-topped cane, which was abandoned now, no doubt because it drew attention to its own necessity, and Damian inclines towards vanity. Although he sat down briskly in the chair Claire had vacated for him, the protest of a joint caused him, for a single instant, to wince. His light, fair hair is grey in places now, and I don't suppose he cares for that either, or that his teeth have shrivelled and become discoloured, nor that the freckles on the backs of his hands form blobs where they have spread into one another, or that the skin of his forehead is as dry as old vellum. But that day there was nothing about his eyes to suggest a coming to terms with a future destined to be different from the past, no hint of a hesitation about what should or should not be undertaken: in that sense Damian remains young.

Even as a boy his features were gaunt, giving the impression then of undernourishment. He was angular, but without any of the awkwardness sometimes associated with that quality. In spite of whatever trouble he was having with a joint, he could still, I noticed that day, tidy himself away with natural ease. As always at the beginning of a visit, he was good-humoured; moodiness – sometimes a snappish response to questions, or silence – was apt to set in later.

If, in terms of having a profession, Damian is anything, he is a poet, although in all the time I've known him he has never shown me more than a verse or two. Years ago someone told us that he once had a coterie of admirers and was still, in certain quarters, considered to possess 'a voice' that should be more widely heard. A volume entitled *Slow Death of a Pigeon* – its contents sparse, Claire and I always assumed, for nothing about Damian suggests he is profligate with his talent – appears to represent all he has so far chosen for posterity. In time we would receive a copy of *Slow Death of a Pigeon*, he promised on one of his visits, but none arrived.

'Well, yes, it was that. Something like it,' he was saying, slightly laughing, when I returned with another deck-chair after Claire had brought out the tea things. He had repeated all he'd told me about his sunstroke and the lack of anything of interest in Vancouver. Yes, he was confessing now, a relationship with a woman had featured in his more recent travels, had somehow been the reason for them. There was no confirmation that the powder-blue suit had been a gift. Damian wouldn't have considered that of interest.

'I thought I'd maybe die,' he said, returning to the subject of his sunstroke, but when I asked him what he'd taken for it, what treatment there had been, he was vague.

'Bloody visions,' he said instead. 'Goya stuff.' In any case, he confidently pronounced, Spain was overrated.

Had the woman been Spanish? I wondered, and thought of dancers, white teeth and a rosebud that was red, black skirts swirling, red ribbons in black hair. I have doctor colleagues who farm a bit, who let the wind blow away the mixture of triviality and death that now and again makes our consulting rooms melancholy places. Others collect rare books, make cabinets, involve themselves in politics, allow gardening or some sport to become a way of life to skulk in. For me, Damian's infrequent visits, and wondering about him in between, were such a diversion. Not as efficacious as afternoons on a tractor or searching out a Cuala Press edition of Yeats, but then by nature I'm lazy.

'A chapter closed?' Claire was saying.

'Should never have been opened.'

Later, in the kitchen, I decanted the wine and Claire said the lamb would be enough, with extra potatoes and courgettes. We heard Joanna's car and then her voice exclaiming in surprise and Damian greeting her.

I carried a tray of drinks to the garden. Damian's small black suitcase, familiar to us for many years, was still on the grass beside his deck-chair. I can see it now.

*

The visit followed a familiar pattern. In the small suitcase there were shirts and underclothes and socks in need of laundering; and when they had been through the washing-machine most of them were seen to be in need of repair. Damian, besides, was penniless; and there was the request that if anyone telephoned him – which was, he said, unlikely since, strictly speaking, no one knew his whereabouts – his presence in our house should be denied.

When we were children, Damian and I had played together at Doul, the grey, half-derelict house where his Aunt Una had brought him up. Doul is no longer there, having been sold to a builder for the lead of its roof, and later razed to the ground. Damian's Aunt Una had drunk herself to death in a caravan. I was actually there when her head jerked suddenly to one side on the pillow, the visible indication of her demise. She'd been, in our childhood, a vague presence in that old house and its lost garden, tall and handsome yet somehow like a ghost of someone else: it was said that she was Damian's mother. People who remembered her advent, with an infant, in the neighbourhood, said the house had been bought for her by the man who'd made her pregnant, buying her silence also.

I learned all that later. When Damian and I were eight his Aunt Una was known to me as his aunt and there was never a reason, afterwards, to doubt that she was. He and I were sent away to different schools – the seducer from the past said to have obliged in this way, also, where Damian's boarding fees were concerned – but our friendship none the less continued. Damian – like a scarecrow sometimes because it was never noticed by his Aunt Una that he grew out of his clothes – was easy company, hard to dislike, an antidote to the provincial respectability I grew up in. We wandered about the countryside; we hung about point-to-points; when we were older we went to Friday dance-halls if one of us had money; we dreamed of romance with Bettina Nowd, clerk in the Munster and Leinster Bank. Abruptly, our ways parted, and remained so for a long time: when Damian, at nineteen, left the neighbourhood he did not return for fourteen years, by which time his Aunt Una was dead and her house gone. It was said he hadn't written to her, or communicated in any way during that time, which was surprising because he was always fond of her. But as I heard nothing from him either it's perhaps less odd than it seems. For Damian, perhaps, the vacuum of people's absence cannot be filled by any other means. During that fourteen years he and I met only once, at Killaloe at the first of his weddings.

'You know, I'd like to see Doul again,' he said the day after he'd appeared in his powder-blue suit. So we went there, where there was nothing to see, not even the caravan his Aunt Una died in. Beneath the brambles that grew everywhere, and the great swathes of nettles, there might have been remains of some kind, but if there were the naked eye could not discern them. When we walked on a bit there were the walls of the kitchen garden, ivy-clad in places, fallen away in others.

'You couldn't build Doul again,' I pointed out when he said he'd like to. 'Not without a fortune, Damian.'

He muttered something, and for the first time sounded disagreeable. There was some kind of complaint, a protest about his continuing lack of means, and then: 'The avenue . . . the gates . . .'

A fragment from a poem? I wondered. Sometimes in Damian's conversation words stand isolated and out of context, as though they do not belong in conversation at all.

'The house,' I began.

'Oh, not the house as it was.'

Claire's spaniels sniffed about for rabbits. As we stood there, the September sun felt hot. Damian believes in the impossible and when we were younger occasionally inspired me with his optimism: that nothing could be easier than poaching salmon, that a bookie or a publican would accept an IOU, that Bettina Nowd had the love-light in her eyes. It was an endearing quality then; I wasn't so sure about its being one that had endearingly endured. I felt uneasy about this talk of coming back. During the companionship of our youth there had never been an attempt to borrow money, since there was none to lend; nor was advantage taken of small politenesses, since politeness was not then readily on offer. The threat of a neighbour with a fly-by-night's presumptions was just a little alarming.

'Who owns it now?' he asked, and I told him: the son of the builder who had stripped the roof of its lead.

The cawing of rooks and the occasional bark of the dogs were the only sounds. It had always been quiet at Doul; that tall, beautiful woman floating about from room to room or picking the last of the mulberries; bees in the honeysuckle.

'What?' I said, again unable to catch Damian's murmur. Still moody, he did not directly reply, but seemed to say that the Muse would not be silent here.

*

I had ceased to practise on my sixtieth birthday, feeling the time had come, although previously I had imagined I could go on more or less for ever, as my father had in this same house, to his dying day. 'What'll it be like?' Damian used to ponder when we were young, the world for him an excitement to investigate after a small, familiar town in south-west Ireland. Both of us, of course, knew what it would be like for me: we knew my father's house, its comfortably crowded rooms, its pleasant garden; we knew the narrow main street, the shopkeepers, priests and beggars, the condensed-milk factory, the burnt-out cinema, the sleepy courthouse, the bright new hospital, the old asylum, the prison. But neither of us could conjecture a single thing about what lay ahead for Damian.

'It's all right, is it?' Damian asked me on the way back from

Doul that day, his mood gregarious again, suddenly so, as if he had remembered who I was. 'Doing nothing these days is all right?'

'Yes, it's all right.'

In fact, it was more than that: all sorts of things were easier in retirement. People weren't patients any more. Met by chance on the street, they conversed with less embarrassment; while privately I registered that Raynaud's was at work or that Frolich's syndrome would not now be reversed. In ordinary chat, awkward secrets were not shared with me; more likely I was shown an adolescent's face and then reminded I'd been the first to see it as an infant's; or informed of athletic achievements in children who had grown up, or of success in other ways, and weddings that were planned. Worries were held back, not coinage for me now, as bad backs weren't, or stitched wounds or blood pressure, the smell of sickness in small back bedrooms.

'Yes, it's fine,' I said in the bar of Traynor's Hotel. 'And you?' I added. 'Nowadays, Damian?'

Again he became morose. He shrugged and did not answer. He stared at the back of a man who was standing at the bar, at the torn seam of a jacket. Then he said:

'I used to think about Doul. Wherever I was, I'd come back to that.'

From his tone, those thoughts about the place of his youth had been a comfort, occurring – the implication was – at times of distress or melancholy. Then Damian said, as if in response to a question I had not asked:

'Well yes, an inspiration.'

He had finished the whiskey in his glass. I went to the bar, and while the drinks I ordered were poured I was asked by Mr Traynor about our son, now a doctor in New South Wales, and about Joanna, who had returned to the town six months ago to work in the prison. 'You'd be delighted she's back here,' Mr Traynor conjectured, and I agreed, although pointing out that sooner or later she would move away again. I smiled, shrugging that away, my mind not on the conversation. Could Doul have been a poet's inspiration for all these years? I wondered. Was that the meaning I was supposed to find in what had been so vaguely stated?

'I thought I recognized him,' Mr Traynor next remarked, his voice kept low, after I had answered his query about who Damian was. 'How're you doing these times?' he called out, and Damian called back that none of us was getting younger.

'God, that's the truth in it,' Mr Traynor agreed, wagging his head in a pretence that this hadn't occurred to him before.

I picked up my change and made my way back to the table where we sat.

'Nothing grand,' Damian said, as if my absence hadn't interrupted what we'd been saying. 'Any little hovel that could be knocked together. There are things . . .' He let the sentence trail away. 'I have the time now.'

I sipped my drink, disguising amusement: all his life Damian had had time. He ran through time, spending it as a spendthrift, wallowing in idleness. Perhaps poets always did, perhaps it was the way they had to live; I didn't know.

'Stuff accumulates,' Damian confided, 'unsaid. Oh, it's just a thought,' he added, and I concluded, with considerable relief, that this was probably the last we'd hear of his morning's whim. After all, there was no sign whatsoever of his being in possession of the necessary funds to build the modest dwelling he spoke of, and personal loans could be resisted. 'Silly old Damian,' Claire murmured when I told her, with the indulgent smile that talk of Damian always drew from her.

*

Then, quite suddenly, everything was different. Perhaps in the same moment – at dinner two days later – Claire and I were aware that our daughter was being charmed all over again by the man she had once picked out as the man she would like to marry. To this day, I can hear their two voices in my dining-room, and Damian laughing while Claire and I were numbed into silence. To this day I can see the bright flush in Joanna's cheeks.

'And are you settled, Joanna?' Damian asked. 'Here?'

'For the time being,' Joanna said.

The prison is two miles outside the town, a conglomeration of stark grey buildings behind high grey walls, which occasionally I have visited during an epidemic. *Ad sum ard labor*, a waggish inmate has carved on a sundial he made for the governor, a tag that is a talking point when visitors are led around. Joanna has worked in prisons in Dublin and in England; she came here because from conversations she has had with me she was aware that rehabilitation – which is her territory – wasn't being much bothered with. It was a challenge that here on the doorstep of the town she was born and grew up in were circumstances that professionally outraged her.

'I remember sharing a railway carriage with a man who'd just been released from gaol,' Damian said. 'He robbed garages.'

In Joanna's view a spell in prison was the offer of another chance for the offender, a time to come to terms with the world and with oneself. She was an optimist; you had to be, she insisted.

'Lonely wayside garages,' Damian said. 'A child working the pumps.'

'Did he say –'

'All he said was that he didn't intend to get caught the next time.'

Beneath these exchanges there was something else, a tremor that was shared; a tick answered another tick, fingers touched although a dinner table separated them. I pushed my knife and fork together; and Claire said something that nobody heard and went to the kitchen.

Joanna is small and dark-haired, and pretty. She has had

admirers, a proposal of marriage from a map-maker, a longish affair with an ornithologist, but her passionate devotion to her work has always seemed to make her draw back when there was pressure that a relationship should be allowed the assumption of permanence. It was as though she protected her own dedication, as though she believed she would experience a disloyalty in herself if she in any way devoted less time and energy to her work. Recidivists, penitents, old lags, one-time defaulters, drug pushers, muggers, burglars, rapists: these were her lovers. She found the good in them, and yet, when telling us about them, did not demand that we should too. It has never been her way to lecture, or stridently to insist, and often people are surprised at the intensity of her involvement, at the steel beneath so soft a surface. Neither Claire nor I ever say so, but there is something in our daughter that is remarkable.

Across the dinner table that evening she became demure. There was obedience in her glance, and respect for every ordinary word our visitor uttered, as though she would blindly have acted as he dictated should his next words express a desire. I followed Claire into the kitchen, carrying plates and dishes. 'I always wanted to,' Joanna was saying, drawn out by Damian in a way that was not usual in his conversation. 'I never thought of doing anything else.'

We didn't speak, Claire and I, in the kitchen. We didn't even look at one another. It was our fault; we had permitted this stroke of fate to stake its claim. The suitable admirers – the dark-haired map-maker, the ornithologist, and others – were not what a retriever of lost causes, a daily champion of down-and-outs, had ever wanted. In the dining-room the voices chatted on, and in the kitchen we felt invaded by them, Claire and I, she tumbling raspberries into a blue glass bowl, I spooning coffee into the filter. 'I remember hearing you'd been born,' Damian was saying in the dining-room when we returned.

It was I who had told him. I delivered Joanna myself; Claire and I heard her first cry in the same moment. 'A girl,' I said when Damian arrived six months later for one of his visits, and we drank my whiskey on a bitter January night. 'How nice to have a daughter!' he murmured when we gazed down at the cot by Claire's bedside. And he was right: it was nice having a girl as well as a boy, nice being a family. Even then, two different personalities were apparent: our son's easy-going, rarely ruffled, Joanna's confident. At five and six, long-legged and determined, she won the races she ran because insistently she believed she could. Oh no, she wouldn't, she asserted when it was pointed out that she would tire of looking after the unattractive terrier she rescued after tinkers left it behind. And for years, until the creature died in old age, she did look after it.

'It was snowing outside,' Damian reminisced in the dining-room. 'Black Bush was what we drank, Joanna, the night your father and I wet the baby's head.'

His fingernails were rimmed: ash from the cigarettes he was smoking, as he always does, between courses. Once upon a time, years ago, he affected a cigarette-holder. He had sold it, he told Claire when she asked, and we guessed it had been another gift from a woman, sold when the affair was over.

'Raspberries, Damian?' Claire offered.

He smiled his acceptance. He placed his cigarette, still burning, on a side plate, and poured cream on the fruit. I wondered if children had been born to him; I hadn't wondered that before. I imagined, as I often had, his public-house life in London, some places he could not enter because of debts, late-night disagreements turning sour. I had a feeling that his travels – so often mentioned – had always been of brief duration, that London was where he had mostly belonged, in seedy circumstances. I imagined lodgings, rent unpaid, possessions pawned. How often had there been flits in the small hours? Were small dishonesties a poet's right? And yet, I thought as well, he was our friend and almost always had been. He'd cheered our lives.

'Damian's tired of London,' Joanna said. 'He's going to live at Doul again.'

*

In the night, believing me to be asleep, Claire wept. I whispered, trying to console her. We didn't say to one another that shock came into this, that we must allow a little time to calm us. We lay there, remembering that not much longer than twenty-four hours ago Claire had said our friend was the tonic we needed. On all his visits we'd never been dismayed to see him, and he couldn't help being older now, less handsome than he had been, his grubbiness more noticeable. He was, at heart, as he had always been. It was unfair to say he wasn't, just because he had cast a spell in our house. We'd always known about those spells. We'd read between the lines, we hadn't been misled.

Marriage was what we dreaded, although neither of us used the word. It was not because Damian had so often confessed he liked to marry that our melancholy threw up this stark prediction; it was because Joanna was Joanna. We might be wrong, we felt each other thinking; a tawdry love affair might be enough. But we did not believe it and neither of us suggested the consolation of this lesser pain. Nor did we remind one another that Joanna, all her life, had been attracted by the difficult, nor did we share it with one another when in the dark we were more certainly aware that there had been no challenge in her relationship with the map-maker or the ornithologist, or with any of her suitable admirers. Perhaps, that night, we knew our daughter a little better, and perhaps we loved her just a little more. She would succeed where other women had failed: already we could hear her offering this, already we sensed her not believing that the failure could lie anywhere but with those other women. 'I'm going to marry Damian,' the childish silliness brightly echoed, and with it our amusement.

Had he come to us this time with a purpose? Claire asked when she ceased to weep. Did he intend our daughter to earn his living for him, to tend him in the place of his childhood, cosseting his old man's frailties? Had his future lit up suddenly on a London street, the years ahead radiant as a jewel in his imagination? 'I'll tell them,' had our daughter said already, planning to sit us down, to pour out drinks in celebration? She would break the news that was not news, and we'd embrace her, not pointing out that Damian couldn't help destroying his achievements. And she would hurry to him when he next appeared and they would stand together as lovers do. We could not foretell the details after that, and quite suddenly the form the relationship might take in time hardly seemed to matter any more: enough of it was there already. 'Are we being punished?' Claire asked, and I didn't know if we were or not, or why we should be punished, or what our sin was.

We didn't want that night to end. We didn't want to feel, again, the excitement that had crept into our house, that passed us by and was not ours. It was not in Damian's nature to halt an adventure that was already under way, not in his nature to acquire from nowhere the decency that would forbid it to proceed. His bedroom would not be empty when morning came, the small suitcase gone, a note left on his bedside table. 'Remember the others?' Claire whispered in the dark, and I knew whom she meant without having to think – the daughter of the Bishop of Killaloe, the widow from upstate New York, the Englishwoman in Venice, and other nameless women mentioned by our friend in passing.

Ill-suited, we said, when we learned that the first of his marriages had fallen apart, and were too busy in those busy days to be more than sorry. We had hardly wondered about the fate of the bishop's daughter, and not at all about the American widow, except to say to one another that it was typical of Damian to make the same mistake twice. And when the Englishwoman left him it was a joke. Old reprobate, we said. Incorrigible.

The first streaks of dawn came flickering in, the birds began. We lay there silent, not trusting ourselves to comment on this past that the present had thrown up. The bishop's daughter – younger than Joanna was now – smiled in her wedding dress, and I felt again the warm touch of her cheek when I kissed it, and heard her reply to my good wishes, her shy voice saying she was happier than she deserved to be. And a face from a photograph we'd once been shown was the oval face of the American, dark hair, dark eyes, lips slightly parted. And the face of the Englishwoman was just a guess, a face contorted in a quarrel, made bitter with cold tears. The shadows of other men's wives, of lovely women, girls charmed, clamoured for attention, breaking from their shadows, taking form. Old reprobate.

'I think I'll go and talk to her.' Claire's voice was hushed in the twilight, but she didn't move, and I knew that already she had changed her mind; talking would make everything worse. Eighty-one, Claire said: he would be eighty-one when Joanna was forty-eight.

I didn't calculate. It didn't matter. I thought we might quarrel, that tiredness might bring something like that on, but we didn't. We didn't round on each other, blaming in order to shed guilt, bickering as we might have once, when upsets engendered edginess. We didn't because ours are the dog days of marriage and there aren't enough left to waste: dangerous ground has long ago been charted and is avoided now. There was no point in saying, either, that the damage we already sensed would become entertainment for other people, as damage had for us.

'I'll make tea,' I said, and descended the stairs softly as I always do at this early hour so as not to wake our daughter. Some time today Damian and I might again call in at Traynor's; I might, in sickening humility, ask for mercy. I heard my own voice doing so, but the sound was false, wrong in all sorts of ways; I knew I wouldn't say a thing. To ensure that our daughter had a roof over her head I would lend whatever was necessary. A bungalow would replace the fallen house at Doul.

The *Irish Times* was half pushed through the letter-box; I slipped it out. I brought the tray back to our bedroom, with gingersnap biscuits on a plate because we like them in the early morning. We read the paper. We didn't say much else.

Later that morning Joanna hurried through cornflakes and a slice of toast. Her car started, reversed, then dashed away. Damian appeared and we sat outside in the September sunshine; Claire made fresh coffee. It was too late to hate him. It was too late to deny that we'd been grateful when our stay-at-home smugness had been enlivened by the tales of his adventures, or to ask him if he knew how life had turned out for the women who had loved him. Instead we conversed inconsequentially.